Independence

Independence

Evan Balkan

The University of Wisconsin Press

The University of Wisconsin Press
728 State Street, Suite 443
Madison, Wisconsin 53706
uwpress.wisc.edu

Gray's Inn House, 127 Clerkenwell Road
London EC1R 5DB, United Kingdom
eurospanbookstore.com

Printed in the United States of America

This book may be available in a digital edition.

Library of Congress Cataloging-in-Publication Data

Names: Balkan, Evan, 1972- author.
Title: Independence / Evan Balkan.
Description: Madison, Wisconsin: The University of Wisconsin Press, [2020]
Identifiers: LCCN 2020004324 | ISBN 9780299329143 (paperback)
Subjects: LCGFT: Fiction. | Novels.
Classification: LCC PS3602.A59557 I53 2020 | DDC 813/.6—dc23
LC record available at https://lccn.loc.gov/2020004324

BL, sleeping under strange strange skies . . .

Independence

1

Paris, South Dakota, May 1976

I was barely a hundred yards from the house when I first saw Lee. He was standing against the Petersens' fence and it was that more than anything else that got my attention. The fence was long, running around the whole yard. It was always a beautiful clean white, no matter the weather. My guess was that one of Mr. Petersen's gardeners scrubbed down that fence every night, and now there was some stranger with his boot on it. Sure, he was good looking and all—the best-looking person I'd ever seen, truth be told, with his dark hair and the way it fell over his light eyes. But the way he looked at me, with that smile of his with its beautiful row of perfect white teeth, he seemed cocky. So I kept walking, all the while he was still looking at me.

Mama never really talked to me much about men except to tell me they're almost always snakes and think of themselves first. Men she'd known seemed to think they owned you the moment the bloom went off. All sweetness and light, as she called it, and then once you're dependent, well, that's the time you can depend on them least. Until her man Hank, that is. She seemed to think Hank was the one different one.

When I got about twenty yards or so away, Lee raised his hand and said hi, still smiling at me.

Considering Mama's opinion of men, and the fact that he was no one I knew, I should have probably ignored him or, at most, just said hello to be polite but then kept on walking. But it was the adventurous side of me that made me stop. If nothing else, it guaranteed that this day wouldn't be like every other. Mama had already set everything off-kilter earlier. I'd caught her on the phone, kind of whispering, and when she hung up she had this big smile on her face.

Hank's comin' home, she said.

I noticed it right away, how she used the word "home."

You mean here? I asked.

Well now . . . she said, and she didn't need to say anymore.

You'll be getting married then.

Lilly, don't I deserve some happiness, after all this time?

I couldn't argue with her. It had been nine years since my pop left so I was sure she got lonely at times. Still, she had me. And wasn't she always telling me that I was all she ever needed? Plus, when she started sentences with my name, it meant she was agitated, so I knew to leave it be.

I'll head over to Mr. Robeson's, I said. Get breakfast.

I walked out the door—and that's when I saw Lee.

Hi, I said, though I didn't smile.

Whatcha up to? he said.

Do I know you? I asked.

He shook his head, keeping his eyes on me. He was handsome, that's true. But I still didn't much like the way he kept looking at me, slowly shaking his head before he said to me, No, miss, you didn't. But I plan to rectify that.

I figured what he meant by that, but still, in the way he was looking at me, like no one ever told him it was rude to look at people like that: I didn't like it. But I came to realize that in some weird way, I kind of did like it, too. There had been other boys who'd looked at me like that

4

before, and I usually hated them for it. But with Lee, it seemed I was of a different mind straightaway.

Didn't your mama teach you it's rude to stare? I asked.

He shook his head again, bent down, picked up a rock, and threw it. Hit the stop sign fifty clear yards away. Right in the middle.

My mama never taught me much, he said. Except maybe how to drink a whole can of beer in five seconds flat.

I laughed. He didn't. I would learn it wasn't meant to be a joke.

You made a mess of that fence, I told him.

He shrugged his shoulders.

You a relation of the Petersens?

Nope. I'm an auto mechanic. Been working over in Carney.

Never heard of it.

Didn't take me but half a day to get here.

Still never heard of it.

Near to the Wyoming line, he said. Shop closed up, so I come here to Paris looking for work. This guy in town told me I might want to try Swensen Petersen. Said he used to be the mayor and owns just about every acre from town out to Eagle Butte, where the Indians live. I told him I was much obliged and then I asked him where I might find this Mr. Petersen. He points me down this street here, says for me to look for the big white house. Called it Paris's one palace—probably the only one in all the Dakotas. I found it easy enough and figured I'd get an early start and try and catch him as he came out.

Good luck, I said. His wife is real ill and no one sees him much anymore. They pretty much just stay hunkered down in there all the time. And when he does come out, he hardly talks.

Lee looked at the house and then shook his head.

Goes to show you, he said.

What's that?

You can have all the money in the world, and it still don't get you what you need in this life.

Lee looked at me like he was waiting for my confirmation. When he stared at me, with those eyes of his, the way his face had of taking me all in, it made me blush.

I guess, I mumbled.

They have any kids? Lee asked.

I shook my head.

How do you like that? Just him and his wife all alone in that big old house.

I'd thought that very thing many times. I often saw Mrs. Petersen on their porch watching the world go by. I always waved to her. She never waved back, but I figured maybe she couldn't because of her illness, so I kept on waving. I wasn't losing anything by being neighborly. Sometimes at night I could see a light on in the lowest level of the house and I wondered if the missus didn't sleep much on account of her condition, whatever it was. Or maybe it was Mr. Petersen awake. I could picture him, in a study or library, at a desk, awake with worry, probably looking over a stack of bills or something. I'm sure there's no fun in being poor, but it never seemed to me that being rich is any better path to happiness. In fact, being rich probably just gives you more things to worry over. And it sure didn't keep Mrs. Petersen from spending her days in a wheelchair anyway.

No doubt about it: give me one solitary room and my working legs over a palace and a steel chair.

What's your name? Lee asked.

Lilly.

Pretty name, he said.

People were always telling me that, I guess because it's a flower, but I didn't see it. Seemed a boring name to me. So I told him as much.

Yeah? What would be a more proper exciting name then?

I don't know. Calpurnia.

What kind of crazy name is Calpurnia? he said. And he laughed and laughed.

It's in a book. Nothing you'd know about.

Now, now, he said, seeing he'd angered me.

And what about you?

Lee, he said, and he did a silly bow.

I could barely keep from laughing.

He walked over to me, leaving his muddy tracks against the white of the fence.

I liked seeing that mud on the fence, I'll admit it. It was like Lee wasn't afraid of anything. It was also like Lee was one thing and the Petersens' fence, and everything else I knew, was another.

He put his hand on my waist and said he was sorry for laughing at me.

Almost any other guy and I would've slapped his face for putting his hand on me like that and in such a familiar place, too. But I let him stay. As I said, it was like he had some kind of power or something. Right from the start. Plus, I wanted to show him that I was no little girl.

How old are you? he asked.

Fifteen, I said.

He smiled again, and this time, I smiled back. And that, I guess, is where everything started.

⁌

There are stories we tell ourselves, and there are stories we tell others. Which one is this, I don't really know. But I do know that it's a story that needs to be told.

Finally, and after all this time, it needs to be told.

New Orleans, Louisiana, November 4, 1992, 5:20 a.m.

I've been telling my daughter all her life that her father is dead. And now, in just a few days, I'll no longer be a liar.

This morning suits the task before us: chilly, overcast even in the predawn darkness, long, as if a promise of daylight is something that will stay on the horizon, teasing, but never show itself fully.

The alarm went off at four fifteen this morning, but I was already awake. I'm not sure I slept even twenty minutes in total last night. I doubt if Lindsey did either. I saw the yellow from her bedside light underneath the door to her room after midnight. I can't fully know what's in her head and I know better than to ask. All I'll get is her usual shrug. It frustrates me. But I remember what it's like to be fifteen. And what she's dealing with is difficult at any age.

So it was in silence that we left for the bus station, not bothering to eat anything, either. Just too early for any kind of appetite and we'll have plenty of time for all that anyway. It'll take us a whole day—some twenty-three hours—for this trip: New Orleans to Sioux Falls, South Dakota. I don't know how I'll do it. There's the matter of length, for one thing. Patience isn't one of my virtues. That's for sure. Even if this trip was for something fun, it would be a struggle for me. But as it is, to go see Lindsey's father, my old soul mate, before he's to be executed, well . . .

I had surgery once. Would be classified as minor—only one day in the hospital. But it didn't feel minor to me then. I was scared witless. What I best remember was going to the hospital that morning in the dark. I had to be there really early and I remember that feeling of driving there, how envious I was at all the other people in their cars, just going about their day, heading to work, no doubt, and how lucky they were to be doing something as simple as that and how so many of them probably hated being up that early and probably hated the jobs they were going to, and how sometimes it takes something like driving to a hospital for surgery—"minor" or no—to be reminded what a luxury simply living a boring life can be.

It's something like that now. We're boarding a bus and it should be fun and exciting, heading to a different state, so far away, but my insides are churning like that day of the surgery. This time, it feels like I need surgery on my heart.

We place our bags of clothes and food above us and settle into our seats. Right away, Lindsey puts on her Walkman and she's lost. A girl of few words these days anyway, once she's got those headphones on, forget it. No getting through. But she'll take off the headphones at some point. Either her ears will start to ache, or the batteries will die—though I suspect she's brought extras with her—or she'll get tired of listening to the same five tapes over and over. So there will be time for me to tell her the whole story. One I've wrestled over for years. Almost sixteen of them, to be exact. The whole of her lifetime.

It's been a week since she found Lee's letter asking us to come see him before the execution, that it would allow him to die like a man. He needed to see her, he wrote. And she wanted to see him. This I came to understand after two straight hours of her screaming at me for daring to keep such a secret from her her whole life.

"How could you? How could you?!" she sputtered and spat while I sat there like a scolded child, her face so red it was purple. I thought she might actually burst something and so I made her sit down on my bed. But she sprung right back up, called me all kinds of terrible names, asked me again how I could be so thoughtless and uncaring, and would hardly listen when I told her that she didn't understand and I tried to explain. Finally, she stormed out of my room, slammed the door to hers, and I didn't see her for the rest of the night.

That was followed by three straight days of dead silence, which was even worse. At least when you're being screamed at, you feel like an actual person and not a ghost.

Then, her demand that we go see him.

"Okay," I said—through a tight jaw and a pounding heart and the chills and everything else a human body can do to itself to punish the one living in it. Like every single part of me was battling with my brain and with the stories I've told myself, convinced myself of, the stories I need to believe. Maybe sometimes there are places I choose to forget or maybe things I add. But now, when I've agreed to tell her, there's a big part of me that knows I shouldn't leave out anything, that it's her right to know. But then there's this other part of me. It's fear; I'm scared she won't understand. Scared she'll think her mother is a monster. And I can't live with that. I've already experienced losing the most important people in the world to me. And there's a piece of you that dies and never comes back when that happens. And I'm afraid there'll be nothing left of me one of these days. I need Lindsey. I need my daughter. I figured maybe these are the stories I would tell her on my deathbed—that's how I've always pictured it. But now my hand has been forced.

There's this other part of it, too, that has me all stewed up. We all need our secrets, those things to keep to ourselves so only we need to live with them, so they don't infect the people we love. This whole thing: is it really more for me to tell, confession as it were, or is it for her? Who knows the line between selfish and selfless until after we act?

But this is her father. She has a right to know. So, I'll have to swallow hard and keep swallowing harder and harder until I either burst from it or manage to cram it all down and go on living like before, as normal a life as I've managed for myself, and for her, too. But she'll have to be told. Hopefully she'll get what she needs.

But how, really, to tell such a story as this? How near and full to the truth do I give her? When I might just lose her should she know everything? I'll have to tell her everything I can and then pray to God she'll understand. Pray she'll still be my daughter. But *how* to tell, when I can hardly understand it myself?

I grip the armrest, close my eyes, concentrate on my breathing and keeping my heart from knocking its way clear out of my chest. I have to do it.

We leave New Orleans behind, heading for my old home, reverse from the journey I'd once made with Lee, before there was a Lindsey. When I open my eyes, I see she's turned away from me. I watch her face in the reflection of the window. Quiet and introspective as she is, staring out at the early morning sky, still black in spots, gray in others, the day trying to come on. I know that face well. Of course I do, as it's my face, too. People always ask us, "You two twins or something?" Makes me laugh still, and blush a bit. Because to me, it's a compliment. But as she gets older, it makes her more and more angry, or embarrassed, or something unpleasant. I can see it in the way her eyebrows move and the way the ends of her lips curve down, this little pouty thing that flashes across her face. I wonder if that's something I used to do. I don't think so. It's more him. I can see him in there.

I take a big breath and then, about two hours outside New Orleans, tap her on the shoulder.

"Here's how it started," I say.

She removes her headphones. She stares straight ahead but she's listening.

"I first saw him outside my house where I grew up. Your grandmother had just told me that Hank would be moving in and it upset me, so I left. I was heading to the store and there he was."

2

Paris, South Dakota, May 1976

Lee nodded, told me he remembered fifteen, like it was some long time ago, though I could tell he wasn't much past eighteen himself.

So you know of anyone looking to hire here in Paris? he asked me.

How would I know about that?

You live here, don't you?

I'm not one who does any hiring.

He stuck his hands in the back pockets of his jeans and looked at the ground like a boy who'd just been scolded. I wanted to laugh. He was funny. Handsome and funny.

Well, I wish you luck, I said. I need to go.

You mind a little company?

Free country.

Lee followed me to the stores downtown, chattering all the way. Got his start working garages in his hometown, he told me, some out-of-the-way place no one'd ever heard of, near where Kansas, Missouri, and Oklahoma all come together. Got a car, he told me also, and a lot of money from the old job. Even got me a monster set of tools, he said.

I didn't see how any of that was my business one way or another and I surely hadn't asked. But I didn't mind listening to his easy way of talking.

When we reached the grocer, Lee followed me inside. I acted like I didn't know him, which, really, I didn't. And I acted like we hadn't come in together, which, really, we hadn't, even though we sort of had. Strangers always got a second look in Paris. It was one of those things about living in Paris, or any small town, I guess, where everyone knows each other: strangers can generally count on being looked after, cared for, given what they need. And yet locals will still look at them with suspicion. You don't know them, you don't know what they're capable of. And Lee was a stranger.

I said hi to Mr. Robeson and he said, Hi, Lilly, how's your ma, like he always did. He looked at Lee and tipped his head in greeting, but he didn't say anything. Just stared at him.

Lee paid it no mind and followed me through the aisles to the refrigerator and when I reached in to grab a bottle of milk, he threw himself in front of me and grabbed it himself. I stood there staring at him and he was staring at me and it all seemed so foolish, and then he looked around and galloped to the front of the store and got a cart and put the milk in and then raced back over to me, almost knocking down a pyramid of cereal boxes, and then he slowly wheeled the cart behind me while I walked down the aisles. Every now and then I looked back at him; he'd put both feet on the bottom rail so he could kind of glide and once or twice his weight caused the cart to tip up in the air a little bit. I wanted to laugh at him, but I hid my face when I felt it coming on.

I got the few things I needed and Lee unloaded the items onto the counter. Mr. Robeson was looking at us like he didn't know what, but still he didn't say anything. I suddenly got a sick feeling in my stomach thinking that Lee was going to take some of his own money and try and pay for my things. But he didn't. Just stood there and took the bag from Mr. Robeson and tipped his head to him in thanks and then we walked out into the sun.

We were outside maybe thirty seconds before Lee said, Hold it. One minute. And he went racing back into the grocer. I was thinking I should walk away, but I stayed. Seemed rude of me to just leave.

He came racing back out holding two vanilla ice cream cones and immediately they started melting in the sun. He ran his tongue over one of them and handed me the other.

Only had vanilla, he said. What kind of place sells ice cream doesn't have chocolate?

I like pistachio the best, I said.

Well, seems we already have one thing in common, Miss Lilly. Pistachio's my favorite, too.

I wondered what were the chances of that and thought maybe he was putting me on. But I didn't say anything. Didn't seem a thing worth questioning about.

You in school? he asked.

Just about finished up for the year.

What's your favorite subject?

I like history.

He nodded.

I liked poetry, too, but I didn't tell him that. He didn't need to know everything. That seemed to me a secret worth keeping. I liked Emily Dickinson the most. I hardly ever understood the meanings in her poems, but I liked to try and puzzle them out and I could spend a whole afternoon doing that. Such a line as this: "Demur—you're straightway dangerous / And handled with a chain . . ." It put a flutter in my chest when I thought of it. It had a different meaning every time I pondered it, depending on my mood. It never mattered to me if I was getting it right or not. She was long gone by the time I discovered her, Miss Dickinson, and what she left behind were just words on paper, and they didn't mean a thing all by themselves until someone like me came along and read them. So in that way I couldn't ever be wrong about those poems, and it kept me reading.

I'm guessing you're all excited about this bicentennial then, Lee said.

What do you mean?

Two hundredth birthday of America. It's exciting.

Seems overdone. Everything done up in red, white, and blue. And here barely not even summer. It's like putting up Christmas decorations in October.

I disagree with you there. A country only turns two hundred once. Seems a thing to celebrate all year long.

I shrugged my shoulders.

Besides, didn't you just tell me you like history?

But the bicentennial is the present. It's not history.

He laughed, shook his head. I guess you're right about that, he said. When you think about it. I'll give you that.

When we got a block from my house, I reached out for my bag.

I can help you all the way to your house, he said.

My mama sees me with you, you holding our groceries, me eating ice cream for breakfast . . .

What about it? he asked me.

Well, that's just it. I don't know what about it and she'll be liable to have questions I don't have answers for.

He looked around, still holding my bag, like he was thinking of running off with it or something, but then he handed it over.

Well, Miss Lilly, he said, I aim to see you again.

At first I just stood there and didn't say anything because I had nothing to say. But then it became awkward standing there in the street not talking. So finally I said, Well, that's your prerogative, and I walked away.

I didn't look back, but I could tell: he was watching me. And I liked that. And I liked also that he aimed to see me again.

Mama could have her man, and I could have mine.

3

The house was nice and cool with the windows open and a breeze coming through. I set the groceries on the counter and started breakfast. Mama came up behind me and ran a brush through my hair, over and over, a thing she'd done ever since I could remember. There were nights we did nothing but sit on a bed or a couch and she sat behind me running that brush through my hair like a meditation or something.

You have beautiful hair, she said.

I never thought of my hair as beautiful. But people told me that all the time, so I guess there was some truth in it. I think it looked a little like straw when I was younger, the color and all. And when it got to be a mess, like after a fitful night of sleep or something, it kinked all up like a spent broom. But then Mama fixed it, running that brush over and over until my hair got soft and untangled again.

When it was just the two of us, before Hank, it sometimes felt like Mama and me were the only two people in the world. Friday nights we'd sit on the couch and share a blanket and watch whatever movie would come on TV on the ABC movie of the week. Sometimes they were good, those movies, but mostly they were pretty dumb. But it didn't matter. Either way we'd have our bowl of popcorn between us and our scratchy old blanket over our legs and I'd feel her shoulder against mine and every now and then we'd both reach into the popcorn bowl at the same time and bump hands and spill popcorn and she'd yell at me like she was mad but she'd smile when she did it and she wasn't mad at all. When it was over and I could hardly keep my eyes open she'd tell me to come sleep with her in her bed. It wasn't like her bedroom was anything more than five feet closer to the couch than mine. But we'd pretend otherwise and I'd get into her bed even with my teeth all filmy from popcorn and fall asleep there for the night.

She never said as much, but of course it was hard for Mama after my pop left. Me, I don't remember it all that well. But it's different when you're older. So I did my best to make things easy on her. She had enough to deal with, raising me and making sure we had food on the table. I could see it in her eyes when she got home from waiting tables at the bar, staying late to clean up and make extra money, being there all night and not getting back all that long before I was getting up for school. She'd usually stay awake the few hours and then come in my room while I was dressing, tell me how grown up I was getting and if she didn't watch it, she'd miss it all. Wake up one day and I'd be a woman. I told her that was silly. Back then, I hadn't even gotten my breasts yet and nothing else to do with being a woman. But she'd say it just the same, every day. She loved me, my mama.

So I held in check that side of me that screamed to get out, go somewhere and do something, so impatient I was for my life to start. It was in my nature to explore and be restless. I always thought it was the best part of me. As for Mama, I think she was of two minds about this characteristic of mine. She always told me that my adventurous side showed I possessed bravery and that was a good thing. There are so many people in this world that are scared of their own shadows, she said, and never take a risk on anything.

The way she would say this to me, standing there with her eyes cast down, what looked like a sad smile on her face, I got the sense she might have been talking about herself. Though she didn't say. Course, she added, that adventurous spirit might also get you in all kinds of trouble.

When Mama met Hank is when things changed. He was nice and all, to her and to me. That wasn't the problem. More that she began to live for him and not only for me and I hated that. Hank drove trucks long haul and so he'd be gone sometimes weeks at a time. Then it was just Mama and me again. But when he was coming back home, she'd start getting all antsy two, three days before. She'd clean the house until everything shined and I was hardly allowed to eat anything or touch anything for fear I'd mess something up. And then when Hank got back it was almost like I wasn't even there anymore. He'd bring me gifts, little knickknacks from the road, and Mama would stand there beaming, looking at me and him and saying things like, Well wasn't that nice of Hank, to have thought of you when he was on the road?

I guess so, I'd say.

But I never asked for anything and it didn't matter to me if he brought something or not. He could've forgotten for all I cared.

Well now, don't act like I never taught you manners, she'd say.

Thank you, I'd mutter.

You're very welcome, Hank would say, and then he'd turn to Mama and say something like, I didn't forget about you, either. And they'd smile and giggle and act like little kids and it was enough to make me want to throw up. I'd excuse myself and let them be alone.

Hard as it was, I did my best to be understanding. I missed having Mama to myself, of course, but I suppose everyone gets lonely now and again. And it must have been worse if you had someone once and then you didn't. As for me, before Lee came around, I never did mind being alone—preferred it in most cases—but then again I never did have anyone to lose besides Mama.

I made us French toast and we ate mostly in silence. Mama kept looking at me, getting exasperated, until finally she said, What's gotten into you?

Nothing, I said.

Well, it doesn't seem like nothing.

Just tired is all. I didn't sleep great last night.

Well, then, get yourself to bed early this evening.

Okay, Mama.

I cleaned up our dishes and afterward I headed out to the porch with a book. I sat there reading when suddenly the sun got blotted out and I heard, Hi, Lilly, what you got there?

It was Lee.

I was surprised by the feeling that ran through me, all excitement and happiness, like I was seeing him for the first time after a long separation. Just like that, my mood lightened and it was enough to make me forget all about Mama and Hank. The sun was behind him and it made a kind of halo and he looked like an angel. The light turned his hair from dark brown to something lighter. And his eyes, those light-blue eyes of his, blue like the sky in January when there aren't any clouds and the air is so cold it hurts you to your bones—his eyes I could see real clear, and they seemed even lighter than the light behind him. He was almost hard to look at at that moment, the way you can see something so beautiful that you want to look away and preserve it there forever, keep it from ever getting messed up with anything else.

Lee took the book from my hands.

Why you spend your time reading poetry? he asked.

I guess I like it.

He nodded, like that was a satisfactory enough answer, and handed the book back.

Until I spotted you here, I didn't know which house was yours on account of you making me stop down the street before. Had I known, I would have knocked.

And how would I have explained that? I asked.

You can't have friends?

No friends that look like you.

19

Mind if I sit?

He sat down on the last step and the light seemed to follow him.

He held his hands together and let them drop between his knees. He looked up and down the street.

Anything to do around here? he asked.

Not much.

Peaceful then?

Boring.

Can I take you out somewhere later?

I paused and caught my breath. But then, remembering myself, I said: I doubt that.

Saturday night, gotta be something to do.

I shook my head. There was no way Mama would let me go out with a stranger, not on a Saturday night. Not ever.

How about tomorrow then? Maybe in the afternoon, after church.

I don't go to church.

No?

No. Used to. But the preacher told Mama that she had to honor her husband no matter what. She disagreed with that, so we stopped going. Besides, Mama says there are too many Lutherans and Presbyterians around anyhow; she calls them the Frozen Chosen. She thinks they can be real chilly toward others, and this includes her own kin. So it wasn't all that hard for her to give up, I guess.

I think me and your mama would get along just fine.

Just then Mama came to the door.

Lilly?

Yes'm.

Who's that then?

This here is Lee. He just came by. Of his own accord.

Mama came onto the porch. She had on her agitated face.

Is there something I can help you with, Mr. Lee?

I had the pleasure of making Lilly here's acquaintance this morning and I thought I'd come by and say hi. I'm new around here, and don't have any friends in Paris and, well, heck, I don't know anyone in the whole state of South Dakota, tell you the truth.

Lilly needs to come in and help me here in the house.

I got up and brushed the dirt from my skirt.

Lee got up, too. It was nice to meet you, ma'am, he said to Mama. To me he said, Lilly, I hope to see you again soon. Still looking for work, so if you know of any . . .

I'm certain she's not the one to tell you, Mama said, and then she pushed me in the house. Once I was in, she turned to Lee and said through the screen door, I don't think you have any business around here with my daughter. She's only fifteen years old.

Then she closed the inside door, too, something she hardly ever did when the weather was nice. On such days, even when we were gone from the house, that front door was left open. I don't think she even had a key to the lock.

Where you know him from? she asked me.

I don't. He followed me to Mr. Robeson's.

Who is he?

Said he was working in a mechanic's shop in someplace called Carney, near Nebraska, I think, and it closed and so now he's in Paris looking for work. That's all I know of him.

You sure that's all you know? she asked.

It was something in the way she looked at me when she asked me that, like she'd already made up her mind that I'd done something wrong or that I was lying to her.

Yeah, that's all I know, I said.

Well, you stay away from him. He looks like the murderin' type.

Oh, Mama.

I can see it in a man, and I can see it in him straightaway, the way he keeps his eyes shaded and low when he talks to you, like he already knows to be ashamed of something he hasn't even done yet.

That's silly.

Let me remind you: I work in a bar and I see all types and I can tell a man through and through after only one look. And that man is no good.

I felt a great anger rising up in me, so sharp and sudden it almost took my breath away and maybe because of it I couldn't help myself and I blurted out: You think you know everything? You used to tell me *all* men are snakes and you got this one pegged, too. But you have your Hank now, and how is it you're able to get yourself the only one good and true man in the universe? How is that?

You watch it, young lady. Hank *is* a good and decent man and he earns himself a proper and respectable living instead of roaming around asking strangers for work.

Hank drives trucks. Lee *fixes* them. Now you tell me—

Enough of that! You stop it right there. That man you're talking about, I'm gonna marry him and he's gonna be your new daddy. So I strongly suggest you watch what you say.

Something changed deep inside me. I decided right then that I hoped I did, in fact, see Lee again—and I hoped it would be soon.

Like I said, Mama could have her man, and I could have mine.

4

I heard it a few times but I was still in that hazy place in between sleeping and being awake. Like I was dreaming real life. But then it came again, this tapping noise, and finally I woke to see Lee outside my window. I didn't know at first if I was dreaming, but if it was a dream it sure felt real, right down to the way my heart was jumping all around and my stomach felt like it had dropped straight into my toes.

His hair and shirt were powdery white from the moonlight, like he was an angel, or a ghost. He looked like part of the world around him, the trees and flowers and the night sky and moon, but also apart from the world, too, like floating above it. When he saw me awake, he didn't smile or anything, like what he was doing was the most natural thing in the world. He just kept pointing at the window.

I got out of bed and went to the window and slid it open, little paint chips falling onto my fingers.

What are you doing here? I asked.

He put his finger to his lips, shushing me. Then he whispered, Come on out here.

I could feel myself shaking as I threw on my old robe. He held my hand as I crawled through the window and I was already outside when I realized I'd left my feet bare, but that really didn't bother me. The night air was cool and clean and when we got away from my house, we walked straight in the middle of the street as if we owned the whole town and weren't afraid of anything.

What time is it? I asked.

Around two.

We walked some more, not talking, and I wasn't sure what I was supposed to be doing or how I was supposed to be acting, but after my heart stopped thumping like a jackhammer, I actually felt something like calm.

Where are you staying? I asked.

I got a room over the hardware store on Main. Think Mr. Olson might let me work in the store, too, at least a few days a week. Said I gotta learn the metric system because of the change and all. I told him I already learned it in school, which isn't true. But, you know . . .

Lee patted his front pocket and said, Gotta keep the money coming in—like he'd got all his money right there in his blue jeans.

There was a path between the Petersens and the next house, where Rosemarie Van Waggoner lived, one I used to take all the time, and I led Lee down it. Once clear of the houses, it was nothing but prairie all the way down to the creek. I felt it on my feet, and it was a good feeling—familiar and safe. The coolness of the hard soil and bent grass, the way it held you up. I'd know it anywhere. In summer the grass went very tall and the ticks were in it and you had to clear your legs of them when you got down to the creek. And the grasshoppers bounced off your shins as you walked by like they couldn't see a thing despite their big eyes. There were plenty of snakes there, too, but they always scattered as you approached and all you ever saw of them was their skinny black tails curving away from you.

The moon made everything on the prairie look like a sheet of ice. And the way it shined like that, it made the creek appear as if some giant hand had laid a ribbon of silk across the land, this straight line cutting right through the prairie. But even in moonlight, I'd have recognized it anywhere. I knew every inch of the place and I could tell the time of year almost down to the day just by looking at the creatures in or near the water, like the crazy-looking tadpoles in their pools; some with their little legs already popped and others with their long tails still and no legs and only starting to get froggy with their rounded middles. It used to make me laugh when I saw them, but I know: we all go at our own pace.

I could tell the exactness of seasons, too, even if the wind tried to change things up with its cold or bringing with it some far-off hint of coming warmth, either too early or too late for the calendar. When I walked certain paths at certain times of year, I'd scatter what must have been a hundred thousand tiny frogs all hatched at long last and taking part in that great journey to some spot their brains were hardwired to know from the moment they were born. I wonder if it's the same with us, too, if we humans are hardwired to always return home no matter where we roam.

The trees at the creek were tall and full of life, with new leaves that caught a breeze that didn't reach us even though we could hear the soft whoosh.

It sure is pretty, Lee said.

I like to come down here when I want to get away.

He laughed, asked me what it was I needed to get away from.

I don't know. Life, I told him, and he laughed again, like he didn't take anything I said very seriously.

Sorry, he said when he saw that he'd angered me. Tell me what you do down here.

Think mostly.

About?

About maybe setting off. Away from here. See something of the world. You know?

I do. I do indeed. Not all that often you meet a kindred spirit, he said.

He took a bit of my hair and tucked it behind my ear.

Where you want to head? Any place in particular?

I've always wanted to go to New Orleans, ever since I was a little girl and I saw people celebrating Mardi Gras on TV.

He nodded. I can see that, he said.

Tell me about your mama, I said.

Why you want to know about her?

You met mine.

My mama is a good enough woman, I suppose. But she suffers, he said. Suffers from all the pains of the world. Tragedies befall some people all the way in China, she gets wind of it, she cries, and prays, and pulls her hair out. And then she says, Nothin' we can do about it anyhow—which is the point, really, and if she knows this already, why does she carry on like she does? But it seems she never remembers that part, and gets right back to carrying on again the next time some tragedy crops up.

What about your pop?

Lee said nothing. Instead, he put his hands in the back pockets of his jeans and turned his face toward the creek and beyond.

What's that? he asked.

What?

Rise over there. This place is level as a flapjack but that one rise there.

Just some feature of the land, I told him.

But it was more than that. I'd spent so many hours at the creek staring at that rise in the distance, the way it piled up from the flatness, the only thing for miles and miles that did, the way sometimes it was black and sometimes purple and other times the same color as everything else, depending on season and my own mood. And sometimes it got swallowed up in the waves of heat that floated up from the prairie when all the snakes and mice and crickets and grasshoppers and everything else laid low in the grass to keep cover from the sun. I'd stare at that rise forever, and sometimes I got frustrated at the way it just lay there like it was mocking me, how it was at once so close, at the edge of the horizon, and at the same time so far away. One time I decided to walk to it. I walked and walked, for hours I walked, and it never came any closer. I swear it, at times during that trek it looked even like it was moving farther away from me. And I had to turn back and it was cold and long dark when I got back to the creek and Mama had a fit for how long I was gone. I'm not sure what it was that fascinated me so much about that rise. But as long as I could remember it had. Maybe it was the way it had of insisting itself on the land. The prairie is all about the long view and distance and a refusal to be interrupted. And yet there was that rise, the only thing like it around. So I couldn't answer Lee's question about what it was, but I knew that I wouldn't have even if I could. I was jealous of its mystery, felt it was something only for me to crack, so I told him I didn't know, that it was only some feature of the land, I guess.

I was quiet and he was quiet except to say that he'd like to come back in the day, see what it was like.

Then he asked if it'd be all right if he kissed me. A nervous sweat broke out all over me. And in my nervousness, I blurted out, I guess so, but you better hurry because I have to get back.

He put his hands on my hips and leaned in. I kept my eyes open but he didn't and before he closed his I could see that the light blue in them had turned light gray in the moonlight. He pressed his lips to mine and held them there, just pressing. I worried about the sweat on my lip. We stood like that for what felt like a long time before he pulled away and said, Maybe loosen up a little bit.

I turned away.

I didn't mean to criticize, he said. That was just fine. We'll keep working on it.

It was my first proper kiss. Well, there had been the time when Rand Keiser kissed me up in his hayloft, but we were really young and Rand was a little touched in the head ever since he fell from a ladder, so that hardly counts. So this was it then, with Lee. And it had me all stewed up inside. All the different emotions and feelings running through me made me feel sick and thrilled and nervous and calm, all at once if such a thing is possible.

But I was stuck on those words, "just fine." I wasn't sure what it was he meant by it and I couldn't find the right way to ask.

But there was hardly any time to think about it anyway. Once it was done, we walked silently back up the path and back to my house, the whole way without saying a word.

Thank you, Lee said. For the nice night.

Sure.

I was about to step up again, so I could get back into my window, careful not to trample the daffodils, but he held me for a moment and asked if he could kiss me again, a good night kiss.

I guess that would be okay, I said, and this time I could see what he meant about loosening up. His lips were softer and that made it easier to let my lips go soft, too, and now I couldn't feel the hard edges of his teeth behind his lips and it felt nice and there was a certain kind of heat I'd never felt before that went through my whole body and even with the cool night air I felt really hot.

But just as quickly, I remembered where we were and that Mama was inside and what if she chose that moment to come into my room and check on me, what then? Hank was set to come back any day, and she'd been nervous and excited and not sleeping all that well.

Go, I told him, and he seemed to understand the urgency in it.

From my window I watched as he jogged out onto the street and then slowed to a walk like he was only out for a pleasure stroll. And then he disappeared down the street and I couldn't even follow the length of his shadow that the moon threw long and deep.

Once he disappeared, I felt a real emptiness.

I wanted to see him again, more than I wanted anything else in the world.

And there wasn't a thing that I was going to let prevent that. Not even Mama.

I closed the window and got back into bed. But it didn't make any difference that it was three in the morning or even later. My brain and the pictures it sent up to me wouldn't let me sleep.

Instead, it was Lee, down by the creek, Lee looking over the prairie, Lee at that very moment, for I could picture him climbing the narrow metal steps behind the hardware store to his own room, walking in and shutting the door and getting into his own bed, and for the first time in my life I felt the sharp pain of being apart from someone.

It was like our two bodies, separated from one another, were just empty pages scattered in the wind. But together we were like a book. A book of poetry—beautiful all by itself, but something that can change in meaning the more you read it.

5

After school I didn't walk straight home. I didn't stay at school, either. I never did. I didn't have many friends at school, and that was fine with me. Early on, I got a reputation as someone who liked to be by herself, a bit of a loner. That was fine with me, too. Mostly because it was true, I did like to be by myself. But people grew frustrated with you if you didn't have much to say and that was especially true after the local girls became teenagers. They whispered about this one and gossiped about that one and I didn't have any interest in it. And because of that, often their whispers and gossip turned to the subject of me. But I'd never cared much about that either; I didn't really need friends, I discovered. Mama was all the company I needed, the way she could chatter on sometimes and I loved to just listen, and then other times she was quiet, for days at a stretch sometimes, and I liked that, too, the way we could sit in silence and not need to say a word and yet feel perfectly comfortable anyway. Even when Mama was at work, there were the cats to keep me company. We had four of them, two who never left the house and two who came and went as they pleased, sometimes disappearing for weeks at a time before we found them sitting on the porch like they'd never left. But, like I said, things changed after Mama met Hank.

So instead of turning toward home like I always did after school, I headed to the center of town. That's where the stoplight was, keeping the cars on Main and Elder from ramming into each other. Used to be, when I was real little, they had stop signs on those corners and when they brought in the light all the townspeople grumbled about it, calling it government interference and questioning why it was they couldn't be trusted to drive their own cars. But there had been a couple of accidents, one so bad it sent one of Mr. Petersen's gardeners to the hospital, and that was why the light went up. But when there was an accident, at least there was some excitement for a day.

There was another reason for that stoplight, too, at least according to what I'd heard: the shop owners demanded it, saying it was good for business to have people not moving there with nothing other to do than look in shop windows while they waited for the light to go green. It would certainly explain why people had to sit for two, three minutes sometimes with no cars at all taking advantage of the opposite green light. But it didn't matter to the old-timers in town, who only slowed down at that light, no matter if it was red, and then went on through. I suppose you might get to a point in life where you don't want to be told anything anymore. Like you're running out of time and so you try and speed things up. It's funny, because I'd always felt that way, even when I was just a little girl. I suppose life's like a circle where you start and end at the same place.

Mr. Olson's hardware store sat at the corner of that intersection, to the right of the beauty salon. I'd gone into the salon once to see how much it would cost for me to get Mama a day there and I didn't have near enough money. I asked about just a nail polish for her hands and I was short there, too, so I didn't do anything else but make Mama a card like I did every year. Still, like every year she cried when she read it and hugged me and told me how much she loved me, that I was the only thing in this world she needed. I know she believed that at the time—maybe she didn't even allow herself to imagine someone like Hank.

But nothing can ever stay the same. That's something no one had to tell me. And that's why on that day I turned one way when every day before I'd turned the other.

When I got to the hardware store, I stopped and looked up. I know what a fool I must have looked, standing there in front of the store staring up and over it, past the metal stairs to the one window, knowing that's where Lee slept at night. But no matter how foolish I might have looked, I stood there looking up anyway, wondering past that window. You couldn't see anything inside of it, at least not from where I was. I considered crossing to the other side of the street to maybe see from there, but that still wouldn't answer the mystery of what it was I was hoping to see anyway. Perhaps just a figure moving past, perhaps to know that there he was and here I was and we were close together, even if we were far apart.

Can I help you, miss? I heard.

It was Lee, standing in the doorway, acting as if I was a real and proper customer.

You got the job here then? I said, and I could hear that my voice had gone a little fluttery. I hoped he didn't notice.

Said he'd try me out for a few days. See how it'd go.

I'm sure you'll do great.

Not much to mess up. Just showing people where to find what they need and occasionally make a recommendation or two.

You need to know your tools and all.

I suppose. But mostly it's just moving heavy things from one corner of the store to another. He don't trust me to man the register yet.

I wouldn't take that personal.

No, I don't.

I know I looked silly, exposed for having no purpose for my presence there, holding on to my school books and twisting my hips this way and that from nervousness and excitement.

32

So, can I help you with something, miss? he asked again, all serious.

I figured he needed to act professional if Mr. Olson came out, so I played along, and after thinking about it a second told him I needed a new spring for our porch door.

Got two kinds. You wanna look them over?

I stepped into the store and followed Lee to a shelf. Here you go, he said. You have a preference?

I didn't answer because I heard a familiar voice: there was Hank standing at the counter, a cup of coffee in his hand, talking to Mr. Olson. He didn't notice me. He stood there talking and laughing and occasionally blowing on his coffee and sipping it.

Miss? Lee said again, keeping on the front.

That's my mama's boyfriend.

Mr. Olson?

The other one.

Guy said he just come in from a long haul. Was all the way out to Oregon, that's what he told Mr. Olson.

His name's Hank and he and my mama been together since the winter. Talk about him moving in. They'll be getting married soon enough. Least that what Mama said.

Your pappy's gone then?

I kind of just dipped my head, a gesture Lee seemed to understand.

Men are a tainted bunch, he said. We seem to be born with a lot to overcome.

Lilly?

It was Hank. He walked over to us and before he said anything, he looked at me and at Lee and the look he gave Lee wasn't a very kind one.

How are you, Lilly? How's your mother? he asked.

She's all right, I guess. She know you're back?

I just got in. Drove through the night and day.

He tipped his coffee to me as if that was some kind of proof.

I plan on heading down there right now, he said. Just needed to stop in, get the truck settled, and order a few parts.

He looked at Lee and it seemed Hank was uncomfortable about something, and then he turned to me and he said, Listen, Lilly, I want to talk to you about me and your ma.

He motioned for me to follow him to a more private space, but Lee didn't let us get far.

Mister, if you need help installing those parts, I'm your man, he said.

You a mechanic? Hank asked.

Yes, sir. Worked seven months out in Carney before the shop closed up on account of the owner passing on.

You work on cargo trucks?

Every kind of engine you can imagine. We saw them all. From trucks to backhoes to brand new '76s. Even had some guy come in once with a '29 Model A coupe.

Well, we'll see, Hank said. He looked again at Lee with a look one can only call suspicion, like there was something about Lee he couldn't put his finger on but knew he didn't like. It was a look Lee was probably used to by then.

The bicentennial was supposed to bring us together, remind everyone we were one country and all Americans and all that. At least that's what people were saying. But those of us who were still young, we knew that it didn't so much matter if the country was turning two hundred, or five hundred, or was still busy being born, older people would always look at us with mistrust. It's a thing I suspect will never change.

Lilly, I'll see you at the house? Hank asked, though his tone wasn't so much asking as telling. Maybe we can talk then, the three of us?

I nodded. He walked back to resume his conversation and coffee with Mr. Olson. I was a little flustered from seeing Hank. I hadn't expected it, and I wasn't looking forward to our talk because I knew full well what it was all about, so I told Lee thanks for your help and walked out.

I expected him to follow me and was sorely disappointed when I realized he hadn't. I stood out on the sidewalk for some time before I felt stupid standing there all alone like that, waiting for nothing, so I started to leave.

I wanted to turn around and look, to see if Lee was coming out of the store. It took all my will not to, but I didn't. Instead, I just imagined it, picturing him there, having stepped from the store into the sunlight, watching me walk away, and him feeling in his heart what I was feeling in mine: that we were meant to be together, something written in the stars, just the two of us.

I couldn't help myself any longer and turned around and I was thrilled to see it was the way I pictured it: he *was* standing there, watching me go, and I imagined another thing, that the crazy thumping thing that happened inside me when I caught sight of him was happening to him, too. The way my heart jumped around in my chest and seemed to take dives into my stomach. It made me feel alive and sick all at the same time, like a deep hunger that no feast could satisfy completely.

It was a wonderful, exhilarating feeling. And it upset me when it turned into a different feeling, a bad one, when I saw that Hank had stepped out on the sidewalk, too.

I didn't like the way he'd crossed his arms over his chest as he watched Lee watching me.

⌁

Mama was waiting for me when I got home.

Where were you? she asked.

I saw Hank, I told her.

Immediately her hands went to her hair, the way they always did when he came walking up the steps to our porch and she stood there behind the screen door watching him come up. It was her habit to open the porch door only when he reached the top step, never when he was just on the sidewalk. I don't know why she did this, and I suspected she couldn't say why either, if she even knew she did it at all—just standing there waiting, her hands all about her head like that.

I'm sure I did some silly thing like that too when I saw Lee. This, I figured, is what love can do to you: make you do dumb, pointless things you aren't even aware of.

He's in town, I said.

She continued patting the curls that hung below her ears and tugged on the ends of her shirt, which had little tails that fell below her waist. It was a sleeveless thing and dipped down in front so that the tops of her breasts showed and these she pushed up with this little shoulder shrug thing she did, another one of her weird quirks when Hank was around.

By now, she'd moved to the door to watch. It wasn't long before he came, either, walking up the porch steps, a clutch of flowers gripped tight at the stems in his fist. He reached the porch and Mama opened the door. He had his hair combed over tight on his head. It looked freshly wet and his shirt was tucked in and buttoned even to the top. He looked like a different person than the one I'd seen in the store. But his eyes were still weary and red and of course there's no hiding a night without sleep.

Hank had the biggest smile on his face, and so did Mama. I felt myself growing sick over it. And that's when I saw Lee, out on the sidewalk and making his way up the porch, not far behind Hank, with a bag in his hand.

I wanted to run through the door to let him in and I was overcome with the queerest feeling, that it could be a nice reunion all around, that it would be Mama and Hank and me and Lee and we would all head to the table and have a fine supper together, like it'd be the most natural thing in the world. But seeing Mama's face like it was, and then the way Hank's face changed first with puzzlement and then with concern and then recognition and then, finally, anger, anger perhaps at Lee's ruining his moment with Mama, I knew to stay put.

Despite the look on Mama's and Hank's faces, Lee kept on coming, as ordinary as could be. He even skipped over a big crack on the sidewalk, and he was looking like an overexcited puppy and I had to let out a little giggle.

That's the boy came round here a couple days ago, Mama said, real low. Messing with Lilly.

He was in the store just now, too, Hank added.

Now Hank turned and addressed Lee directly: Thought I'd said I'd let you know about those truck parts, son.

And I'm looking forward to that, sir. But this visit here ain't about your truck.

Lee opened his bag and pulled out two springs for the door. He turned to me.

You never did pick which one, he said. So I brought them both. I can take back whichever you don't use.

Lee brought new springs for the porch door, Mama, I said, as if he hadn't already said as much and it required further explanation. No one else was talking and that kind of tense silence made me nervous. So I continued talking to fill the space.

The springs are so the door won't keep slamming the way it does, I said. That's why Lee's brought them.

I see that, Mama finally said. Well, this ain't exactly the best time for this, she added, saying this directly to Lee.

Well, ma'am, I brought along a screwdriver, too, so I can just get this set for you out here and you don't need to worry about me at all.

She said this ain't the time, Hank said.

I could feel the air getting thick. I still didn't know Lee very well so I didn't know what he'd do next. But in some ways it felt to me like I knew Lee inside and out and every which way and so I knew he was not about to just turn around, say, Yes, sir, and walk away. I wanted the thickness to go away but I didn't see how that was going to happen with Lee there and yet there was a part of me that wanted Lee to stay right where he was and say whatever he needed to say because if he did in fact turn around and leave, I knew there was a chance I was going to try and leave with him and I couldn't even begin to imagine the scene that would bring.

Lee put down the bag with the springs and the screwdriver and reached into his back pocket and pulled out a pack of cigarettes. He banged the pack against his closed fist and one of the cigarettes showed its head and Lee pulled it out with his grease-stained fingers and put it to his lips. He got it going with a gray steel lighter with a flip top, and only talked after he'd inhaled and the smoke lingered with his words.

Well, he started, Miss Lilly here came by the store—you saw her— looking for a spring for the door. Now, anyone can see that old spring is busted.

He pointed and we all looked at the white spring with the rust all over it hanging loose from the door, only two of its four screws still left and holding it onto the wood even though we all knew already it was busted and none of us needed to look at it to confirm that.

But she left without choosing which spring, Lee continued, and so because I want Mr. Olson to see I'm a good worker and understand the importance of customer service for repeat business, I came here with the springs and I'm offering to go ahead and make the fix for you folks. I sure don't see anything wrong in any of that.

Hank looked at him, then looked at me. But I didn't say anything. I stood there like everyone else until he looked away. He took a step toward Lee so that they were real close to one another and he placed his fingers on Lee's chest and he said it again:

It ain't the time, boy.

Lee smiled, real big and wide, as if he'd just heard the funniest joke, and then he started to laugh a little. But because he laughed the cigarette popped out of his mouth and because Hank was standing so close, the cigarette landed on Hank's shirt. Little sparks of fire came from it all the way through its journey down Hank's shirt to the ground where it came to rest, still lit.

Hank didn't bother to figure out if this was an accident or not. He looked at the smoking cigarette at his feet, then at the little black marks

38

of ash on his shirt, and without a word pushed Lee hard. On account of where he was standing, Lee fell backward off the top step and in trying to regain his balance threw up his arms but could clutch at nothing to suspend his fall and he went over and onto the grass.

When he landed, he grabbed at his knee. There was a good-sized tear in his jeans and I could see a deep red wound visible too, where the blood had started to pool up. Lee looked at his knee, then looked at us up on the porch. If he was hurt, he hid it well. Nothing on his face but surprise. Finally he got up, straightened himself out, and brushed himself off. All this took a few seconds, but it felt like centuries. He said nothing. Everybody waiting for the next thing and sensing there were no good ways for the next thing to be born into this world. And Lee still standing there, saying nothing.

Finally, he looked at me. Only at me. And it was as if he knew that in doing that, it was a more defiant act than anything else he could do or say. He had shut out the rest of the world, and the only thing in it worth anything to him was me, and me alone. Hank and Mama and that house and those springs still sitting there in that white bag on the porch, none of it mattered at all. And with that message sent, he turned and walked away.

I could tell that his knee was hurting him because he wasn't bending it all the way but he kept on walking as if that little sudden limp was a thing he'd had his whole life. He reached in his pocket for his cigarettes and seeing them all bent and mashed up, tossed the whole pack to the ground.

They say it's the little things. Mama most likely loved Hank in part because when he came back from the road and brought his little gifts and combed his hair across his head, those things probably mattered most to her—little things. Sure, at the end when you look back on a whole life, I imagine you only remember the big events. But they don't come around too often. It's the day-to-day things, the little things, that make up life. The things that when they're happening they don't even stand out to you. Lee could've fought back, screamed, yelled. He could've stood up for himself. But instead of that, he didn't say a word and just walked away and that was about the bravest thing I'd ever seen because he'd swallowed his pride on account of me.

It was a little thing that took the place of a big thing. And I knew it then, if I hadn't already known it. It was as if what my heart had been telling me, now my head was telling me, too: that I was in love with Lee and because of that it was easy for me to watch him walk away all bruised like that because I knew he'd be back. I just knew it. His look had said it all.

After he'd gone off, Mama turned to me and told me that I was not to see Lee anymore, period, and Hank said to me, You hear your mama?

I'm not deaf, I yelled, and I stormed into the house and straight to my room but not before I called out, And you're not my daddy, either!

They must have considered the matter closed because they didn't follow me and they didn't say a thing more about it and in fact I heard the porch door slam soon after and they were gone.

I thought of the bag of springs sitting there. It made me sad and I started to cry to think of something that had come into being with a specific purpose and then was left without being put into its intended meaning. I still feel this way and this goes for people and things and it tore me up sitting there on my bed imagining those springs. It felt like they were part of Lee himself, just lying there having come to no purpose.

I went to my window and looked out. The light was starting to fade. I couldn't see anybody out on the street and so it seemed Mama and Hank were long gone.

I was sure they thought they'd settled the matter and Lee was off now and wouldn't be back to bother me anymore because Hank was around to protect us. It was easy to let them think that because I knew better. I knew Lee would be back for me and I knew also that the next time he left my house, it wouldn't be in a cloud of dust or blood. And I knew another thing, too, decided it right then and there: the next time he left, I'd be leaving with him.

6

I guessed that Mama wanted to come talk to me, give me some of her hard-earned wisdom as she liked to call it. But the fact that they'd left without her coming into my room told me that Hank most likely suggested she just leave me be, that I needed space and time and that I'd soon enough come to my senses. There was some logic to that, I suppose. Though sometimes I felt like they didn't know me at all.

I figured maybe they'd left a note for me at the kitchen table. But there was no need for that as I knew where they'd be going. It was a ritual with the two of them that every time Hank came back into town they went straightaway to the bar where Mama worked so she could show everyone he'd returned. Mama liked going there when she wasn't working so someone else could wait on her for a change. The girls who worked there treated it like some big event and Mama sat at the bar and smiled and took it all in and had a few drinks while Hank swapped stories with the other men. I knew they'd be gone most of the night.

So I was still standing there in my bedroom, my head both blank and too full at the same time, when I heard the door open again. I assumed it was Mama and that she was torn up about the events of the day.

But it was Lee. He didn't even bother to knock. Just came right in. I couldn't say as I was shocked exactly, but I didn't know how to act or what I was supposed to do. Considering all that had happened, and the way I'd been feeling, it seems I would have jumped up and grabbed him and kissed him, joyful that he'd come back for me. But it wasn't like that. Instead, I sat there feeling paralyzed, out of breath even.

How'd you know which one was mine? I finally managed to ask.

Only three doors and the other two were open.

My heart was racing so much I couldn't have said anything more if I tried.

Well, come on then, he said.

Still I just sat there, sweat popping out on my forehead.

He decided not to wait for me and went straight to my bureau, opening the drawers like it was his room and not mine.

You got a suitcase? he asked.

I pointed to my closet and he went to it and pulled out the hard green case that used to be my pop's. He placed it on my bed, opened it up, and threw in a few of my dresses off the rack.

Sleeping bag? he asked.

I pointed to the shelf at the top of my closet, and he grabbed this too—the same sleeping bag I'd had since I was a little girl: blue faded denim with a soft inside and only midway up my chest by that point. Still, it was all I had.

You may want to get your undergarments yourself, he said.

So I did, but in a hazy state, and my toothbrush and hairbrush and some blue jeans and T-shirts and my socks and shoes and some unmentionables—items for my monthly. I only had half a box, so I took some of Mama's too. Just in case.

True, I'd dreamt about and wished for this moment, but now that it was actually happening, it all felt so unreal—too unreal. What didn't help was how little time it took to get my things. Maybe if it took me longer, it would have allowed my head to catch up with the rest of me, which seemed to be moving on its own without any orders from my racing brain. But I was awake enough to realize how little I actually had to take along. But so long as what you have meets your needs, it's all you ever need. Of course, this only goes for material items. As for everything else, well, sometimes the entire universe isn't enough to satisfy. I knew that, even then.

I went to the kitchen and found Lee rummaging through the drawers. He appeared wholly unsatisfied by the contents until he found some candles, which he threw in the case, and then Mama's flashlight too.

Well, that's that then, he said. Let's get out of here.

He started to close up the case.

Wait, I said, and I got my poetry books and put them in too.

He shook his head but didn't say anything about it, and we started down the hall.

Go ahead, I said. I gotta pee.

He went, moving quickly even with that big case, and when I saw him go out the door, I passed the bathroom and went to Mama's room.

I stood there a minute, taking it in. The little nightstand next to the bed with the lamp and her magazines. An unfinished sock, still with the knitting needle attached, on a chair in the corner. A tub of cold cream she used to rub on her knuckles and dab under her eyes every night. The quilt at the end of the bed, and the frilly pillows leaning against the headboard. A pair of her ratty old slippers tucked neat under the bed where she got in at night and out in the morning. Not much else.

I sat on the edge of the bed and listened to that familiar old squeak I heard at night when she was restless. I leaned down and took a big sniff of her pillow—that shampoo of hers that smelled like fresh-cut flowers— and I felt it then, the tears I knew were coming. And I came close to telling Lee I wasn't going anywhere. But I heard him back in the house, and he was hollering after me, Lilly, come on now, and I got up to go with him, like all my will from barely ten seconds earlier had gone. Disappeared like it was never there. Like I had no power over myself.

But before I went, I grabbed a pen and a piece of paper from Mama's dresser and wrote out a quick note, *I'll be fine, Mama. I love you*, and I placed it on her pillow.

There was more I wanted to say, but I didn't know what it was and I suddenly felt very rushed like there was this big wave or something sweeping me along and if I didn't move right that moment I might drown in it.

Case is in the car, Lee told me when I rejoined him.

Just before I walked out of the house, Herman, one of the cats, wrapped himself around my leg, raising his tail, and I scratched him behind his ear. He looked up at me and meowed, as if saying good-bye.

I walked out with Lee onto the porch. The light was just about gone now and the day's last shadows were blurring across the porch and the first hints of stars were starting to take shape in the sky. Lee stopped, standing there looking agitated, and then said, Dammit, hold on one second. He reached down for the bag of springs and pulled one from the bag and took the screwdriver that had been left there too. Then he pulled the two screws from the old spring and quickly put the new spring in.

Nothing Lee did ever only had just one purpose. He replaced that spring because he said he would, and he often told me a man isn't worth a thing if he can't be taken at his word. But I knew also that Mama and Hank would come home and maybe they wouldn't notice that spring right away but when they went to close that door, they'd know, even before Mama found the note I'd left. They'd know who'd been there and what it meant that I was not.

While he was putting the spring up, his jacket lifted and it revealed a gleam of metal.

What you need that for? I asked him.

What's that?

Isn't that a gun you got there?

And so what if it is?

What were you intending?

He finished tightening up the screws, tested the door, and then, grabbing my hand and leading me down the porch steps, said, I come back here with the aim of one of two things happening: either I was shooting that man dead or you're leaving with me.

That scared me, it's true, but not enough to stop me. He continued to the car and went around and opened my door for me. But right before he closed it, he said, Or both.

◦—

I didn't look back at the house as we drove away. I didn't want to see the flower garden or the tree in the side yard where Pop had bolted the swing and where, when I was a little girl, I would sit and pick flower petals and let my feet dangle and I would mark my height by where my feet landed until one summer they sat flat on the ground and after that I didn't sit on that swing anymore. And before I even knew it, we were beyond the house anyway and heading toward the center of town.

We passed the bar where Mama and Hank were and I slumped down in my seat but still looked anyway and I could see people moving about inside through the windows. But I couldn't make out anyone definite. There was no reason for me to be hiding anyway because anyone looking out at the street wouldn't see much more than an unfamiliar car going by.

About that gun . . . I said.

Protection, he said. You never know.

We passed the grocer and the hardware store.

Aren't you going to get your things?

Already in the back, Lee said. Bedroll. My clothes. Tools. Cans of food and three big gas cans, too, all full up. Plus, I got us a big tarp I took from the store.

You swiped it?

Lee looked at me.

45

I left there before I had a chance to get paid for the work I put in, he said.

What do we need a tarp for anyway?

We wind up sleeping outside some night, you'll be grateful for it.

If such a thing was inclined to bother me, there was little chance of turning back even if I wanted to. Before I knew it, we were heading out of town and it wasn't long before it was nothing but fields recently planted with corn and wheat and soybeans, I could guess, and there wasn't the slightest sign of people apart from the blacktop and the occasional car that passed.

Where we headed? I asked.

Away from here, Lee said, and he kept on driving. Just as darkness came on full and complete.

Jackson, Mississippi, November 4, 1992, 8:32 a.m.

The bus sits awhile at the Jackson station and so we take advantage by using the restroom inside. The one on the bus is still all right, best I can tell. But still, I want to limit my exposure. Besides, I need a break from all the yammering about the election. Most folks seem angry about it, but I don't understand the fuss; Louisiana went for the winner after all. It was weird to see that map on the news, this straight line right up the country, this side of the Mississippi all blue for Governor Clinton, and that side, my old side, where we're headed now, all red for President Bush. Me, I didn't even vote. I had to work that day, and, honestly, I couldn't get excited about it either way. But part of that, I know, is because things like voting I've always thought were best left to those with more normal lives and concerns, people who didn't feel that they had a debt to pay or otherwise owed in some way.

Lindsey's gotten off first and she makes her way without waiting for me. She doesn't even look back. I know she's still ticked at me, probably will be for years to come. It hurts me, the not talking, the hardly acknowledging my existence. But there's a part of it that's a relief too. When I started telling her everything, she just sat back, arms folded across her chest, headphones over her neck, and just watched me, those light eyes of hers boring into me. I'll never forget it.

I have some hope that this will be an unburdening, that some force will reach down inside me and rip it all out, this stone that's been sitting there for almost two decades now. But I know I'm fooling myself. There will be nothing easy about this and when I climb unsteadily off the bus and grasp the handle on the door, I can see my hand shaking and while I would love to chalk up my shaky limbs to being knotted up on the bus, I know what's really going on. I'm finally telling her the things I've kept to myself.

Back on the bus after our bathroom break and stretch, we decide to eat. Lindsey's still not talking much, but as we sit at the Jackson station chewing our muffins and bananas, she doesn't put her earphones back on.

"I've never seen you reading poetry," she finally says, a big chunk of blueberry muffin in her mouth. It's as if she's challenging me, calling me a liar without calling me a liar. It's a thing she's started doing in the last year or so.

I know better than to rise to the bait, though. "As you get older, you don't have time for things like you did when you were young. It's true what they say: boredom is a luxury only the young can afford. Who has time to sit and read books of poetry when you've got a daughter to raise?"

She scrunches up her face. "You can go back to your poetry if you want. Don't blame that on me."

"Didn't say I was blaming anyone."

Of course, I have plenty of time to read and in fact I do most nights if I'm not too tired that I conk out the moment I get in bed. It's more to the fact that the romantic, dreamy side has pretty much been knocked out of me. But she doesn't need to know about that.

47

"How come you've never gotten another boyfriend, like Grandma did with Hank. I mean, come on, Mom, don't you ever need a man?"

I look around the bus, aware of the close quarters and do we really need other people hearing this? But then I realize I'm just making excuses. I've been mostly whispering and with the empty seats around us, I'm sure that no one can hear me. And no one seems to be listening anyway.

"I doubt you want to hear about all that stuff."

"I know how things work."

"I know that. It's just that my guess is you'd think it kinda gross hearing about your mother and, well, all that sex and private stuff."

She shakes her head. "I don't care. I'm not a little kid, you know."

I just stare at her. I can hear myself saying this same exact thing to my own mother when I was Lindsey's age. Funny how that works. She's me and I'm her. But I don't tell her the truth of the matter, which is that I'm terrified to give myself so completely—my heart or my body— to another person. True, I'm older now and can better judge things— mostly myself—but you never know, do you?

Instead, I say, "Well, after your father, I just never found the right guy. And I've never been all that interested anyway. I've been perfectly happy with just the two of us. Some people need others in their life. You know, with intimacy and all. But I don't know. Seems I had all I ever needed. That could change, someday. But I've never been in any real hurry for that."

"Maybe after I've moved out."

"You planning on moving out?"

"When I'm older."

"You don't want to ask me about that gun? I figured that might be of interest to you."

She shrugs. "Not like he pointed it at you or anything. Forced you to go along at gunpoint."

To be able to penetrate the mind of a teenager. Does she really not care? Or is that her way of telling me, "Mom, you ain't so cool?"

It worries me some, her attitude about guns, like it's no big deal. There isn't a gun in our house and as far as I know she's never been around one. Guns in New Orleans mean something very different than guns in my old South Dakota. New Orleans has violence problems, though our neighborhood is nice and quiet, thank God. But still, a gun in our neighborhood or in our house could come to no good. Back where I grew up, everyone had a gun. Because everyone hunted. And even if you were that rare person who didn't hunt, you had a gun anyway. I remember there being several in our house and they seemed to be just in their places untouched and unloaded. I never had any interest. So when Lee had that gun on him, it didn't seem such a big thing. And I'll admit this, though not out loud, not to her: after he said he'd have used it on Hank, I know I should have been more scared than I was and called the whole thing off. But if I'm being completely honest, it excited me a little too.

"You want me to go on?" I ask.

She shrugs her shoulders, like it doesn't matter one way or another to her. But her earphones are still off, so as the bus gives a little tug and we pull away from Jackson, heading toward Memphis, I continue.

Shakiness or no. Terror or no. I continue.

7

May 1976

It was only when I woke that I realized I'd fallen asleep and that we'd stopped. I looked over at Lee and smiled at him.

He smiled back. I was watching you, he said. Just watching you sleep.

He shook his head a bit and blew a stream of smoke from his mouth. Maybe the prettiest thing I've ever seen, he said.

What time is it?

I have no idea.

We here?

Where? he asked.

Well, that's what I'm asking.

Honey, we ain't nowhere.

Why are we stopping in nowhere?

By way of answer, he leaned his head toward his window and pointed up. That's why, he said. Look at that. Hardly even needed the headlights.

I leaned down in the seat so I could see what he was pointing to. And there was the biggest, fullest, yellowest moon I'd ever seen, like it owned the universe, smiling down on us.

Lee opened his door and jumped up on the hood and held his hands out for me. Come on, he said.

I joined him.

That old man so close we can just about tickle his underside, Lee said, and then he put his hands together to give me a boost and I stepped on and then up and steadied myself by placing my hands on his shoulders. He grabbed hold of my waist and lifted me as high as he could.

Go 'head, he said.

I stretched my hand and then my finger and closed my eyes and imagined it best I could and I can swear it to this day that I touched the moon, all huge and bright and filling up the whole sky like there wasn't a thing else in the heavens.

I touched it, I touched it, I yelled out, and a feeling like an electric shock ran through me. I could feel it blast its way through my waist and into Lee's hands and he felt like heat on me and there I was, the link between him and that beautiful man up in the sky and I felt for the very first time that I was a part of something much bigger than I was or could ever hope to be.

I stood there smiling, all giddy with myself, before I realized Lee was shaking a bit with the effort and so to relieve him I told him I was ready to come back down.

We sat on the hood for a long time, staring at the moon and not saying anything, our hands holding each other's. The warm late spring air was on our faces, the smell of oncoming summer was in the air, and our shoulders were leaning in against each other—the whole world around us ours and ours alone.

We sat like that until the moon got smaller and then disappeared behind some clouds, the occasional brightness shining through before the clouds took it over completely and there was nothing left but darkness.

Once we were back in the car, instead of putting on the seat belt, I scooched over a bit on the wide seat and lay my head on Lee's leg. I could feel the rumble when he turned the key and revved up the engine a few times before he pulled the shift into gear.

Where are we going? I asked, excited at the prospect, whatever it might be.

Away from Paris.

Figured that already. But where to, not where from.

Well, you always wanted to see New Orleans, ain't that right?

I nodded, smiling. So wide I could feel my face ache.

Well then, New Orleans it is.

You know the way to Louisiana then? I asked.

Yeah, sure. South.

But we were nowhere near the interstates. We weren't even heading toward the highways, best I could tell. Lee had been taking the smaller roads, the two-lane ones with nothing but field and prairie stretching out on all sides.

Gonna take forever, I said, unless we get ourselves to a more proper road.

I was immediately sorry I'd said it. I didn't want to be a pain in the neck, but I couldn't help myself. I was teasing him a little, but it wasn't as if there wasn't truth to what I was saying.

Your mama's man no doubt knows every inch of these roads for a good thousand miles outta Paris, Lee said. And you can bet he'll be out there in that truck of his scouring the highways. Most likely calling his friends on the CB too, have them on the lookout for us.

I suspect you're right.

So for a few days at least we keep to these roads where the trucks are less likely. It'll be fun. For now, keep our heads low until they believe we're good and gone. Could be in Canada for all they know. Hey, he said, you know that the U.S. border with Canada is the longest demilitarized border in the world?

52

But what about New Orleans? I asked.

It ain't going nowhere, he said. And off we went, down the dusty two-lane road once again. Besides, he said, we've got all the time in the world.

⌒

The pink light of dawn was creeping up when I lifted my head from Lee's lap and looked around, trying to collect myself. It was only flat land going on forever, it looked like, with the straight road scratched out of it like an arrow. Dirt road and fields and nothing and no one else beside. It took me a minute to remember the events of the previous day. It felt like something I'd seen during one of those movies of the week or something and then fit into my own life. I tried to put all the pieces together: Lee, Mama, Hank, Paris. It had only been a night, but it felt like I'd lived half my life in the past day alone. It was a strange idea to get used to, but an exciting one, too.

I rubbed my hands over my eyes and swept back the hair that had fallen into my face, pinning it behind my ear, a habit I'd had since I was a kid and a thing Mama used to tell me made me look like a boy. Keep that pretty hair in front, she'd say.

Now that my head was clearing and a new day was coming on, the first day in this new part of my life, I thought about her, about what her night must have been like when she came home and realized I was gone. But I did my best to push it away, remind myself that Hank was there to comfort her.

Lee was fast asleep, leaning against the window, his hair down about his face. I left him there like that and quietly stepped out of the car. My arms and legs needed some serious untying. Lying like that for the past however many hours had left me achy and sore, so I stretched myself out and breathed in the fresh morning air. I walked out to the prairie to pee. It felt like I was an animal or something, hiking up my dress and taking down my underwear out in the open. But there was no one

53

around so there was no real reason for vanity. When I was done, I stretched some more and took in the long view across the grassland, how it went on forever, and the sky above was just this giant bowl. The only thing interrupting was the car where my man was sleeping.

A slight breeze chilled me, reminding me of those early fall mornings when Mama first started working nights at the bar and she'd sleep in and I'd leave the house early so as to not wake her and head out back and inhale the new day and wait for her to get up.

And then, before I knew it, I was crying, the tears coming just a few at a time at first and then, as if beyond my control, a whole mess of them and it wouldn't stop. There was no way around it: my heart ached for what I'd done to Mama, knowing how she must've been feeling, how empty that house must've felt without me there. It was the first night since I was born that I didn't sleep in my house; how that must've hurt her. I wiped at my face to get all the tears off but then gave it up and let myself sob and I was grateful Lee was asleep for I wasn't sure he'd understand. Besides, I didn't want him thinking he'd gotten himself mixed up with some little girl who couldn't control her emotions. When my crying fit was over and I walked back to the car, he was just then waking up.

Hi, he said.

Good morning, I said, hoping my face was clear of the evidence of my crying.

He nodded, still a little zoned out.

You know where we are? I asked.

He rubbed his eyes and I could see the blur in them, the way he needed to look this way and that, puzzling out the mystery of how we'd landed here, like some alien ship had beamed us to this empty place and left with no explanation.

We ain't nowhere, is all he said after a good look around. We ain't nowhere.

Well, where to now then?

He stepped out of the car and surveyed some more. Road behind, field to the left, field to the right, road ahead. His gaze barely flicked at each direction except the last one, where he fixed his eyes.

Looks like the road heads that way, he said. And we're already pointed in that direction.

He said this as he banged the hood a few times with his fist for emphasis.

And that, I guess, settled it. So we both brushed our teeth with the water and the toothpaste we brought, spitting the suds onto the dusty ground, which made us both laugh, and off we went once again. It felt like a real adventure and I was happy for it and I was happy also that I managed to get in a good cry. Like all good cries, it made me feel much better. Just needed it out of the system.

The feeling of excitement and adventure continued during the day, even as the hours ticked by without anything and we ran through what passed for towns around those parts: a few spread out farmhouses, grain silos, a single intersection with a couple of storefronts, houses with window boxes filled with geraniums, small packs of dogs loping up and down the sidewalks unattended.

Where do these people eat? I asked. No restaurants at all, or even grocers, it looks like.

They're farmers, Lee said, as if that explained it all.

Soon we stopped at a big empty field with tall grass.

Let's have a picnic, Lee said.

He went to the trunk and when he opened it I could recall hearing a rattling much of the night and could see now what all that noise was. A dozen or so loose tools lay scattered in the trunk next to the cans of food and gas. For someone who appeared to take pride in his few possessions, it seemed strange to me that Lee would have those tools laying there all scattered around and loose like they were. And the smell of them: strong and sharp and metal-smelling, like grease, like he'd never bothered to clean them.

Don't you have a case for them or something?

If I did, I'd have them in there.

I pulled out my sleeping bag and saw it had a big black scuff of grease across it. Look at that, I said, trying to no avail to wipe it off.

Lee rummaged around the trunk, pushing aside our suitcases and his bedroll and several pieces of torn newspaper—lord knows why he had those in there—and collected up some long pieces of thick rope he had and then gathered up the tools and wrapped the rope around and around them until they were all tied together. He cut off the end with his knife and then tied it off. Why he hadn't thought to do that earlier, I can't say. But it was all part of the contradiction in Lee: he could appear at some moments like he'd be prepared for about anything the world could throw at him, like he was born on edge and just waiting for problems to arise so he could fix them, even in those cases when the problems were of his own making. And other times, like with the tools, he could be careless. It was one of the things I liked about him, I'll admit. Made him unpredictable and I liked to be surprised.

Lee laid out the tarp and we sat there in the grass and ate the peanut butter sandwiches he'd brought from Paris.

Birds hopped from the tall hard milkweeds and left them bouncing in their wake and when they flew off, they sent little black seeds floating through the air and sometimes the whole sky filled with them and it was a beautiful sight. The birds were singing, too, and I imagined their song was just for us. The sun was high in the sky and the smell of the air was thick with perfume. It was a time of the year I loved, full of life, everywhere you looked.

So what are we gonna do? I asked finally.

I knew I was asking too many questions, but I couldn't help myself. The excitement was all in me, and Lee didn't seem to mind it anyhow.

Well, I suppose you could say we're doing it now, aren't we?

That's no kind of answer.

We take it one day at a time.

That's no kind of answer either, I said, smiling wide at him.

Well, Miss Lilly, Miss Hard to Please, I suppose we'll do what people do. After New Orleans, we'll find someplace warm where we can settle down. I'll get myself a job and you'll have our babies.

That right? I asked.

You know it.

He went to put his hand on my waist but then stuck out his finger and tickled me till I felt almost sick and I told him to stop.

He did so, but all that close contact had aroused the friskiness in him, and he started kissing me all over and running his hands over my chest and legs.

Stop, I said. Not out here. Anyone can come along.

All right, Lee said, and he didn't seem put off or rejected by this.

We folded up the tarp and put it in the trunk with the other things and got ourselves back in the car. Once we were settled into the front seat, he started up again, putting his hands and fingers in my underwear. I liked the feel of it. But I stopped him once again.

I'm not ready yet, I said, and I slid out from underneath his hands.

No? he said, and he did so with enough hurt in his voice that I felt sorry for him. I wanted to fix things and I liked how he wanted me the way he did. It wasn't that I didn't want to. It had to happen some time or another and I wanted it to happen with him. It was just that in the times I'd thought about it, I sure hadn't pictured my first time to be out in a field on a tarp or in the front of some car. Besides, I was scared. I'd never done it and I didn't know what it would be like. I'd heard it talked about before, at school, in the bathroom and such, and I'd heard some girls say how much it hurt and others talked about how there was a lot of blood.

When then? he asked.

I shrugged. But then I told him, We'll know when the time is right.

It seemed that he understood this because after another moment or two, time I took to readjust my underwear, he put in the key, pulled down the gear shift, and revved up the engine.

Okay, he said. Let's put her going then.

I wanted him to know it wouldn't always be this way. But I wasn't sure how to say that out loud, so I put my hand on his knee and rubbed back and forth, almost like I was petting him.

That ain't helping, he said.

I understood and stopped.

In due time then, he said. I'm sure it'll be worth the wait.

If I hadn't have known it before, I knew for sure then that I had a good man in Lee and I wished Mama and Hank could see us together and the respectful way he had about him.

And when I looked over at him, at the cool way he had of holding one finger low on the steering wheel when he drove, like he had the whole world under control, I felt that fluttering in my chest again and I also felt like I might have been the luckiest girl in the universe.

8

We spent the day going from one place to the next with what felt like no fixed reason except the way the road pointed. It was a freedom I'd imagined as a little girl and I was surprised and happy to find it had come to me already. We consulted no maps, but instead moved on with nothing other than hunch, and whenever we reached a fork or someplace that required a decision, we always felt the same about which way to go, like we were two people thinking with only one fixed mind. When the driving got too much, we stopped. Simple as that. No regard to time or place.

We found ourselves a spot near a forest and set up a makeshift camp. Lee had been in the Boy Scouts and had learned all about how to survive in the woods and so we were hardly in that spot an hour before he had rainwater catches set up and a trap for snaring rabbits or squirrels. Lee said that he was doing it for practice, that we still had plenty of food from Paris. I pitched in by clearing a space for us to pull up the tarp and lay out our bedding. It was a silly idea, cleaning out a patch of woods like that, but it made me feel as if I was contributing. It was also my job to collect firewood. I knew that for a fire it was best not to collect wood off the forest floor but rather to break off dead branches from the surrounding trees so it would be dry—the only thing my pop taught me that I remembered. But at least there was that, that the one thing he taught me had come in handy to know.

Lee complimented me, told me I had a knack for finding the best kindling. He headed off deeper into the woods to see what he could find while I put the final touches on. I stood back and took it all in: our bedding laid out under the full branches and our bucket full of water hanging on a low branch. There was something about it not quite homey enough. Of course, we were out in the woods, so that shouldn't be surprising. But still, I couldn't quite put my finger on what it was that was missing. Remembering we'd passed a big patch of wildflowers, I circled back and collected up whole handfuls and I took some of the frayed ends of Lee's rope and wrapped it around the stems and tied it all off. I made a pile of dirt and swept it up so that the flowers could stand upright. When Lee came back, I showed him the flowers, called it our new home, and waited for his reaction.

But his reaction was nothing other than to stare at those flowers and not say one word. Instead, he looked at them and at me as if in contemplation of something grand, and then he simply turned around, said, I'll be right back, and walked off.

I didn't understand it, but it sure made me feel silly for going through the effort, and I worried again that he thought I was just a dumb girl and maybe he was having second thoughts about me and about us and about what we were doing out there.

Turned out Lee had gone back to the car. He returned with two of the candles from the trunk and when he got back to where I was sitting and still feeling bad about things, he took some of the dirt, poured a little water on it to stiffen it up, and then stood the candles up on either side of the flowers. Now it's home, he declared.

That night we ate our pork and beans straight from the can over candlelight and flowers.

We lay down together and he kissed me and I kissed him back and I knew I was getting close to doing more with him. But I wanted it to be special, and he didn't push the issue and so we fell asleep on account of having missed out on much sleep the night before.

The next morning, very first thing, Lee climbed a nearby tree with the rope looped around his neck and when he got to the first high branch that was thick and sturdy, he tied the rope around it several times. He did this twice, about three feet from each other, and then got a piece of thick wood and spent a solid hour hacking and sawing it into the size he wanted with his knife and the tools he had. He threaded the rope around the sides and tied it off with some kind of intricate knot and from this he made me a rope swing.

Go ahead and try it, he said, standing back, his shirt and hair soaked through with sweat.

It was sturdy and held my weight without a problem. I didn't have the heart to tell him that the wood he'd used for the seat was knotty and stuck into you when you sat on it, so I told him it was perfect and I spent the next half hour making my bottom so sore I could hardly feel it for the numbness, but I swung and swung and told him I loved it.

We scoured the forest edge and found whole acres of honeysuckle for breakfast. We took a full hour or so, biting off the tips of the flower and sucking in the nectar, again and again until we had a pile of spent flowers at our feet and our jaws ached, from the effort or the many drops of what Lee called edible sweetness, I don't know. And then, because no amount of nectar can fill a person up, we enjoyed a feast of wild strawberries too, which Lee had discovered and called alpine strawberries, when he'd gone off to "take care of business," as he said.

He picked a whole handful of berries at a time, taking the ripest and juiciest ones and handing them to me like they were my due. We blew on them each before we ate to get off the bugs or whatever else was there we couldn't see, and that noise, that constant blowing noise, became like a lullaby to me. It's a noise I can still hear in my head to this day.

It was one of the ways Lee had of saying he loved me without even having to say it.

⌒

We stayed one more night in that place and we had canned corn and peanut butter sandwiches for dinner.

Afterward, I was collecting firewood and Lee was off checking the traps when I heard him yelling for me to come quick and at first I was scared for the sound in his voice. It wasn't something I recognized. So I went running to him and he was calling over and over: Lil, come quick. Lil! And I kept running and even though he sounded so close, I couldn't see him anywhere until it turned out I was right underneath him and he said to me, Look at this!

I looked up and there he was, halfway up a tree, sitting on a branch with a big stick in his hand.

Look, he said, pointing.

I didn't see anything, and I told him as much.

There, he said.

Still, nothing.

He took his stick and poked at a big hollow where two branches came together. As soon as he did that, a dozen or so bees came storming out and circled around his head and he had to swat them away and it wasn't long before he cursed one of them for stinging him.

Leave them alone, I yelled.

You kidding me? he said. We're gonna feast on honey tonight, baby girl. Those flowers and berries ain't nothing compared to what these guys have for us.

You're crazy, I told him. No way those bees are gonna let you get at their honey.

We'll see about that, he said, and took off his shirt. He wrapped it around his hand, the one holding the stick, and started poking the stick into the hollow, pushing it this way and that, and it was but a second before a hundred angry bees came swarming out of there and they were buzzing all around his head and I could see some of them landing on his bare chest, but he kept fighting and soon enough he'd scooped the nest out of the hollow and it came tumbling over a branch and fell to the ground. Lucky for him, too, for something in those bees' brains told them to follow the nest and so they quit Lee and he was able to come down from the tree. In the meantime, I'd run off a bit because the nest had fallen close to where I'd been standing.

Lee joined me on the ground and I could see red welts on his neck and chest. A couple more on his arm, one on his leg.

Hurt? I asked.

I'll be all right, he said. I could tell he had adrenaline running all through him and I knew, but I didn't say, that once that settled back again into his veins, he was gonna feel those stings something fierce. I'd once taken six stings at one time after unsettling a nest and it was the worst pain I ever felt. Of course those were wasps, but Lee must have had ten stings.

Now what? I asked him.

We were both standing there, looking at the nest lying on the ground and a whole swarm of bees in and around it, fired up and crazed.

Go fetch some water, he said.

I'm not your slave, I said, teasing him.

Come on now. Look at me, he said, angry, pointing out the welts, only then realizing, I think, that he'd even had so many.

No one told you to do something so foolish.

He stared at me. Please, he said, half asking, half telling.

I went off and got him his water. While I was at it, I poured a bit of the water into the soil to make some mud and then scooped up a big chunk.

When I returned, he was standing there still keeping his distance, with that stick still in his hand and his shirt wrapped around it, watching those bees as if ready to fight them off should they come after him.

Here, I said, handing him the water. Then I took the mud and dabbed it over his stings. It was an old trick I'd learned when I was a girl; it eases the heat and even helps to loosen up the stingers if they're still under the skin.

He let me stick on the mud and then he took the water and poured it all over the nest. A whole bunch of the bees managed to fly away, but most were stuck where they were. Silly as it might sound, but it tore at my heart to watch them struggle and drown as those little pockets in their honeycomb turned into prisons. I couldn't even imagine it: them doing what they do, protecting the hive, making their honey like nature had taught them to do, and then out of nowhere some huge force so much stronger than they were wiped them out, so many of them at once, and there was nothing they could do about it.

So it was with a real sadness in my heart that I didn't admit to out loud that we retrieved the nest and took twigs to scoop out the dead bees.

Lee said, Be careful. Even though they're dead, the stingers can still get you.

Any kid knows this so I didn't know why he felt he needed to tell me. I didn't say anything but just looked mean at him. I was still upset over it all. But it was not really him I was mad at. More like mad at the world and the way it works sometimes and feeds on the powerless. It didn't matter anyway if I was mad because he was too busy with his portion of the honeycomb to even notice.

And I will admit this, too, once we got all those bees out and we took the dripping and full honeycomb back to where we'd set up camp, I'd forgotten my troubles about the episode and instead enjoyed the sweetness of the honey. Lee told me it was a primal thing, like cavemen and all, that human beings crave sugar the way we do, that it went back to a time when we couldn't get energy so easy and so we developed a need for sugar that lasts to this day even though by the time we came around we could find it in little cubes in any old roadside diner. True enough. I could recall several times as a little girl dipping a teaspoon into the sugar bowl Mama kept for her coffee and swallowing it whole until she got mad and hid it from me.

And so after a while, even though he was covered in welts and mud, we sat with our backs against a tree and ate that honey and I even allowed a laugh and a few smiles and we let it drip down our chins and cheeks and kept at it until our teeth ached.

Yes, there are forces larger than we are and at any minute they can strike you down. For those bees it surely meant a bad end. But for me and Lee, in that moment, it felt like something or someone had decided to put us together and set us out on our own, that whatever force there was out there, it was one that was looking out for us. And because we were in love and were made for each other and soul mates, it must have been a grand and benevolent force working on us and we'd ride it out together.

And I can say it honest: life was very, very good.

॰

The next day, we were on the road a long time and all the adrenaline and excitement of the previous days had worn off in a tangle of poor sleep, heat, and boredom. There was nothing to see but the same thing every mile—fields and fields, soon to be bursting with corn, oats, rye, wheat, alfalfa—a landscape that the Great Plains are known for, I suppose. Despite my pleasure at being out on the road with Lee, I was plain bored. The only thing that broke it up was when we drove through the sad Indian reservations where everyone looked beaten down and even there the only thing to see of any interest were automobile graveyards, whole collections of dead and rusted out cars all jumbled together.

Can I? I asked, reaching for the radio.

Fine by me, Lee shrugged.

I turned and turned the dial but got nothing other than staticky talk, and nothing interesting about it: the primaries and upcoming presidential election, the chances for the Vikings in the next football season, and of course so much about the bicentennial. When I tried to turn from that, Lee told me to leave it. So I was bored all over and turned grateful only when our driving put us out of range of any station and we had no choice but to turn off the radio again.

At first, I felt a nervousness when the radio was off and all we could hear was the silence of our thoughts. I had it in my head that if we were a couple now, we should have had lots of easy talk. That's how couples are, I thought, or should be anyway. But then I told myself that the closest of couples are those that can be silent with each other. They don't need chatter to fill the space that's already filled with the presence of themselves. It was amazing to me that we'd already reached that point, there only a few days out of Paris. And so I felt better, and I decided not to take Lee's quiet as a sign that he was tired of me or anything.

Anyway, it couldn't all be perfect all the time. I knew enough to know that. But soon enough, we'd make our way south and I was sure that in New Orleans we'd have more fun than I could even imagine. I came to regard going to New Orleans as our very reason for being. I knew I needed to be patient, but I could almost feel it, out over the horizon somewhere, waiting to embrace me and Lee with open arms.

But for a little while longer, I'd have to endure the in between, being in the car for hours on end until everything hurt and the road and its endless sameness was a burden. At moments like those, I got stuck way inside my own head and couldn't get out. Back when I was still at home and I got like that, I used to like to find a place, down by the river, or on my old swing, or in the armchair set by the window in my house, and be alone with all those things rattling around in my head. Sometimes I enjoyed that feeling, but other times I was screaming to get out.

It seemed Lee understood all that, understood it without my even needing to say a word about it. Without any warning, he simply pulled the car off the road and made a beeline across the prairie, bumping all the way, testing out the shocks, I thought, the dirt piling up in huge clouds behind us, flattening the grasses and no doubt scattering millions of unseen prairie creatures. I didn't ask what it was he was doing. Instead, I just waited for the answer. And it wasn't long in coming: he skittered to a stop near some lonely trees pushing through the otherwise empty prairie as if God himself dropped them there on accident and decided to leave them be. Lee got out of the car and hopped on the hood and patted the spot next to him, a signal for me to join him. The hood was hot from the engine running all day and even though the day was warm, the heat of the car felt good, like it was alive and the third member of our little party.

The sky on the far horizon looked like someone had taken a sharp knife and sliced it right down the middle. It was blue as a robin's egg for quite some distance before us but then it was black as night. There we sat and watched that blackness roll on into itself and within minutes we were treated to one of nature's true miraculous shows. Far off on the horizon, stretching well across the Plains, a violent lightning storm had its way with the earth. Just an enormous black cloud and these yellow and white streaks shooting from it every which way and easily a dozen streaks every thirty seconds or so, and the amazing thing, the thing that I couldn't get over, was that we watched all this while remaining in complete comfort on the hood of the car dry as a bone. The storm never did reach us but rather spent itself out far from us, as if we were living in some kind of cocoon or something. This was the image in my mind, so I couldn't help myself and finally broke our long silence and explained to Lee what a metaphor was and told him this about the cocoon and he looked at me and said, You must think I'm stupid. Who doesn't know what a metaphor is?

And so now I knew to not make any assumptions about what Lee knew and what he didn't. And in any case, it was a lesson that sometimes the best thing to do is keep the thoughts inside and just take pleasure in what's in front of you. Not everything in this world needs a comment to it.

That night, we set up our tarp strung from the branches of the trees and lit a fire and made ourselves comfortable. We were getting pretty low on the food we brought with us and so soon we'd need to start either catching food—Lee'd had no luck with his traps so far—or visiting stores to buy it with Lee's money. But that would mean taking to the bigger roads and towns and I didn't know if we'd been gone from Paris long enough for that. But for now, my belly was full and I was comfortable. It was nice, just us two under the tarp, and we were silent with each other. As we'd now edged up against the start of summer, cold was hardly a problem, not even at night. And even if it was, we had each other to cuddle up next to. Lee put his hands on my cheeks and he kissed me real gentle and then he put his hand on my knee and I let him keep it there. He started to rub it back and forth and I felt a heat running through me.

But just like that there was a blinding flash and a mighty crash and the storm from before seemed to have finally caught up to us. It was a doozy and despite the short distance we had no time to get back to the car. So we huddled up under the tarp as the rain came on and at times that rain was so strong it hardly mattered that we were under the plastic for it felt like the wetness was reaching under the tarp and there was nothing to do but sit and ride it out. Couldn't even talk to one another for the noise the rain made beating on the plastic.

When it finally let up, we got ourselves out from under the tarp and took off our shoes to walk around in the rivers of mud. We let it squish between our toes and Lee ran up and grabbed a branch above my head and shook down all the rain that had collected on its leaves and gave me a good soaking—the parts of me that weren't already soaked, that is.

I ran after him and we went in circles sliding all over the mud and when he slipped, I finally caught him and jumped on top of him and we kind of fake wrestled—at least I gave it my all while he only pretended to—and eventually we wound up in a torrent of kissing and he got on top of me and pinned my hands to the mud, softly, and kissed me harder. He ran his hand up my dress and over my panties and then he put a finger inside me before I even had a chance to figure out what was happening, and when he pulled it out to position himself and take up my dress all the way and pull down his pants, we both saw that he'd got blood on him. He looked at me before he whispered, Yer bleeding. I pushed my dress back down and got up and walked back to the tarp. I didn't know it was that time of the month. Either it had come early or I lost track or in the excitement of everything, I'd plain forgot. Either way, it spoiled the mood.

Ain't nothing to be ashamed of, he called after me.

Never said I was ashamed, is all I said. But that was the end of that. I took care of it back under the tarp and in private, but it had put a damper on things.

Eventually he rejoined me and without any words to each other we did our best to try and get comfortable. But with everything wet and then turning chilled and, well, with everything else, I don't think either one of us slept a wink that night.

9

We drove for hours and hours in lord knows what direction, stopping every now and again only so that Lee could fill the gas tank from one of the cans we brought along or for us to eat from our dwindling food, or to stretch. Before we knew it, it was dark and then it had been dark for hours, and finally Lee stopped the car by the side of the road.

What are we doing? I asked.

I think that's enough for the day, he said. I'm plum beat.

We're not just gonna sleep right here, are we? In the car?

Why not?

Can't we find someplace else?

Where, do you propose?

Some town somewhere around here, I'm sure.

You've been in this car with me the last ten hours, haven't you, and seen what I seen. And what I haven't.

And so that's that?

Let's at least make the best of it, he said. He reached behind him and grabbed two of his shirts and handed one to me.

Here. Ball it up and put it behind your head for a pillow.

He did the same and almost instantly he was asleep.

Maybe it was the position he was in or because of the dust of the day coming through the open windows as we drove, but he started snoring away like an old man. I couldn't help but laugh because it was kind of cute and I looked forward to telling him about it the next day, ribbing him for it. I figured he'd deny it for sure, but I knew what I was hearing.

I was hopeful that in the morning he'd feel it was safe to get out on the main roads, on our way, finally, to New Orleans, and we could pass through some proper towns along the way, with restaurants and grocery stores and even motels, where we could get ourselves clean and get some rest in a real bed. Besides, even though that constant driving was no fun at all, it was only when we were moving that it felt to me like we were on our way to something grand, like pioneers heading toward the ocean or some other promised land. And the longer we sat idle, the more of that treasure that was rightfully ours would be lost. But it was a silly idea, I realized, because at least since we set away from Paris, we weren't really heading *to* much of anything, but rather away.

I was glad for Lee that he was sleeping, but no such luck for me. Instead, I stayed awake just about the whole night waiting for the light of dawn. I tried my best to sleep, but my mind wouldn't stop playing tricks on me. All night long, I saw things, shadows, jumping all around, on the side of the car, or in front, little flitting things like bats, but every time I tried to catch up to whatever it was I couldn't, and I wondered what creatures of the night were around or if it was all in my head.

But I heard noises, too, and at least once I could swear it, I heard something big bump up against the car. *Lee*, I whispered, frozen with fright, but he hardly even moved and after a while I realized that while I was waiting for it to come back, I was waiting for nothing because it never returned. Still, it was enough to spook me and I told myself that the moment dawn arrived, I was waking Lee and telling him we needed to get on our way already and no more of this sleeping by the side of the road.

71

But at some point I did finally manage to nod off and I was sorry for it because I had a terrible dream where I was one of those trapped bees and there was water all around and I was trying to break free of it, trying and trying, but I couldn't get free and there I was struggling and at some point I realized that Mama was there, and she had her hands out to me and she was crying and I was crying and she was trying to help me but she couldn't until finally I woke in a burst.

I sat there a few moments, trying to collect myself, and it was a hard thing because I had a real weighty feeling still pressing on me. Even though I was awake now and I saw where I was and who I was and what I was, it was like I was still one of those bees from the dream. It was a queer thing, I know, to even compare, because I was not a bee and no huge hand of God or something was going to toss water on me, but I could feel what those bees must have went through, taking their last squirming attempts at life, wriggling in their honeycombs, drowning the way they did.

Ever since I was a little girl, I'd had this feeling that at any moment something big and way beyond me would descend on me with no warning and there I'd be, struggling and wriggling, trying to get out from under something so much bigger than me and so much stronger too, that I'd be powerless to escape. And I felt it then, at that moment: not me, not Mama, not Lee, not his gun, would be able to get me out of it. It felt, at times, like it was just waiting for the right moment. I could feel its presence. I had hoped that now that I was with Lee all of that would come to an end. But it seemed that wasn't the case. Not yet, at least.

The moment a hint of morning came on, I tugged on Lee, woke him, and told him there was no way we were sleeping in the car again.

Well, what do you want me to do about it?

You find us some place else to sleep.

I know what he wanted to say, which was some version of what he already had—*What do you want me to do about it?*—but he didn't say a word. I can only imagine how I looked and I'm sure that I didn't look that morning like someone to be messing with.

In the light of day, we could see that where we'd stopped wasn't far from some woods, running as far as we could see in both directions.

I had my druthers, I'd sleep in those woods, I said. If there's a river there, we can bathe too.

You'd do that? he asked.

You've seen where I grew up.

I seen the shower in your house.

And you've also seen the creek where I took you. I can't count the number of baths I've had down there. On summer days, I'd march down there with soap and shampoo, and get right in. There's nothing like it.

The wonders never cease, he said, smiling at me and shaking his head. Well, let's go check it out then, shall we?

By now, the sun was up all the way and the day had broken fresh and warm. We set out across the grass toward the woods and soon enough found the river, just inside the tree line, like I figured. It was maybe twenty feet across, good flowing, deep and fast. Looked even like it was spilling its banks a bit and I figured those storms had fallen there too — or at least somewhere upriver. I dipped my bare feet in and felt the chill straightaway. Like ice. Beautiful wonderful ice and even though I'd hardly slept at all, it woke me right up. It was a gorgeous place, full of sunlight and big rocks that pooled up the water and then sent it on its way in ripples and foam. Just like that I felt happy again, happy to be in this beautiful place with Lee, and I could pretend we were on our honeymoon or something and the river was ours. Amazing how it is that things can change so fully and so quick.

I walked over to Lee and kissed him hard on the mouth and threw my arms around him. I love you, I said. I was surprised to hear myself say it. But it just came out.

What's bringing this on?

I've never said that to you before and so I'm saying it now.

Lee smiled at me.

Well?

Well, what?

Aren't you gonna tell me you love me back?

You know I do, baby.

You still haven't said it.

All right then—I love you. I love you, I love you, I love you. How about this?

He cupped his hands over his mouth and screamed as loud as he could: I LOVE YOU!

Then, from somewhere unseen in those woods, came a response: *I love you too.*

We both stared at each other, our eyes bugging out, wondering what on earth.

Finally, Lee yelled out, Who's there?

He put one of his hands in his pocket, where he kept his knife, and the other hand went behind him, to the back of his pants. Ready, just in case. It was times like these that I understood why Lee had that gun with him. He wouldn't ever allow anything to happen to me.

He called out again: Hello?

Hello! came the response.

There was a little path cut along the river and we followed it a bit, slowly, checking things out, and it wasn't long before we came across three fishermen. They were lined up along the river with their long poles, one of them yanking a fish out of the water. Sunlight caught the silvery scales as the fish twisted and turned on the hook and the man got it off and tossed it into a bucket. There was a fire going and three medium-sized fish stuck on sticks cooking above the flames.

The men stared at us kinda funny as we approached, like we were kids hooking school or something.

One of them said hello as we came closer. He was older than the other two, with deep lines in his forehead and around his eyes. Looked like he'd had a lifetime of worrying over something.

Lee put his hands back in front of him. Morning, he said.

Morning.

The other two didn't say a thing, but rather just looked at us and one of them was a huge guy and when he saw us he started making these terrible strange noises, like moaning, and getting really high pitched. I could hardly believe high sounds like that could come from someone so big. He had to be six foot and a half easy and approaching three hundred pounds. And wasn't he a sight: he started hopping up and down and flailing his arms and he continued that moaning. I was sure he was touched in the head some way, but the other guys were clearly used to it because they didn't even react to it and soon enough he stopped.

The older man said, I suppose your amorous declarations were for your lady here, and not us then?

Lee smiled at him. You got that right, mister.

I figgered.

Good fishing around here then? Lee asked.

Best in the county.

The man saw we had nothing with us but the clothes we were wearing and said, You gonna try your luck without poles?

We're just passin' through, Lee said.

The man took off his hat. He had a white patch right above his forehead whereas the rest of his hair was jet black. I'd never seen anything like it.

We were just about to have us some breakfast, he said. You're welcome to join us.

The smell of cooking fish was all over and I was hungry—we both were—so Lee accepted, saying, Much obliged, and I was glad for it.

The man grabbed two more fish from his bucket. He put each one on a rock and hit at their heads until they stopped flopping. Then he poked sticks through these too and put them on the fire. Soon, there were five cooked fish, the skin broken open and lots of beautiful white meat bursting out. We all sat down and took the meat off in chunks and then sucked at it delicately so as not to swallow any of the tiny sharp bones. It very well might have been the best breakfast I'd ever had.

Through the whole meal, I watched the big guy as he ate. He was calm, as if all he needed was food. But several times, he got up without a word and started walking away. And each time, the older man yelled at him to come back.

Gotta watch this one, he said to us. He likes to wander.

The old man wiped his hands on his pant legs. You say you're passing through. On the way to where? he asked.

The others seemed content to let him do the talking for all three of them as they hardly said a word—not only the big one, who didn't seem capable, but the other one, too. Just nodded every now and again.

New Orleans, I said.

Lee looked at me sharp and not altogether pleasant.

That's quite a place, the old man said.

You been there, Pap? one of the younger men mumbled.

In '52. With your mother.

They all went quiet, as if this bit of information carried with it something painful.

The Negro influence, the old man resumed, finally, looking at us. That city, it's got the Negro influence to it. It ain't like around here.

Well it ain't no place I'm fixin' to go then, the one guy said.

Didn't say good or bad, the old man said. Just different.

Well, we ain't going there anyhow, Lee said.

No? You just said—

Maybe someday. Far on down the line. But for now, I got a job waiting for me in Oklahoma. Oil.

I looked at him, but he kept his eyes from mine. On purpose, I could tell.

I'm Lee-roy, and this here's, uh, Violet, he said. We're planning to get married once we get enough money together.

Well, ain't that nice. Marriage is a beautiful thing, the man said. Assuming you got yourself the right woman. These here are my two boys. Mama's dead these ten years now.

Well, I'm sorry to hear that, sir. I truly am.

It's the way of the world, I'm afraid. Nobody's guaranteed happiness.

We sat in silence, pushed there by a private sorrow of this man's and his boys' that he'd made public and invited us into.

Well, he said finally, slapping his hands on his knees and getting himself up, I suppose it's time to get back to the river.

He and his boys kicked at the fire until it was smolders and then they went back to the water and picked up their poles.

We're mighty obliged, Lee said.

The man swatted at the air, saying it was nothing.

Mind if we sit awhile longer? Lee asked.

Suit yourselves.

So we stayed where we were, watching the men pull more fish from the river and putting them in their buckets and soon I'd fallen asleep from my lack of it during the night, plus the comfort and peace of everything and it was well into the afternoon before Lee woke me.

Liable to sleep the whole day away, he said, smiling.

It felt good, like much of the difficult parts of the previous days had washed away. I didn't feel like getting back in that car, though, and I told him as much.

Maybe we stay here tonight then, Lee said. Find a nice spot, make a fire, lay out our bedding. Can bathe in the river, too, just like you like to.

It sounded like a dream and so I told him, yes, I'd like that.

Well, then, let's find us the right spot.

We thanked the men again for the fish, whereupon the old one gave us more to take for our supper, and we thanked them yet again and took our good-byes.

They were nice, I said.

Sure were.

I like them. That one fella, though, I don't know.

Aw, probably just some kind of retard, Lee said. Harmless.

Lee, why'd you make up that story about us?

Which is that?

Our names, that stuff about Oklahoma.

We don't need too many people knowing too much.

New Orleans is a big city, I told him. Besides, I'm not a liar.

But he just repeated: We don't need too many people knowing too much. And I can do the lying for the both of us.

Fine, because I'm not interested in lying to people, especially strangers.

Honey, you let the rough stuff fall to me, okay?

I frowned at him. I didn't like talk of any "rough stuff," whatever that was. But I figured so long as Lee was always straight with me, that was the most important thing. Anyway, there were more immediate matters: namely, finding a good spot to stay the evening.

We came upon a little sandy spit near the river and down an eroded bank where the trees barely held on with their roots exposed. It would only be a matter of time before the land underneath them would disappear and the trees would tumble into the river. There was something about that I found comforting. It wasn't only us who would come and then go, all evidence lost. It's that way for all God's creatures, even the trees. And that's as it should be.

We'll set up here for the night, Lee said. It looks as good a spot as any.

He was right. Still, despite it, I was not altogether comfortable.

There are people around, I told him.

Just those fishermen. They're not coming back here at night, and we'll be up and gone early.

Lee told me to collect some firewood and he'd go back to the car to get the tarp and the bedding.

I'll put the car in that high grass, too, he said. Keep it from too plain a sight. Don't need anyone poking around.

I watched him go and then began collecting the wood. I walked from tree to tree, snapping off small dead branches, before an enormous heron startled me. It was hardly twenty feet away and I hadn't even seen it there. It made a swooping sound, its great wings batting at the air, almost like the very sound of silence itself, and then made its way along the river, so low its wings rippled up the surface, before it flew out of sight. I watched its path and then the river itself, running swift in some places, hardly moving in others, and I was all so taken with it. I could never get tired of a place like that, with the sunlight bouncing off the water and how the branches of a weeping willow, batted about by the breeze, threw both light and shadow across the surface. I forgot about collecting wood for the moment and went down to the bank so I could watch that glorious show. The sound of those heavy branches dragging themselves across the water, the rustle of the leaves and the swoosh of it, and the way the sunlight broke and splintered and rippled, it was just beautiful. Water bugs skimmed across the surface and I imagined those little ripples must have been like ocean waves to creatures so small. And above them the dragonflies darted this way and that and it was all so peaceful and beautiful it almost made me want to cry.

I was glad for the moment to be alone and enjoy it. But I allowed myself only so long down there. Besides having a job to do, I know how these things go: it's better to take in the beauty of something and lock it up in your brain before something comes along to spoil it. So I dragged myself away and got back to collecting the wood, humming tunes to myself while I did, a habit I tried not to do around Lee for all it would drive him crazy.

I got a nice little pile going before I realized there was noise besides my humming, and it was coming closer. It was a strange noise, kind of in and out, going high and then grunting low and it seemed somewhat familiar to me but I couldn't quite place it.

Lee? I called out.

The noise got more distinct and I knew then what it was. I froze, letting the wood in my hands fall to the ground. I wanted to call out for Lee again, but my voice left me. I was paralyzed, just standing there, waiting. And then he came, that man from earlier, but he was alone and when he saw me he got all excited and his arms went up again and he was shaking his hands and moaning and he started hopping up and down. My voice returned to me and I called out for Lee but he was probably too far away.

So I started yelling at the guy.

You leave me alone! I yelled. You're gonna get in big trouble.

He looked at me like he didn't understand me or didn't care.

My man will be back any second now and you better not be here when he does, I yelled.

He cocked his head at me like a scared dog. We were just standing there, staring at one another, maybe twenty feet apart. The trees started swaying and I was trying to keep the guy in focus, but he was going in and out and I tried to call out for Lee again but nothing came. It felt like the world was spinning too fast for me and I could barely hang on.

Suddenly he got this real mean look and he lunged at me. His hand struck my face and I went down. He was on top of me and he had his huge hands on my leg and he started pushing up my dress and putting his hands all over me and I was screaming and screaming and I could hardly breathe. It was like the weight of the whole world was on top of me and there was nothing I could do, no way to break free of it. I punched and kicked best I could. I scratched at him, but it did nothing. His hand was here and then there and his weight pressed on me and the leaves spun and I tore at his hair and the earth below me pushed up from that side and I was pinned in between two things with no give and no mercy and it was like a terrible nightmare, one from which I had no chance of breaking free.

But then the guy started bobbing his head this way and that like he was ducking hornets and it was only then that I realized Lee was behind him whacking at the guy's head with a big tree branch. At the same time I was still scratching and kicking and I wound up kicking him between

80

his legs and this, in combination with Lee taking whacks at his head, got him off me. I crawled away toward a tree, where I sat against it and cried.

Lee was standing over the guy when he got up and in one easy swing the guy knocked the branch out of Lee's hands.

Lee backed up, said to the guy, You'd best just hold it right there. Neither of us wants this going any further. Just get yourself on out of here before it gets any worse.

But he gave no indication of understanding and after a moment to clear his cobwebs he jumped at Lee. But he slipped on some leaves and took a tumble that would have been funny if it all wasn't so dead serious.

Lee watched as the guy got himself off the ground and took another lunge and that's when Lee pulled the gun from his back and held it out in front of him.

Mister, I'm gonna tell you one last time, he said.

But the guy still didn't seem to understand, or to care, and he took a swipe at Lee yet again.

You're out of warnings, Lee said, and he pointed the gun right at the guy's chest.

The guy yelped and seemed confused. At first he just stood there. But then he picked up the stick that Lee had had and held it out in front of him and despite everything it made me sad that this man—there was clearly something wrong in his head—believed that a stick and a gun could be used to the same effect.

So there they remained in a standoff before Lee finally lowered the gun and muttered, This is ridiculous.

But then the guy tossed the stick at Lee and jumped at him, with more coordination than I would have thought possible, and he banged into Lee's arms and the gun went flying, skittering through the leaves. It slid straight to me, bumping into my feet.

It sickened me, the way it shined with the wet from the grass and the barrel like an open oily mouth. Its blackness looked plain evil.

He and Lee were on the ground wrestling and the guy was getting the better of it, so I needed to do something. I got up and grabbed the stick and I started whacking at the guy, but I wasn't doing a great job because I was afraid I'd wind up hitting Lee, so mostly I was dancing around them as they rolled back and forth, the guy trying to squeeze his hands around Lee's neck and Lee scratching at his eyes and face. I got one good crack at him, right in the back of the neck. That caused him to rear up so he was straddling Lee and that's when Lee kicked him off.

Get the gun, Lee yelled.

I did it without thinking. The guy was up now and coming straight for me so I lifted up the gun and pulled the trigger.

I've never heard anything so loud.

It echoed across the whole woods. But once that echo died away, it was dead silent.

I had a feeling like coming to, waking up from something and stepping into the living world from some fantasy place. But then I was on the ground, on my knees. The gun had fallen from my fingers and was sitting on the grass. Lee was standing there staring at me. And the man was standing there too, looking first at me, then at Lee, and it was a long time—it felt like forever—before he and Lee, and then me, too, realized that I'd missed. I'd sent the bullet deep into the woods, where it had probably lodged into a tree.

I was still standing there, not moving, falling back into that other world where I couldn't hear anything or see anything or even feel anything. Just standing, dumb. Even as the man ran toward me and even as Lee dove on the ground and grabbed the gun and rolled over and shot that man straight in the belly.

He made a terrible sound, like he'd been punched real hard and the air was leaking out of his lungs. He looked down, at the red splotch on his shirt getting wider and wider, coming up from his stomach.

And then, like rising from the depths of hell itself, he let out a roar that spoke of terrible vengeance and pain and that was more than enough for Lee, who fired three more times at him until his body fell out from under itself and he crumpled silent and dead onto the leaves.

Lee got up. I was crying. And that man wasn't moving.

Finally, Lee gathered up his courage and went over and poked at the still body with his foot a few times until satisfied and then came to me. I'd crawled over to a tree and was sitting against it, the bark digging into me. I could feel every square millimeter of it, like all my senses had gone from numb to high alert. It seemed even the echo of the shots still rang through the woods, bouncing off the leaves, leaving behind a great big silence as everything shooed away from that great noise.

You all right? Lee asked. But I could hear in his voice that he was not all right. When he reached down for me his hands were shaking.

I nodded. I'm all right, I told him. But I wasn't.

You all right? he asked again, as if he hadn't heard me.

He hadn't enough time to do what he was after before you got back, I said.

Lee's voice and hands were still shaking and he kept looking back at that body like it was gonna jump up and grab us or something.

My hands were shaking now too, and I unclenched my aching fingers.

Come on, he said. Let's get out of here.

But I didn't move.

Come on, he repeated. If they're around, those other two had to hear that and they'll be coming soon enough looking for him.

We started to make our way out of there, gathering the other things Lee had brought back with him. He was calmer now, more together. But when I took one final look at that dead man, I started crying again like a little girl.

Lee didn't slap me in the face to calm me, like they do in the movies. That would no doubt have made me even more upset. Instead, he looked around as if what happened hadn't and maybe it would all go away if we only willed it that way. But then he pulled himself together and grabbed me by the shoulders and gave me a slight shake, and said, It's gonna be all right, but we gotta go. Now.

We began walking up the path and then without either of us saying anything or I believe even realizing it, we were jogging and then running full speed, running as if we believed you could run from your past and there he was, that man, a part of our past now that promised to never go away. But I knew better. There would be no going back for me. I was one Lilly when I left Paris, and now, just days later, I was a different person altogether, a person maybe capable of anything, a person who experienced things way beyond her. Had anyone told me that before, without any specifics as to what that meant, I'd have seen it as nothing but good. But experiencing things, being capable of anything, well, it cuts both ways.

When we got to the car, Lee threw everything in the back and we jumped in and he started up the engine and we got out of there, skidding away and speeding off. We drove, not saying a word, and he smoked cigarette after cigarette while we moved on through the night in silence and by the fifth or sixth cigarette his hands were no longer shaking so much and he seemed to be Lee again. We needed to keep going, get ourselves as far away from that place as we could and only hope that the man's companions didn't find him for another day or two at least, a time in which Lee and I might be three states away.

I thought about that man's father, and how he had already lost his wife, and . . . well, I had to cut off that line of thinking. Otherwise, it would have been just too much to bear.

Give me one of those, I said.

Since when do you smoke?

I didn't answer, so Lee gave me one, lighting it up for me on his own.

I inhaled and it burned straightaway. I coughed a fit. It tasted terrible, but also good in a weird way. I could feel the smoke curling around my insides like some alien filling up the empty spaces. But soon enough, my head was spinning and I was leaning out the window to throw up.

Whether from the cigarette or from what had happened, I can't say.

10

We put as much distance between us and the scene of it as we could. Lee took the roads faster than usual and for the first few hours turned down ever smaller dirt tracks until we discovered that we'd come to the end of the line: the road just stopped, in the middle of absolute nowhere.

Why on earth dig out a road that leads to this, Lee said, waving his hands at the empty prairie.

Maybe they never got around to finishing it, I said.

He was jumpy and I was nervous and we were neither one of us ourselves. For now, we didn't talk about it.

But there was no escaping it.

What else we didn't say but rather came to simply realize was that we'd actually stumbled upon a perfect place to lay low until the morning and let whatever was going on over that dead body play itself out far from where any person would think to look for us. We put down the tarp and the bedrolls and sleeping bag and huddled up together and slept right out in the wide open with the stars twinkling and the night insects chirruping.

I don't know if I've ever had a more peaceful night in my life, before or after. Funny thing to say, considering, and I can't say how it happened that way, but it's true. Like it had hit me that, yes, I might be into something now much bigger than myself, but there was a certain pride in that somehow, all mixed up in the shame and horror of it, too. But I had a bad feeling that idea probably wouldn't last so long, that the pride of it would disappear soon enough with only the bad taking its place.

The next morning, early, we circled back the way we'd come until we hit a paved road and this time turned in the opposite direction.

Keep your eyes out for some place to eat, Lee said. I'm starving.

I was still okay that morning, almost as if the dawning of a new day had somehow pushed the event into some distant past that might not have even been a real thing but rather some sort of shared nightmare, a bad dream we managed to both have together. And because we were in it together, it seemed to me that the burden of it was cut in half, to be shared by the both of us. Besides, I told myself, I needed to be strong for Lee; after all, he was the one who had to carry the weight of the actual killing. The least I could do for him was make it so he didn't have the extra responsibility of having to keep me calm, too. Now that it was a new day, we acted as if we could simply turn our faces forward and resume a kind of normal life. Breakfast, for one. We were on the lookout for breakfast. As normal as could be.

But it was a long time before we saw any place we could stop. Instead, more road and dust and prairie, for hours. But then finally we drove straight into a town, there with no warning: it was called Duvray, and it had a diner just outside the main square. Where Lee parked the car was right next to a park with plenty of shade trees and benches and so we stretched ourselves out for a few minutes and watched the townsfolk congregate, with mothers talking to one another, and their little children swinging and playing in the sandbox and climbing all over these big stone turtles they had spread around. Some of the bigger kids got on the seesaws and pumped so hard they tried to throw each other off and next to them littler kids went back and forth on these painted animals on huge springs. We both sat and watched like we'd stumbled upon the biggest city in the world or something, such was the effect of where we'd come from. But there was another thing that kept us there, and it wasn't something either of us acknowledged. But I knew it anyway: the longer we sat at that park and acted as if everything was normal, and watched ordinary people getting about the business of their lives, we could pretend that we were just part of the landscape also. That everything was perfectly normal with us, too, and there wasn't a dead man left behind and even if there was, he would mean nothing more than a stranger in a cemetery.

But after around a half hour of this, we remembered our hunger and headed to the diner. The whole place was decked out in red, white, and blue, like the rest of town.

You think this is safe? I asked as we settled ourselves in.

He nodded. But let's not stick around, he said.

We gorged ourselves on pancakes and eggs and bacon and juice and coffee.

During the meal, me and Lee just looked at each other a lot, catching eyes and not saying anything. We knew it was there, so there was no reason to talk about it. Instead, we ate. We stuffed ourselves as if the more food we put in, the less of a hole there might be in us created by the fact of it, that unmistakable fact no matter what we might have told ourselves otherwise: the day before there had been at least one more person walking this earth and then there wasn't and that was on account of what happened. There was a good excuse behind it and I told myself that I wouldn't worry over thinking otherwise, but still, it was there and I couldn't know if I'd be able to keep it inside like that forever. So instead of talking about it, we ate, ate like we hadn't had any food in a week and even ordered some pie to go.

Lee drank his coffee black as it comes while I mixed mine with heavy milk and lots of sugar. He watched me tossing in my three cubes and he smiled the way he always did when he thought he was above something he didn't understand and said to me, You waiting until the spoon stands up straight? No, I said, and that's about all the talk we had for each other.

I didn't really have the taste for coffee at that time and so all that sugar was the only way it was palatable to me. Mama made coffee every morning and from when I was a little girl I used to wake to that smell, and its scent was like the smell of safety because it would pull me from my sleep and as I'd be coming to, that smell reminded me of where I was and that I was under covers and there could be snow or rain outside and it didn't matter. I'd drop my feet to the floor and if it was winter I'd put on my fuzzy slippers and go to the kitchen, where Mama would be with her chipped coffee mug and a magazine, slowly flipping the pages in such a way that I believe she was only looking at the ads and not really reading anything, maybe imagining herself as one of those people in the ads who always looked so happy with this thing or that or in that place and not in Paris. So when I was probably five or so I insisted on trying some of her coffee even though Mama warned me I'd hate it. I whined for all heaven to have some and boy was she right. I took one sip and immediately spit it back into her cup. And because I'd been eating a blueberry muffin, bits and chunks of that fell into the coffee and she had to toss the whole thing.

I told you you'd hate it, she said, angry at me for ruining her coffee. But in later years, it became a joke between us. It was only around the time Lee came into my life that I'd tried it again and I could tolerate it, so long as I had enough sugar and the bitterness was taken out of it. And this morning, I could hardly get enough of that coffee and that sugar.

Well, you kids sure was hungry, the waitress said when she refilled our coffee cups.

Yes, ma'am, we sure were, Lee said.

She snapped her gum and winked at us. I could tell right away she was a decent person who'd never done anyone any harm. I used to think that was pretty much how the world was divided up: those who do harm and those who don't. At least I was brought up to think that way. But I was coming to understand things might not be so simple. Which camp it was me and Lee fell into, for example.

But as for the waitress, I could tell she was a kind soul and never hurt anyone. She kept a permanent smile on her face and she did this thing with her hair, a big swoop of it she had rising toward the top of her head into a tight bun, where she pushed her pencil in there and it stayed put and then she'd pull it out again when she needed it.

Whenever you kids are ready, she said when she laid the bill on the table. I had this weird feeling that Lee was going to say we needed to run when she wasn't looking and skip out on the bill, so I was relieved when he pulled out his money and put down five dollars. I didn't know how it worked in that particular diner, but I imagined the waitress got nothing if people ducked the bill and maybe she even had to cover what was lost herself. I couldn't abide such a thing with this waitress, I liked her so much.

I knew from Mama that a waitress didn't make much money. Enough to get by, and I would guess easily enough in a place like Duvray, but still. It's hard work, waitressing, hard on the feet and back and sometimes, especially in a place where people get to drinking, like where Mama worked, it can be even harder because not everyone treats you with respect and there's almost nothing you can do about that.

Lee finished his last few bites and instructed me to do the same.

I'm full, I said.

It might be awhile.

Full is full.

So he ate my leftovers, too.

And then we got ready to leave and that nice waitress told us to take care of ourselves and we promised her we would. Once we were outside, I realized I was staring through the window, watching the waitress as she ran from table to table, filling coffee cups, dropping checks, pushing in her pencil, smiling. I had this crazy idea that I wanted to stay, park myself in a booth and watch her all day and then go home with her at night, help her take off her shoes, even pour her a tub of hot water to soak her feet.

Come on, Lil, I heard Lee say. We gotta move.

And so we left Duvray behind like it never was.

When you wake up in the same place every day and you do the same things and the only changes are too slow to take notice of, the days pile one on top of the other without any true meaning. When you're living the life Lee and me had set up for ourselves, you'd like to think it'd be different. There are places and people that come into it and then leave as quickly and so you realize nothing really means anything there either because there's not the time for it to. It's a funny realization, and one I wasn't so sure I was all that happy about learning. But, still, one has to learn about the hard lessons of life eventually. In the end, even the most trying days turn into normal when they're over.

∽

I don't know how many miles of those roads Lee had traveled before, but I can say for sure I'd never been there, wherever we were. Before then, I'd never been more than fifty miles from my childhood home, and that was for the funeral of a great-uncle I'd never met and who lived three counties over. But it was getting later and later and Lee showed no sign of stopping anywhere. Of course, there wasn't really anywhere to stop and so when he pulled the car to the side of the road, I figured this was it then. But still, I couldn't help myself.

Aren't we going to try and find a motel? I asked. Considering.

Considering what?

What happened last time.

Well, on account of what happened last time, and what we left there, makes about as much sense as government cheese we start showing ourselves in places like motels, places people might be looking. Bad enough we ate in that diner.

90

He got out of the car so that even if I wanted to respond, the conversation was over. He went to the trunk and pulled out the bedding and then came back and handed it to me.

It isn't cold, I said.

Not yet.

But I'm not even sleepy.

Well, that's fine because neither am I.

Why'd we stop then?

He didn't say anything, just smiled and inched over to me and started kissing me. It felt good so I kissed him back and soon his hand was on my knee and inching its way up my dress.

No, not yet, I said, and I gently pushed his hand away.

He sat back where he was, looking like he'd been scolded.

I'm trying my best to be real patient, he said.

I told him I was sorry. The memory of that man and what he was trying to do to me were still too fresh in my mind and I needed a little more time. We can still kiss though, I told him.

I almost said sorry again, but he was already balling up his shirt and putting it against the window and leaning into it. He readjusted a few times, punching at the shirt a little to get it right.

I wanted to say something to make it better, tell him that we'd make love soon enough. But I couldn't find the words.

After another minute, he told me he had to go take a leak and went off into the fields and he was gone awhile. No doubt he was sore about everything and wondering if he'd gotten himself mixed up with a silly girl. It was just that I wanted the first time to be something special and not like this, so soon after the incident at the river and all. I know it must have been hard for him, especially as we'd been out on the road a week, and I imagine it's true what they say, that it's harder for men than women, generally speaking. But I couldn't. Not yet.

So when he returned I didn't say anything more about it. He seemed a little better about it anyhow, less frustrated, and soon enough he was asleep.

91

I sat awake for a long time, thinking things over. I wondered how it was that I felt so safe with Lee. Before I left home, if I imagined something like this trip and how it started, I'd have thought I'd be awful lonely without Mama and scared of what was coming next, especially true considering the episode with that awful man. I'd be sure I'd want nothing more than to make Lee take me back to Paris, where I could crawl into my bed under the covers and wake in the morning to that coffee smell and to Mama in the kitchen. But I was surprised at how much of that turned out to be wrong. For one thing, if I went back home, it wouldn't be me and Mama, but me and Mama and Hank and while he was all right enough, his presence in that house changed everything. When he stayed over, they usually went out for breakfast and left me behind and it was the same discussion every time: Mama said, Let me make you some eggs and toast here, and Hank would say, Let someone else wait on you. I got money and no better way of thinking to spend it than on you, and she'd smile and giggle and let herself be pampered, which I surely couldn't blame her for. But then there I'd be, making my own breakfast, or skipping it altogether, and even if I wanted coffee to sip at and then spit out, I wasn't even sure I'd know how to make it right.

I couldn't make it out so it was like Hank or Mama pushed me away. It was more to the fact that I was getting older and maybe Mama wasn't so crazy when she said she'd blink and then I'd be a woman.

She was right in that some of the things that happen only to a woman's body had happened with mine and there were feelings I had that told me I was not a girl anymore and when I looked over at Lee, there was this thing that went on where for the slightest little moment I could hardly breathe. Like my heart was bouncing around inside my chest and while I couldn't say for certain what was going on in there, it sure told me something. And what happened down by the river cinched the deal. Lee was a stranger not so long before and I suppose without either one of us even saying it, he'd become my boyfriend, even before we'd left Paris, but now, because of what happened and the secret we shared, it was much more than that. Now, I realized as I watched him sleep, I knew we had a deeper bond between us, something dark and terrible but something that would be our secret to keep and to link us to one another, no matter how ugly a secret it was—one that I suspected would be there even until the day we died.

11

We were another three or four days driving around, stopping wherever we could to get gas or food or stretch our legs between the long empty spaces. At night, we found the best places we were able and warmed ourselves by a fire and slept the best we could. Some nights it was easy; others I could hardly catch a wink of rest. Sometimes, thoughts of that man came back to me suddenly and I had to reckon with the fact that it was no bad dream but rather a real thing and I marveled at how I was at peace with it the first night after. But more and more that peace seemed to elude me in the dark and quiet hours. It was hard to sleep, and because it was hard to sleep, I realized how uncomfortable I was. In the morning, I woke up with dirt in my hair and an awful taste in my mouth and I hated it.

But you can get used to anything, and as the days got on, we adjusted well enough and eventually the bad thoughts became less, even at night.

One of the biggest problems had become boredom once again, which, all things considered, is a pretty good problem to have, I suppose. I'd only taken two books from home—one Dickinson and one

Whitman—and I'd read them both ten times through already. Without those as a distraction, there was little else to do but think.

I started to think of simple things I'd never given any thought to before. Clicking on a lamp, for instance. You never consider the miracle of that when it's available to you. But sleeping outside, when dark comes on and there's nothing to do except live with it, or else run through the effort of making a fire and sometimes it rains and it's no use even trying, that's when you think of it. A fire isn't an even kind of light anyway, so you can forget about reading even if you haven't read the only things you have a bunch of times through already. So you think then of clicking on a lamp. A simple flip of a wheel or a push of a button, what a luxury that is.

There were other things I missed. We had a chair back in the house in Paris that sat near a window. And for part of the year, the coldest part, the sun rested right on that chair for an hour or so in the morning. And on those mornings, I soaked up the sunlight and read my poetry.

I missed that chair and I missed the warmth of it, the way I closed my eyes when the sun rose to my face and the whole world was bright behind my eyelids. And then when the sun moved off my face, I could open my eyes again and watch the stardust dancing in the light. The whole world seemed so still and peaceful at those moments, like all the planets had stopped and somehow the center of the universe was me in that chair in the sun with my book of poems. At least for that hour, anyway.

I think it might have been on account of missing things such as these, but there were days when I woke up in the foulest mood and I couldn't break out of it.

When I got in one of these mean moods, Lee tolerated me well enough. He just let me be, knowing I'd come back eventually. He was almost always in the same mood, just about all the time, and he hardly ever got a holler tail. He thought a lot. But even if those thoughts were bad ones, ones that haunted him, or worries he might have had or regrets over things that couldn't be changed like all people have, you'd never know it to look at him. He could just as well be thinking about why the sky was blue than about that dead man we left behind.

To try and help kill the boredom, I fiddled with the radio dial whenever I could, hoping to get hold of some good music. We could get stations in when we came near towns, but the music was always the same and far more often than not, I hated it. I got so sick and tired of those same songs over and over. It all seemed so top layer that stuff. I suppose some of it was catchy enough at first. That "Right Back Where We Started From" was all right in the beginning. In fact, the first few times Lee and I heard it we'd sing it at the top of our lungs and laugh, but after a dozen times of that it lost its novelty altogether. There was also that "Welcome Back" song from a TV show I didn't ever watch, and some dopey remake of "Shop Around" by a duo I'd eventually come to understand was called the Captain and someone-or-other. Teal, I think it was. At first, I liked "Silly Love Songs," by Paul McCartney's group after he left the Beatles. But I grew tired of that, too. Now, as summer started coming on stronger and hotter, as if it was meant to coincide with intolerable things, that awful old "Afternoon Delight" song was on almost every time we turned the dial. You couldn't get away from it.

None of it did a thing for me and I was relieved when Lee turned the radio off. As far as the music went, nothing could compare to what Mama had introduced me to when I was very young. She'd done it with-out sitting me down and saying, Hey, Lil-Bear, you gotta hear this. In-stead, she just took the albums out of their sleeves and set them on the turntable and, depending on circumstance or her mood, I guess, either danced by herself in the middle of our family room or swayed at the kitchen sink. One record she wore out completely was a Mother Earth album, played it over and over and over again, a hundred times a day it seemed like. Most especially this "Down So Low" song. To this day it gives me the chills to hear it.

And whenever one of those awful songs came on the radio that seemed like the musicians or the singers were barely putting themselves into it, I got to thinking once again about Mama and the way she would stop whatever she was doing when "Down So Low" came on—just stop, close her eyes, and sway. Lost to the world, giving herself over to that singer with a voice a mile deep. It gave me the shivers to hear her and I knew, even before I knew what love was or what it could be, that you didn't get that sound in your voice unless you've lived it some, unless you've suffered something fierce, and it seemed to me that my own mama was living out her suffering every time she put on that song. And yet the way it rose and rose and that woman sang her heart out, bleeding right there on the track, I could see the uplift in it, too.

I took my cues from Mama then. That's probably why I hardly remember the time after Pop left, and I think that's because I made a decision then to forget it and forget him, like it looked like she was trying to do when she'd listen to those songs.

Of course, there were times this proved hard. I do remember that. Whenever the thoughts of his leaving got bad, I would do this thing where I'd hold my nose and breathe out real hard, like clearing my ears, and imagine a bubble or something growing from me that would push everything away and keep everything that was on the outside out there and then it would be only me inside and nothing could get to me. I'd imagine things like mosquitos or something trying to get in and my bubble was like a flame where they'd come close and then fly away quick and then try it again, only to be pushed away each time. It was a silly thing, I know, but I was only a girl then.

That was a hard time for Mama, too, no matter how strong she wanted to be. She tried to hide that fact, the hardness of it, and I suppose it was easy enough for her—or at least possible—on those days I went to school and she'd only have to act as if everything was okay for an hour or so before I left. But on weekends, that was harder. I'd be up before her and she'd often not even have any words for me except to ask if I'd gotten myself breakfast and maybe apologize for not getting it for me and I'd tell her it was okay. Then she'd lay herself on the couch and drink probably a dozen cups of coffee and read magazines until late in the day when she'd have to go off to the bar to work. I can't even recall her ever eating anything.

One time I heard her in the bathroom. It was a weird noise, not one I'd ever heard from her before. She'd left the door a little bit open, and from where I stood I could see her through the crack. She was sitting on the floor with a tissue box at her feet and tears all over her face. There was snot running down and clinging to her chin and I couldn't believe it, how my own mama could look like a little girl.

I thought I should go in and try and make it better, but I didn't know how to do that, not at the age I was then, which was seven or eight, I think, so instead I ran away from it. I went back to my favorite armchair and wrapped myself in blankets and closed my eyes against the sun and watched how the light against my closed eyelids made these amazing shows when I'd move my eyes up and down and to the sides. Like the way paint looks when you mix it with water, how they mingle but don't join up.

When the sun quit my face, that's when I'd open my eyes and watch the dust dance and sparkle and twirl around in the air and it occurred to me that it was everywhere, that dust, all the time. It was only when the sunlight poured in could you see it, but it was there all the time. I took great comfort in that, in the idea that with all those pieces of moon and star having traveled who knew how many years and how many millions of miles to get to my little house in Paris, well, it made you think that whatever problems you had in this life maybe weren't so big after all, and that went for Mama, too.

After Pop left, we got a puppy. I suppose we did it to try and forget our troubles by having a new distraction. I can't remember how we got it, but I think maybe a neighbor's dog had a litter. I can barely recall a big cardboard box with a bunch of clumsy furry pups, nipping at any finger stuck near them with their tiny sharp teeth. The rest of it I can't remember except that one of them was in our house and how quickly it turned into a peeing, pooping, howling, mewling mess of a creature and Mama became too exasperated to keep it. There she was, on her hands and knees, cleaning up after it, her hair a wild mess about her head, cursing and yelling and one time sprinting out back into the fields after the thing had broken loose and galloped toward the creek.

But before we gave it away, I remember it sharing my sun spot with me, how that little thing flopped its furry, soft-boned body down next to me, and the way the hair felt against my skin, and then how it got hot to the touch and, overheated, rose up on its little unsteady legs, wobbled over a few feet out of the sun, and crashed onto the floor, its tongue rolling out of its mouth. Two big veins appeared under its eyes and only went away when it cooled down. I'm not sure how it is I remember that so clearly when I can't recall anything else about that dog, not even its name. For all I know, we hadn't even gotten around to giving it a name before we gave it away.

I can't remember missing it, either. But I'm sure I did. I was a kid and it was a puppy. I probably cried for days. It's funny that I can't say the same thing about my pop. But like I did with him, I might have put thoughts of that puppy outside the bubble, too, and that's the reason I can hardly remember it. It was a way of coping with things and it made it so I didn't spend too much time worrying about the fact that I had no daddy at home anymore.

So I had my way of dealing with things and Mama had hers. And for her, that music was a great comfort. I used to take that favorite album of hers and stare at it for hours sometimes, trying to puzzle out how the little woman on the cover could have a voice like she did, how she could sing about being down so low and you felt it, believed her, how that tiny needle spinning on that record could loose something that could shake my Mama to her soul—and raise the flesh on my whole body besides.

I heard that voice a lot when I was with Lee, when the radio was off and silence filled the car, when the thoughts of Mama threatened to become too much. I was beginning to understand what took her over in those days when she'd stand and sway with her eyes closed and sing along, her voice rising and falling with the singer's, and she'd be lost to this world for the four minutes that song ran. She'd only come back to the life she'd been destined to live when the needle found the end of the record and it cracked and popped and then lifted itself to a rest in its arm—back to washing the dishes or dusting the shelves or whatever it was she was doing.

One time, after the song was over, I went to her and put my arms around her. Mama? I said.

Yeah, baby?

You're a good singer.

Thank you, baby.

I mean, you're really good.

I always wanted to be a singer. Ever since I was a little girl. Like you.

Why can't you?

Well . . . girls grow up. And they become women.

So?

So, I guess there comes a time when you have to put all those silly dreams aside, she said.

It made me cry to hear her say that. But something in me told me to do my crying in private, that the last thing Mama needed was to see that she'd made me cry, that telling me how the world works—that kids grow up and dreams die—made me fall into a deep sadness that lasted for days.

These are the things I thought about as me and Lee drove the long and lonely miles, the days marked more by sun and speed and wind than the regular markers that make up most people's lives. I knew it wasn't a normal course we'd set ourselves on, but it seemed the only one still possible to us.

And so it was, and so we went. And we stayed on course in part because we were still young enough to have our dreams.

But I can say this: the relief I felt, two weeks after we'd set out from Paris and almost a week since we'd left that man at the river, when Lee finally declared it safe enough for us to stay a night at a motel, that relief was immense. So we drove into a town called Haysville and headed to the Pine Bluffs Motel, with vending machines, color TV, and a swimming pool. All for seven dollars a night.

12

Lee parked the car down the street a bit from the motel.

Wait here, he said, I'll get us a room.

Why can't I come with you? I asked, thinking that maybe he was ashamed of me or something.

Look at your hands.

There was some dirt, sure, under the nails. But so what?

What's wrong with my hands? I asked.

I don't see a wedding ring and my guess is no place is renting a room to two unmarried people, especially when one of them looks as young as you, he said and then walked off.

While I was waiting, I adjusted the rearview to see myself best I could. I looked a fright, my hair knotted up from the wind and lack of a bath. My eyes looked tired and raw and the spray of freckles across the bridge of my nose had darkened up on me. There were times I hated the way I looked, but Lee told me all the time how pretty I was, and Mama used to do the same, so maybe I wasn't all bad.

After a bit, Lee came back to me, his hands in his pockets, striding over and looking both ways as he walked like he did and I couldn't help but smile.

I'm gonna grab our stuff and go in, he said. Room 212, second floor. Give it a few minutes. Door'll be unlocked. And try not to be so obvious about it. Small town hicks'll probably throw us out if they know we're in there together.

I waited about ten minutes and then headed up. I climbed the steps and walked right in. Easy as pie. No one even around to take any notice.

There was Lee sitting on the bedspread, a shiny rose pattern, spread out like he'd been in there for a year already. But his hair was wet and his clothes were changed.

Whatcha think? he asked.

I like it fine.

I poked around, checking things out. Not much to it, though: in the bathroom there was a little tub and sink, all wet. I made my way over to the TV and turned it on. The TV we had at home was black and white, so this was a sight. Of course, about the only colors on all four channels were red, white, and blue again. And of course Lee got all excited. But this time I didn't roll my eyes at it, though, considering we were not all that far off of July Fourth anymore.

There was a desk next to the bed and a lamp on it. I opened the desk drawer and there was a Gideon Bible. Otherwise, just a tiny closet and that was it to the whole room. And even though I'd grown up in a house ten times the size, the place felt like luxury to me considering the last couple of weeks and how we'd been living.

From the TV came the sounds of a soap opera. I turned to watch, taken in by the colors—so bright and shiny, yellows and browns and oranges like you usually only see on fall leaves.

A commercial for Ford trucks came on, with some Farrah Fawcett look-alike and then a bunch of people all smiling and dancing while a song for "Freewheeling Ford" played and these people in their trucks and vans all looked so happy and carefree and me and Lee laughed at it because we, too, had been out on the open road and it sure didn't look anything like that. And then I started getting hungry watching commercials for Golden Grahams and Hidden Valley Ranch and Three

Musketeers and Cap'n Crunch and Campbell's Chicken Noodle-O's soup and a really stupid one where some kids chased after a leprechaun trying to get his Lucky Charms.

People sure do eat a lot of cereal in this country, huh, Lee said. He pat the bed for me to sit down.

But first I went to the bathroom and closed the door. I looked at myself in the mirror again. I was grimy for sure, but I'd allow that, yes, maybe I was kinda pretty—at least underneath all the grime. I let my hair out of the knot I had it tied in and it barely moved. I took off my filthy clothes and threw them into the sink. Later I'd use the soap that Lee'd already taken out of its wrapper and scrub all our clothes. But all I wanted at that moment was that shower so I could scrub myself. The feeling of hot water against my bare skin when I stepped in was like nothing else. The pure pleasure of it. I turned it on even hotter so that I could barely stand how hot it was. It felt like it was scalding the filthiness right off me and after a few minutes of this, my whole body was beet red from the heat and from my scrubbing.

I'd lately come to like the look of my own body. I could see the womanness in it, the way my hips and breasts had started to curve out and I could understand better what Mama meant when she used to say that a woman's body is God's most beautiful creation.

When I was done with the shower, I didn't put my dirty clothes back on, of course. Instead, I walked out of the bathroom naked as the day I was born. I couldn't help but laugh when Lee's eyes went wide and it looked like he could hardly breathe as I sat down next to him and kissed him. He kissed me back and before I fully realized what was going on, I was lying back on the bed and he was above me and it felt like a lot of tension that he'd held inside himself was now coming through him. My brain seemed to shut off and I could feel my body giving itself over to him and allowing things to happen of their own accord.

He slowly ran his fingers up my legs. I took a big inhale of breath and he kissed me some more, on the mouth and then my neck and then my ear and I could feel my skin getting goosefleshed. When he put himself inside me, at first it felt like I was being stabbed, but not with something sharp. It didn't feel all that great, in truth. But it wasn't bad either and there was a weird battle going on in me between down below and the rest of me. As he went in and out, it hurt, and when he got certain angles I needed to pull away a bit, but then at other moments it did feel good. The rest of me was reacting in a good way: my breasts were hard and my arms were full of goose bumps and when he kissed my neck it drove me crazy. And I did like the way he was making the sounds he did and telling me he loved me.

He started to go real fast and I rubbed my fingers down his back and whispered in his ear that I loved him, too, and now I settled into everything and felt all right about it. In fact, I was so happy we were able to share this, happy at how close we were. It was one more way that me and Lee were one—and it felt that way, too, like we were two people but one body, all mixed up in each other. But then he was jumping off me real quick and letting it go onto my stomach and some of it went all the way up to my neck and started to run off. All I could think was that the smell was like when pear trees come into blossom, that heavy, sickly smell that from a distance is kind of nice but up close can make it hard to breathe.

Sorry, sorry, he said.

It's okay.

He got off the bed and went to the bathroom and returned with a towel in his hand and said that it was for wiping myself off. While I did that, I started feeling self-conscious. I wasn't ashamed. I knew this was coming and I wanted it. And when it was to happen, I didn't want it to happen with anyone but him. But now that it was over, there was a weird letdown feeling. Like I would have expected to feel completely different, like a whole new person, or fully a woman now, or something. And yet I didn't feel any of that. I felt vulnerable, sitting there naked and cleaning myself off while he watched. Maybe I expected too much.

105

Sex was a thing everyone my age talked about practically all the time—at least the kids at my school did. But now that it had happened, I couldn't see what all the fuss was about. I certainly didn't mind it, but to tell the truth, as I got dressed, the biggest feeling I had was that I was glad it was over with. That it was done and not something I had to wonder about anymore. It was nice enough, sure. But if it didn't happen again for a while, I was okay with that, too.

13

Afterward, we took a little nap, wet hair and everything. Lee fell asleep before I did and it didn't take long before our breathing synced to one another. It was a queer thing, and I couldn't explain it, but every time we lay down together to sleep, eventually we inhaled and exhaled at the same exact moments, our chests rising and falling together. I told Lee about it once, the first time I noticed it.

That right? he asked.

Yeah.

Means you and me, Lilly-Flower, we operate on the same wavelength.

I sure didn't need any convincing of that.

When we woke, we went out to explore the town a little, me first and then Lee leaving after to lock the door.

We met out on the street near the car and walked from there. Lee was not very talkative and he kept his eyes off of me. I hated to think that things had changed because of what we did together. We stayed quiet until, as we were passing a little pharmacy, Lee said we should go in.

Once we were inside, he walked away from me, almost like we weren't even a couple. I wasn't sure why things felt different but a deep sadness came up in me because of it, so to distract myself I looked at the makeup displays. I especially liked the blue eyeliner they had. I never wore much makeup before except for those times when I played dress-up with Mama and she'd let me use some of hers. But mostly it didn't interest me. Least not for myself. I did like to watch Mama as she ran that little curved brush of hers on her eyelashes and curled it upward. It was funny that she couldn't do it without keeping her mouth open while she put it on and I would tell her to do it with her mouth closed and she'd try but she just couldn't keep it closed and we'd both laugh.

When I was real little she would sometimes make up my face and tell me how grown-up I looked. I think she liked the idea of it, that maybe I could turn into her best friend or something as I got older, but then when I actually did get older, she seemed to get sad at the idea, always telling me she wondered where the little girl had gone. Could be that was why I never took any interest in wearing makeup, that I knew it might make her feel worse.

But of course every girl wants to look pretty now and again and because of what happened in the motel, I was feeling more and more like I should be doing lady things like wearing makeup and earrings and starting to think of myself as more of a woman. Maybe if I did that, Lee would get back to his old self again and there wouldn't be this queer feeling between us.

I put down the makeup and grabbed a pair of silver ball earrings that I thought might look nice on me someday. I held one against my ear and checked it out in the little mirror they had on the counter. Behind the mirror at the end of the aisle, Lee stood there looking at me. He was smiling finally, which filled me up. No matter how many times I looked at him, I almost couldn't ever believe how handsome he was. It was a funny thing, how his being so handsome had actually turned me off at first, like he knew it and could charm his way into anything. But now that he was my man, and I was his girl, I loved how handsome he was. I liked to just look at him and I wanted to show him off to the rest of the world.

You ready? he asked.

You're the one wanted to come in here, I said, putting the earrings back.

When we were outside, he said, Wait here, I'll be right back, and he ran back in and I stood there on the street and watched the people going by. It's a funny thing how when you're somewhere else, someplace not your home, and you don't know what's here and what's there and you're not going back to any home-cooked meal or your classroom or anything you know well, how everything seems so unfamiliar even though it's all the same stuff pretty much anywhere, and the people look the same, too. It was just that in Haysville they were saying hello to each other because they all went to the same places: the same shops, the same schools, the same church, and none of them was saying hello to me because they didn't know me and there was no place for me to go. You know it, and everyone else seems to, too: you'll be gone soon and this place may as well have never existed.

All right, Lee said when he got back outside. Once clear of the store, he reached in his pockets and pulled out the makeup and the earrings I was looking at.

Here you go, Lilly-Flower, he said.

That's so sweet, I gushed. Course, I don't have my ears pierced, I told him.

No?

He looked at me, then took both my ears into his hands like he didn't believe me. Funny how he never realized that.

Well, he said, we can take care of that.

Yeah?

Sure. Easy enough. All you need is some ice to numb it and then poke it through.

I was relieved he didn't suggest we do it right then and there because the idea of it alone hurt to think about. And if I said as much, well, what would he think of me? Capable of sleeping out, going from day to day and taking on whatever came our way, acting like a woman at some times and tough as a man at others, but scared of a little prick in my ear? For now I slid the silver earrings into my pocket and said thank you and we walked on, exploring the rest of Haysville, which didn't take long at all.

A bank, a movie theater, grocer's, two stoplights—double what we had in Paris—a park, two bars, church on the outskirts of town, a barber-shop with its blue-and-red rotating pole, a department store. The motel. Not a whole lot else.

So we ate at the one place to do so, it appeared, and then went back to the motel, him first and then me after.

I suggested we go swim in the pool some, that it had been ages since I swam in a pool.

You bring a bathing suit? he asked.

I'm sure we can find some in town.

Lee wasn't saying anything about it, acting all funny again instead, looking at me and then down to the ground like he had something heavy on his mind but didn't know how to spit it out.

What is it? I finally asked. You've been driving me crazy all morning.

He pulled something else out of his pocket. Condoms.

I got them in the pharmacy, he said. So I don't make a mess of things again.

I could feel myself blushing. I liked that he wanted me like that and I gave him credit for his considerateness. Of course I knew where babies came from—I was no child—and while I would have trusted him to do what he needed to do to prevent all that, he was taking precautions and that was sweet of him, so I said okay and got onto the bed and we did it again, only this time I liked it much better. This time, it felt like our two bodies had joined and we were connected not only down below but in our hearts and heads, too. He kept his forehead pressed against mine and our fingers wrapped around each other the whole time.

I had the idea that the more we acted like that and did it that way, the less real that guy at the river was. If he was gone, what we were doing there, in those moments we made love, was somehow putting more life and energy back into the universe. It was a thing I told myself afterward, in any case, as we lay there in each other's arms, just lying there quietly holding each other. But, truth is, thinking about it made me, well, think about it.

Lee . . . I said.

Hmmm?

We never talk about it.

What's that, baby doll?

His voice was deep and tired sounding.

That man. At the river. We never talk about it.

What's there to talk about?

I don't know. I just think we should talk about it.

I disagree.

He got up and went to the bathroom. On the way back out, he turned off the lamp that had been on and that, combined with the fact that the curtain was drawn, made the room real dark even though it was still daytime.

He got back into bed and soon after I could tell by his breathing that he'd fallen asleep.

Eventually, I fell asleep, too, and we never did go get those bathing suits.

⌒

The man was yelling at me. Though it wasn't really yelling. More like gibberish. And I was trying to understand him, trying my hardest, but it was like in a language I couldn't understand and I just kept asking him, What are you saying? What are you saying? But I wanted to understand. I needed to. I knew that if I could only understand him, then everything could work out. We'd be on our way and he'd be on his. And everyone would get to live their lives. But I couldn't understand and his gibberish turned to moaning and screaming and he jumped at us and the gun went off.

111

I bolted up in the bed, my chest and forehead soaked with sweat.

What is it, baby? Lee asked. He put his arms around me.

A dream. A nightmare.

You okay?

I nodded. I got out of bed and went to the bathroom, where I ran water and cupped it into my hands and splashed it all over my face and neck. Lee was back to sleep when I came back out.

I nudged him. Lee, I said. Lee.

Yeah?

Let's get out of here.

He squinted at the alarm clock, saw it was eleven forty.

Leave now?

I can't go back to sleep.

We got dressed and took a walk around town. It was dark and quiet, no one about. But when we turned a corner, we saw a bunch of people at the movie theater.

There was a midnight showing of a movie called *The Omen*, so we went in.

It turned out this was a bad choice. After an hour or so, I begged Lee to get out of there because it scared me something terrible. I knew it was only a movie, but it got to me anyway. All those animals terrified by that little kid, all except some huge dogs that hung around their house and then there was a scene where Damien, the main character, went completely crazy when they tried to take him into a church. I knew it was silly, and I could handle about anything—in truth, most scary movies I found pretty stupid—but there was something about devil movies that terrified me and I didn't know before we went in that *The Omen* was one of those kinds of movies. It wasn't so much what I was seeing on the screen but rather my fear that it would all come back to me later on. If we watched the rest of that movie, I would have had trouble falling asleep and I knew that if I was lying there awake on account of that devil flick I was gonna want to be home again or I'd replay what happened at the river yet again, torture myself with thoughts that

112

it could have turned out some different way, no matter how many times I tried to convince myself otherwise.

So after I begged Lee, we walked out of the movie.

Sorry we wasted that money, I said, slipping my arm around his.

It was only four dollars.

In those days, that was pretty spendy, almost what our entire huge lunch had cost. But he didn't seem to mind and I realized another thing: after what we did in the motel, Lee was as happy as a clam for a long time afterward.

Look at this, Lee said, pointing to a piece of paper tacked to a telephone pole. It was a notice saying Help Wanted.

What's it for? I asked.

Caretaker.

Here in town?

It's got an address.

Lee tore it off and carried it to the movie lady who sold tickets. Excuse me, ma'am, where is this? Lee asked.

Mirabile. Just outside of town. Old man lives there. He's blind and almost deaf. His wife passed. Son is a hotshot who lives in San Francisco or New York or somewhere. He's a doctor.

That a fact?

It is.

Lee folded up the notice and put it in his pocket.

Why are you taking it? I asked.

This could be a gift from heaven. Come on. We'll go first thing in the morning.

Hey.

What's that, baby doll?

What about New Orleans?

It ain't going nowhere.

We had a plan.

He started down the sidewalk.

Sometimes plans change, he said.

14

Just as I feared, I had trouble sleeping. Not so for Lee, who fell asleep the minute we got back. I tried to watch TV, but there was only one channel on and it was some old Western that was pretty stupid. Without realizing it, I drifted off and when I woke to gray static, I got up and turned off the TV, watching as all the lines of it collapsed into themselves and then formed into a little dot that got smaller and smaller like being sucked into a drain and then disappearing. The TV in my house was like that, too, and I hadn't known that color TVs did it also.

I didn't get back into bed right away. Instead, I went to the window and pulled the curtain so I could see outside. What I had thought was moonlight coming in was a lamppost shining on the pool. A few ducks floated on the water but otherwise the whole pool was empty of everything except a pop can someone had left behind. I looked back to Lee. He could sleep anywhere and through anything. It was a gift I wish I had. But I couldn't turn my brain off. I was afraid to try and go back to sleep because I knew that what awaited me was counting troubles when I should have been counting sheep.

There was no phone in the room, which was good, because I'd have been tempted to pick it up and call Mama collect. I hadn't yet, of course. Apart from the fact that I'd really had no opportunity to do so, something told me it was not a great idea. I did want to talk to her, tell her I was fine, but I knew she'd ask me where I was and I was afraid I'd be powerless to not tell her and next thing I knew, the moment she hung up that phone, she and Hank would be in his truck on the way to get me. And I didn't want that. I felt safe with Lee and in the morning we were gonna go out to that farm and see if we couldn't stay there awhile, acting as caretaker to an old blind and deaf widower. I wasn't happy we were delaying going to New Orleans yet again, but Lee was right: it wasn't going anywhere.

So I crawled back into bed and put my arms around Lee and nuzzled against him. And even though it was hot in the room, the heat of him on top of it felt good. I managed to smile. Tomorrow would be a new day.

⌒

In the morning, we took a ride out to the Mirabile homestead. It was easy enough to find, about five miles or so straight down the road out of town. A man out walking his dog told us how to get there, pointing straight ahead while his big shaggy overexcited mutt kept jumping up on the car and managed once to swipe me across my face with its tongue. It felt funny and I laughed, but soon enough I realized the stink it left me with.

Don't worry about it, Lee said as we drove there. Old man barely has any ears or eyes. You think his nose works all that well?

Actually, it probably does if those other things don't work. They say when you lose one sense, the others get heightened because of it.

That don't make any sense to me at all, Lee said.

He turned down a dirt road from the main one and took it slow up a gravelly drive toward a big white farmhouse.

Looks like this is it. It's no wonder this guy wants help, Lee said.

It was true, the place hadn't been kept up all that well. The paint on the main house had come off in huge sheets and flakes and the porch was full of it. As for the porch itself, there were boards threatening to break through completely. One of the shutters from the window nearest the door was missing, too, and another window, on an upper floor, was nothing but a big piece of plywood nailed over it.

We walked to the screen door. The screen had peeled off in one corner and dangled when we opened it. Behind it was a wood door with glass panes and Lee put his hands to one of the panes and looked in.

Can't see nothing, he said.

I cupped my hands to it, too, and looked in and it wasn't that I couldn't see anything—I could see the staircase going upstairs, some rugs on the floor, a fireplace off to the left, and a hallway straight ahead that looked like it might lead to the kitchen—but I knew what Lee meant: there was no sign of any person anywhere.

Lee knocked. Nothing.

We looked inside again and still nothing. He knocked a few more times, hard and loud. To no avail.

Well, what now then? I asked.

The man *is* deaf. Let's look around.

We stepped off the porch and started our way around the house. There, off to the side, was a car with Illinois plates, but still we didn't see anyone. Beyond the house, the land went on forever, a huge empty field as far as we could see. Off to the right was where the barn stood and a silo next to it and several smaller buildings we could guess were livestock stalls. There was a henhouse, too, and a pigsty, but that was empty of everything except mud and a trough full of brown rainwater.

Hello? Lee called out.

Still nothing.

We made our way over to the barn, where we were surprised to see three cows standing there staring at us, their necks inside harnesses. No noise or anything. Just standing and looking stupid. Course, they might very well have thought the same of us.

Well, someone's got to be around then, Lee said.

Just then a man came around the corner with a bucket in each of his hands. He was wearing blue jeans and big black boots way up to his knees and a flannel shirt smeared with mud. His blond hair was a mess with what looked like feed of some kind.

Hello, he said.

Hi, there, sir. I'm Jason and this here is my fiancée, Marie.

The man looked at us like he could see through that as easy as water. But then he put the bucket down, took off his glove, and said, Nice to meet you, shaking Lee's hand. Barry, he said, referring to himself.

Lee took the notice asking for help out of his pocket and unfolded it.

We saw this in town, he said.

Barry nodded. Help me with this? he said. He pulled up a little stool next to one of the cows and placed a bucket underneath its udder. He leaned his head against the cow's big side as he started to pull the teats and the milk came squirting into the bucket with a hollow metal sound.

Another stool over there, he said, pointing with his chin. I've already applied the udder wash.

You want us to milk these two? Lee asked.

Isn't that what you're here for?

Well . . .

If you're going to be the caretaker for this farm, you certainly need to know how to milk cows.

I'm sorry, you the current caretaker? Lee asked.

My father lives here and he needs someone to take care of the place. He's old, but I know better than to try and get him to move.

Oh, you the New York doctor?

Barry lifted his head from the cow's side and looked at Lee.

I'm a trial lawyer in Chicago, he said, and I need to get back to my practice.

He looked around the barn, shaking his head.

The very reason I left here, he said, smiling to himself, and here I am at it again. Then he pointed again at the stool. Please, he said.

I'd seen this done before and it looked like there was nothing to it, but I'd never actually milked a cow and when I pulled up my stool and put my hands on the udder, I was surprised by how rubbery the teats felt. I followed Barry's example and tugged and pulled. I could see him watching me as the cow started taking little steps back and forth.

Make sure your motion is more rolling, Barry said.

He got up and came over and moved my fingers a little as he told me: Make a ring with your thumb and index finger. Good. Now, tighten the index finger and bring it in toward the palm. There you go.

It was easy enough. Soon I had milk squirting into my bucket and I was even liking the feel of it, even though my forearms started aching. I noticed Barry looking over at Lee.

He's the carpenter, I said.

Yeah. I'll get that porch and whatever else all firmed up for you within a day or two, Lee added.

Let's go meet Dad, Barry said. I'll finish this up later.

We followed him to the back door of the house and inside to the kitchen. It was a lovely little kitchen, with curtains on the window above the sink, a little corn cob pattern on it. There was a stove and oven, a little white refrigerator. A couple of the cabinet doors looked like they were barely holding on, and some of the drawer slides looked like they needed repair.

I can fix these right up, Lee said, wrestling with the drawer.

Me and Lee operated on some kind of wavelength separate from everyone else in the world, just like Lee had said. So often it was the case I was thinking the very thing he said. It was like that breathing thing we had.

Wait here, Barry said, and after a minute he returned leading an old man. But when I say leading, I only mean to say that Barry said things to him like, Watch the chair, Just to your left, things like that. He said it loud, but the old man could obviously hear him because every time Barry gave an instruction the old man said, Yeah, yeah, I know. Been living in this house since well before you was born, to which Barry rolled his eyes at us and shook his head.

Dad, he said, this is Jessie and Marie.

Jason, sir, Lee said, and he went to the old man and shook his hand. Marie's my fiancée. I'm twenty-one and Marie here, she turned twenty last week.

Well, happy birthday, Miss Marie, the old man said.

Barry gave us that look again and I wondered why it was Lee insisted on this, on lying that way to people first thing, that in this case it might very well ruin our chances of staying on. But Barry said to his dad, We were thinking they can help around the house, get things fixed up, take care of you.

So Lee hadn't ruined anything and it reminded me that more often than not I could trust he knew what he was doing. He had more experience in the world than I did.

I don't need any taking care of, the old man said.

Come on now, Dad. You deserve some rest. You've been working all your life. Let someone else take care of you for a while. There's certainly no shame in that.

No, sir, Lee added.

That's a job for kin, the old man said.

Dad, we've been through this. I can't just up and leave my practice. There's a reason you worked every day from dawn to dusk to send me to law school. You want me to turn my back on that now, now that I've got a flourishing practice? Besides, I'll come back whenever I can, as I always have. It's just that now I can feel a little more secure knowing you've got someone here looking after you.

It sounded to me like this was a conversation they'd had a hundred times and that Mr. Barry was putting it on more for us than for his dad.

This Marie, she a pretty one? the old man asked.

I loved his spunk. Figured when Lee got to be an old man, he'd be just the same.

Prettiest you've ever seen, sir, Lee said.

Say? the old man replied, cupping his hand around his ear.

He said she's the prettiest you ever saw, Barry said, and then added, And I can attest to that.

He winked and smiled at both of us.

Dad, he said, we're gonna go out back so I can show them the outbuildings. You stay here.

And where else would I be going?

We followed Barry and I couldn't stop smiling. I loved the idea of this. I could tell right away that the old man was mostly playing at being crotchety and I predicted that if we did stay on that he and I would get along fine.

The pay is only a small stipend, Barry explained as we walked a narrow trail toward the back fields. One hundred dollars a month and that's for the both of you. But you'll have a place to stay and food to eat. He's an independent man and he likes it that way. So I'd only want you to make sure he has what he needs, even if all he needs on any given day is to be left alone. Not too much to it.

Sir, Lee said.

Barry.

Yes, sir, Barry. If you don't mind me asking an impertinent question.

I looked at Lee, surprised he even knew a word such as that one. I couldn't say as I knew what it meant.

Go ahead.

I wonder. He's your pop. You don't know us. Why leave his care to two strangers?

Barry looked off into the distance, out over the fields he must have run when he was a kid, back when they no doubt gave up something other than just spent cicada shells.

I'm a lawyer, Jason. Sometimes I defend criminals. Murderers. Rapists. The worst of the worst.

I can't imagine that's easy.

No, often it's not. But in the United States of America, everyone is entitled to fair representation.

Yes, sir.

My point is that over the years I've come to know people. Often I know people first look at them. I've become known among my colleagues as something of an expert in choosing jurors. One look at you two, and I know a few things. Things you give away about yourselves without even knowing it. Your ages for one thing; you're younger than you say, miss, he said, looking at me. And for another thing, you two aren't engaged to be married. That's a ridiculous notion. She's not even wearing a ring.

Well, I haven't gotten around—

I'm not asking for any explanation. Frankly, I don't care and it's none of my business. What you two look like to me are two young kids out on an adventure and needing a break from it for a time. I don't expect you to stay here very long. But you're unlike every other person who's come here inquiring about this job. Everyone else is old. Not like my dad old, but getting there. They want something to do, fill the time, feel useful. People from town who already know my dad. That's a problem; he'll never tolerate someone like that, someone he used to have some authority over in years past, by virtue of being a community elder. It'll be constant tension and soon enough he'll toss them out. We've been down that road before. But not you two. No way. You two staying here will probably convince him that the idea itself isn't so bad. Then, we can go from there. Understand?

Barry turned to me and said, Don't take offense at this, miss, but the idea of having a young woman in the house again, that alone will keep him happy enough. And you, he said, turning to Lee, I believe you that you'll fix this place up. I have no doubt about it. Because I see in you a young man who's bursting with energy, someone who can hardly contain it and looking for a place to put it.

Well, you got me pegged all right, Lee said, smiling.

It's true, I added.

So there you go. Keep the place up. Keep the cows fed and milked. The hogs and chickens are gone. You'll have a food allowance and can get your goods at the grocery in town. You give them my name. They'll keep the tab, let you know how much you have left each week. And take a break from whatever road you're on. Slow it down. Take it in. The farm life isn't one for me anymore. Heck, I couldn't wait to get out of here. But there's something to it all right. It's hard work. But the day ends early and sitting on the porch after a day working and a hearty meal and watching the sun go down and breathing the clean air and listening to the night insects, well . . .

I was smiling again. I couldn't help myself. And Lee was smiling, too.

It certainly did sound nice. But it was more than that. I loved the idea of settling down for a bit, of not getting into that car day after day and logging more miles to nowhere. The promise of that alone would have been enough. But listening to Barry, it was as if he'd sold us on some temporary paradise. And I couldn't wait to get started.

Jonesboro, Arkansas, November 4, 1992, 12:55 p.m.

It's a hard thing to find the balance in how I talk about my mama and how I missed her when I was gone and how, if I'm telling the truth, there were times when I didn't miss her at all. Lindsey looks up to me, even admires me sometimes, though she'd never say such a thing. But I can tell. She's no dummy and she knows it's not the easiest thing in the world raising a child by yourself.

I want her to admire me. I mean, of course I do. So when I talk about being out on the road, taking off with Lee at the age of fifteen, I want her to respect me for it, for having that kind of independent spirit, a thing she never sees in me these days and has never known of her mother. But I also need her to see the folly in it. So I want her to know that I missed my mother and I suspect Lindsey would miss me, too, if she left. But I don't need her to focus on the fact that while sometimes I was paralyzed by how much I missed Mama, other times I didn't give two damns and was more than happy to be away.

But that seems to be of little concern to her, anyway. I figured she might have questions about the sex, considering she'd asked me before about why I didn't take boyfriends and didn't I need a man. I guess hearing about it for real now, about her own mother, maybe it is kind of gross to her. Weird thing is, I don't mind talking about it. Why hold it back? I'm pretty sure she hasn't had sex yet herself, though of course that is coming someday, and probably soon enough. It's certainly not something she's shared with me, and I wouldn't expect her to.

When I told her about the motel part, her eyes widened a little but then fell back to their usual sleepy-looking state, as if she either didn't care about it or was way beyond any shocking. All she asked about that part was, "Is that when I came about?"

I love the innocent way she had of phrasing it: "came about." It was even enough to hold off the sick feeling of getting deeper into this story and the hardest parts about it. It was a good way for her to get the question across while steering clear of the weird stuff: her mom in a motel room losing her virginity. But I'm a firm believer in presenting it as nonchalantly as it's possible to do; if you take the mystery out of it, it doesn't seem like such a huge deal. And if you go the other way, telling her over and over how she can't do it and how she's not ready, she'll want to run out and see what it's all about. I mean, if your mother tells you not to do something, isn't it an essential part of growing up to go out and do that very thing? Surely was for me. Besides, it's all natural and nothing to be ashamed of anyway. I remember as a little girl sitting in the bathroom while Mama showered—for the warmth of it, the way the steam filled the room and I could run my hands through it and create patterns in the mist—and seeing through the glass that dark patch between Mama's legs and seeing also the shape and bounce of her large breasts.

She didn't draw attention to any part of her body, but neither did she hide anything. I'd sit there on the floor and when her shower was done she'd step from it and get her towel and not bother to hide any parts of herself or tell me to scat. And so I knew long before it happened to me what to expect when a girl's body turned to a woman's.

But Lindsey appears disinterested. There was the killing, of course. But there's nothing shocking in that part of the story anymore because when she discovered that her father was awaiting execution, I already had to tell her why.

"Well, someone had died," I explained. "And I figured it was easier for you to think that your father was simply gone than to know that the state decided that he was a killer." This I told her that first night as she yelled at me for my thoughtlessness. "I see now I was wrong and I'm very sorry for that."

"You're damned right you were wrong, and damned right you're sorry," she screamed.

But now she asks me a question she didn't before: "Did *you* think of him as a killer?"

The question stuns me and I have to catch my breath before I answer. It's weird because this is the very question I have pondered for ages, in different forms, at different times, and I come up with different answers, or shades of answers, every time. It's *the* question, in some respects, the only one that matters, and it's the very thing that has me all stewed up now. It was one thing for me to wrestle with it inside my own heart and head, to toss and turn nights and forget about it altogether on others, deep in the stresses of raising a daughter by myself. But I know I have to face it—it's getting closer, all coming to a head, like some far-off train that you hear only as a whisper before it chugs and chugs and bears down on you and there you stand, blinded by its light, paralyzed, nowhere to turn, before . . . bang!

There's the truth and the near truth. And the truth of *that* is . . . I don't really know for sure. In all my wrestling, I've never landed on an answer that will stick. And for now, at least for a few more hours, I don't know how to answer her question, *the* question, hers and mine together now, and keep any commitment I might have to the truth.

After a moment, I say: "No, I didn't. He did what he had to do." This is one of the answers I've told myself over the years and so it seems as good as any now.

"Do you think about him?" she asks. "That man?"

This is an easier line of questioning. This is about someone else now, someone who is no part of our lives anymore. "I do. Not all the time. Sometimes I go months without so much as a little thought. Then, other times, it wakes me up at night. It makes me sad, I can tell you. I feel like it wasn't his fault, that he was wired some such way and couldn't help himself."

"But it doesn't make it okay to victimize other people, and that's what he was trying to do to you."

"I'm glad you see it that way," I say and just like that there's this huge weight coming off me. It's such a cliché, I know, this idea of a weight pressing down. But it's true. Her telling me she understands relieves one of the fears I've lived with my whole life, that my own flesh and blood would come to see me as an evil person for my part in what happened. But she seems to understand it, at least this part of it. In fact, with the way she's moved her body toward mine, where before she'd been leaning toward the window, her back to me almost as much as it's possible in a bus sitting side by side, she seems almost, perhaps, even sympathetic now. Maybe it's just that she thinks her mother is cool or something, someone not to be messed with. She doesn't say this, but she does shift herself so she's facing me. She even puts a finger on my knee.

"Any other questions you have about it?" I ask.

"Actually, I do."

"Okay."

She looks me directly in the eye, fixes me there and doesn't turn away.

"I'd like to know how it is that he's in jail, about to be executed, and you're here and free and always have been?"

There it is. Just like that, everything is back to where it was. Even worse, actually. I can feel my cheeks burning. I can hardly swallow. Sweat breaks out all over me, popping out on my forehead and chilling my back.

I almost want to strangle her. There's no other way about it. It's an amazing thing, to at once love your child more than anything else in the universe—I'd gladly lay down on train tracks in front of a speeding loco-motive if it meant saving her—and yet at this moment, I could abso-lutely kill her.

"And if I weren't," I finally manage, "where would you be?"

She just shrugs. Of course she does—the freedoms open to a teen-ager unburdened with the demands of being responsible for another person. To have that again . . .

"Go back to your music, Lindsey."

I turn away from her. I need a break from her, from this trip, from my life. And yet I'm stuck on this bus and we've got so many hours to go. I just feel like dying. Why does she do this to me? What is it with teenaged girls and their need to injure their mothers? Is this payback for putting my own mother through what I did? Well, I can say this: it al-lows me to feel less obligated to the whole story. She wants to injure me? Fine. But then she doesn't get everything, and just when I had been willing to give it to her—the hardest thing in the world.

I close my eyes, try and let some calm wash over me, take me away someplace where the thoughts don't ping-pong around my brain and burn up my stomach and where I'm not made to feel like some mon-ster. What does she know about it anyway? Of course she can needle me and poke at me and make it out so that her father is the victim. Of course. I'm the only one who ever punishes her, who makes her clean her room, who gets after her to complete her homework. It's not him, and because it's not him, and never was, she can imagine he's a saint and her nagging old mother is the sinner.

But then I feel Lindsey's hand on my leg. She rubs it a second, then says, in a real quiet voice: "Tell me about Barry and his dad."

It's her way of apologizing, I believe, for being so hurtful. Still, I want her to actually utter the words, "I'm sorry." But I know that's not coming. And if I push it, she'll be lost to me for the rest of the trip and the truth is, I need her. As angry as I am, and as hurt as I am, I need her. Otherwise, I'll continue to pay for it for the rest of my life. And is that fair? Should I have to pay until the day I die?

Well, maybe, I remind myself. Maybe I do. Maybe that is fair. This whole thing is for her—that was the deal I made, with myself and with Lee.

Once again, I take a deep breath. "I enjoyed living at Mirabile," I say. "Very much."

15

June 1976

Barry showed us around the house while his dad—we'd soon enough come to know him as Mr. Chester—sat at the kitchen table occasionally barking orders that Barry ignored. Things like, Go check the cows, and See that Arlene in town has that feed order. Barry would say, Sure Dad, but then not do whatever it was that was asked of him. It seemed they were empty orders mostly, shouted out of routine.

I've moved my dad down here, Barry said, showing us the room where Mr. Chester had been sleeping.

The stairs are difficult for him now, he explained. There are three rooms upstairs, Barry continued. Whether you take two of them or stay together in one is your business and not something I'm going to fret about. You may want to tell him you ran off to town and got married. Otherwise, you two in the same room, he might not like. Me, as I said, I didn't care one way or another. I live with a woman not my wife myself, so . . .

I smiled at Lee. I loved the idea of staying with him like an actual married couple, but I held onto the idea of taking that other room, too, just in case I might like some private space.

Phone's in the kitchen, Barry said, continuing our tour. A shiver went up in me. Knowing there was a phone right there where we'd be staying, it did occur to me that at some point or another I'd most likely call Mama. The idea scared me because whenever I pictured such a thing, besides not being able to resist telling her where I was, I could see myself whispering into the phone and Lee coming in and I'd have to hang up straightaway and that would make it seem like I was in trouble but that I didn't want to say that outright and I knew Mama would be sick with worry. But there it was, that phone, and I couldn't imagine I'd be able to stay clear of it forever. How I'd work that out I didn't know, but it was there and the idea of it stayed with me as we followed Barry up the stairs.

But we didn't get much beyond the first few steps before I let them go on without me. I couldn't go any further because I was stopped by the framed photographs on the wall heading up. It was Mr. Chester, no doubt, but he was a young man in these pictures and very handsome. And with him was his wife, Barry's mother, and she was young and beautiful, too. I couldn't stop looking at them as I made my way up, one step at a time, and with each new step a new picture, a few years in the future, until Barry appeared, and the pictures ended at the top of the stairs when Barry looked to be around eighteen, a young man himself.

Of course I knew that people got old and died. But it was impossible to imagine it really because me and Lee had never been anything but ourselves and who we were was still very young. And my guess was Mr. Chester and his wife probably felt that way too, once, that they'd never get old. Not really anyway. They probably couldn't imagine that they'd be anything other than the same people working the land and keeping the house and raising their son and he'd never turn into a middle-aged man. And I was sure that Mr. Chester, when he was the age he was in that first picture, there with his wife—it could have been me and Lee in that picture, for all the similarities—I was sure he never could have imagined himself as someone who couldn't see anymore and could hardly hear and whose hair would turn pure white, what little left of it there was, and his head would be spotted with age. No one can really imagine such a thing for themselves.

Lee and Barry were going from room to room, and I could hear Barry telling Lee the handle on the toilet in the hall had to be held down for a few seconds when you flush. It occurred to me, listening to them, that they would probably never believe such a thing about themselves either, all that business about growing old and dying. And who would? Why waste time on it? I mean, toilet handles are important. But if we were all going to end up blind and deaf and needing looking after, would we even care about toilet handles and all the rest of it? Probably wouldn't care about much of anything, really. In that respect, it's only what's here and now that matters. I knew that's not the way things work, but still, it was an idea that haunted me the rest of that day and I even came close to telling Lee that I wanted to leave and not come back. That we should just keep moving, as if moving would be the thing that would keep those thoughts from becoming realities and keep us from ever getting any older. I couldn't help but think about that man at the river again. Unlike Chester and Barry and everyone else, he'd never grow old. But once again, I beat back thoughts of this, as if it had all been just some dumb old movie or something.

But still, all I could say was I was tired when Lee kept asking me what was wrong, what had gotten into me.

And I still claimed tiredness that night as I settled into bed early while Lee and Barry sat downstairs and went over the final details of our employment. I stayed in one of the spare upstairs rooms by myself, everyone agreeing for propriety's sake that Lee and I should sleep apart, at least for the time. I was glad for that, and luxuriated in having my own room again. Though of course it wasn't my room and apart from my case, opened now on the bed, my small collection of clothes all jumbled up inside, there was nothing of me in there.

It was clearly the missus's room. There were lace doilies all over it, covering every piece of furniture and even the bedspread itself. I wondered if this had been a hobby of hers, knitting lace doilies, and I decided it must have been because I didn't see any tags on any of them to indicate they were store bought, and so I pictured her, sitting in the rocking chair opposite where I stood now, killing the hours knitting those doilies. There was a little clock in the room, too, and it ticked away the time and I couldn't even imagine the number of ticks that had passed in that room, from when she was the young woman in those pictures through to her having her son and knitting her lace doilies and getting old and then dying. And still the ticking went on.

After a time, it drove me crazy and so I pushed open the windows and let the noises of the night insects take away that awful ticking.

~

In the morning, we all sat down to breakfast together—me, Lee, Barry, and Mr. Chester. It almost felt like we were a family or something, the way the conversation ran so easy and we ate and helped ourselves to seconds and Barry made the same joke about my spoon standing up in my coffee that Lee had made in the diner in Duvray.

Mr. Chester was in a much better mood than the day before. He still acted a little ornery but did it mostly as jokes. Barry was right: he seemed to like the idea of having a woman in the house again because he kept saying, where is Miss Marie? Honey, let me touch your hand. And when I reached out for him and felt his hands, he purred like a kitten. I didn't like the way it felt at first, the way his knuckles and bones stuck out this way and that, and the way the veins seemed to have come loose from everything else under his skin and rode around in there like they had minds of their own. But I soon came to realize that Mr. Chester had earned those ugly hands of his, that he'd touched and worked so many things over the years and no doubt used those same hands to caress his wife's cheek and hold Barry when he was a baby and so in that way his hands, gnarled with age and covered in dark spots, the skin all papery smooth and loose from the bone, were actually pretty beautiful hands when you looked at it the right way.

After breakfast, me and Lee watched Barry drive away in a cloud of dust for his home in Chicago and we stood there on the porch and waved like we were an old couple ourselves and he was our son and then laughed at the idea when we walked back inside. It was a thrilling feeling. Like we'd just bought our own new house or something and Mr. Chester was an elderly grandparent we'd decided to take care of. I was feeling much better about everything and decided that our staying on was a good idea after all. And it was that very day that we got to work, and worked hard, straight on through to supper. I scrubbed the whole house up and down, starting in the kitchen, while Lee worked on the porch. When we finally called it quits for the day, the house was shining from top to bottom—minus the mess of a cellar; that would have to wait for some other day. It was a good day's work, and I was proud of it and could hardly wait for the next day. I went to bed that evening feeling good for myself, and good for the world.

It was a funny thing, and it was one of the few thoughts I managed before I fell asleep: I'd left Paris in part because it didn't feel like enough excitement for me, and then what was it I was looking for all along? That same feeling of boring security, and here I found it, in a stranger's home, with the man I loved snoring down the hall from me, and me in my new room under the watchful gaze of the kindly ghost of Mr. Chester's dearly departed. She was in that room; I could feel her spirit in her doilies and her clock and the little framed watercolors on the walls that I imagined she'd gone to some flea market years and years earlier and took home and placed on these walls herself, helping to make this house her home. And there I was in that same room and the only thing I did before falling asleep was get up and straighten one of the pictures that had gone crooked on the wall and I told myself that she'd like the idea of me sleeping in this room, under the sheets she used to scrub and hang out to dry on clotheslines behind the house.

I fell asleep to pictures of her sitting in her chair with her delicate knitting needles near the window watching as the wind caught those sheets like sails on a boat, here in the middle of the country and so far away from any ocean or sea.

And what followed was deep and dark and wonderful sleep.

16

Lee made occasional runs into town to get food or lumber supplies and every now and again I went with him for something different to do. Usually it was just in and out, to get what we needed before heading back. But sometimes we stayed longer, maybe saw a movie or sat on a bench and watched people go by. You could learn things in town, like the fact that Mirabile sat right on the Nebraska line and in fact, when we sat out on the back porch, we were looking at Nebraska, though of course there was no sign anywhere to tell us that.

There wasn't much to see in town or on the way there but I liked the way the prairie spilled out in every direction from the road and the sky sometimes looked like it went on forever without interruption. It was now late June, and it got hotter and hotter and it hardly ever rained. The effect on the crops and the troubles it gave the surrounding farmers was clear enough. So many of the crops looked burned, used up and slashed like something terrible had happened. A man at the feed store talked about how people were struggling because of it. Of course, he did that thing that all old people do whenever they get to talking about how bad something is in the present: they tell you how it used to be so much worse and that the present day is nothing in comparison. I suppose it might be true, you live long enough, but I couldn't imagine that was any consolation to anyone young enough to not know about it and who was struggling at that moment.

The yields this fall will be low, the man said. And folks will have to tighten their belts.

I certainly wouldn't have argued with him even if I was inclined to. He had only one eye, and another man—came in regularly, I could tell by the easy conversation between them, mostly grunts and nods—he had two of his fingers missing at the top knuckle. You wonder sometimes what kind of hard life these people had. But it did seem to give them authority about things.

I was glad for Mr. Chester that he didn't have to worry about that, that he had saved enough money over the years and had a son who made money that he could send and that he'd be all right regardless of drought. In any case, he no longer had the crops out there to pull in. Still, it did occur to me how sad it was that there were so many other people, not as lucky, who worked a whole lifetime just so they might get a little bit of comfort in it at the end, and then sometimes even that wasn't enough or it didn't come through the way they planned—just like the Swensens I knew back in Paris.

But we were in a position to help Mr. Chester in this way by continuing to fix up the place around him. To that end, Lee got the porch pretty well fully repaired in barely a week's time. Did the railing, too, and even made small repairs to the rocking chairs that sat out there to catch the night and the world going by. Of course, nothing ever did go by, but there was a nice peace to that, too.

There was still plenty of work on the house to complete: repairing the gutters, sealing the windows and doors, patching up the sides of the barn. Occasionally Lee asked for my help with these jobs. But in that heat, it was hard. It seemed there was no in between: we either worked until our clothes were soaked through or we laid around doing nothing under the shade of a tree waiting until the heat broke and reveling in our laziness. When it got like that, I just sat there and listened to the sounds of insects and birds until they became as ordinary to me as breathing. All except the great rattling of the cicadas, which was a constant around us, an incredible amount of noise that I never got accustomed to.

But I'd come to know the birds and their calls even if I didn't know the names of any of them. There were black-and-white ones with yellowish heads and some with beautiful yellow breasts and black spots on the sides and then there were my favorites: several times I'd seen a bunch of them, walking around each other, strutting in little circles, with their feathers up over their heads like ears and their wings raised and these great orange sacks on the side of their heads, all circling around each other and moaning at one another. I never knew if they were getting ready to fight or mate or what, because they never seemed to do anything at all except walk around each other moaning like they did. Lee said they were stupid birds, brains the size of peanuts, but I reminded him that everything's got a purpose, everything in life.

Yeah? he said. How about cockroaches? Or chiggers? Or leeches? What purpose they serve?

I didn't like when he got like that and I had no problem giving him a piece of my mind or telling him he was out of line.

Everything's got some purpose, I told him, even if I can't answer what that might be. Everything on this earth.

⁓

It wasn't so much the case that I still had lots of work to do after that beginning burst of it when we first came to Mirabile, but what work I did have, I generally took care of in the early morning and then left everything else for the next day. Sometimes, the mercury soared to and beyond a hundred even before noon. We had a radio in the kitchen, and I turned it on for Mr. Chester from time to time, which I surely didn't mind except that it had to be turned up really high so that I could hardly stand to stay in the same room. They said on the radio that it was the worst heat wave in the Midwest since 1959.

Barry called to make sure we were getting on okay.

Just fine, Mr. Barry, I told him, twirling the telephone cord around my finger.

You making out all right in this heat? he asked.

Yes, sir. We are.

If things get intolerable, you can find relief in the cellar. It's cool down there no matter how hot it is above.

After we hung up, I went down there. He was right. I hadn't been before except once, and then I only went halfway before I turned back around. The crickets who'd taken up residence were so loud they could almost drive you deaf. It was a creepy-looking place and I had no business down there anyway. But now, with the promised coolness, I went the whole way.

The smell hit me first: a musty odor of old mothballs and age and perhaps water that had come in and dried up several times over. There was only one light, a dim bulb you had to pull the string to after making your way around in the dark to get to it. It was such a weak light that even when I got it on, I still could hardly see anything and what I could see was mainly just a bunch of shelves crammed with stuff I couldn't name if I wanted to. All kinds of strange contraptions, useful on a large working farm, I suppose, but whose function escaped me entirely. There was one thing that looked like a cross between a coffee pot and a toaster and maybe parts of a bicycle. I couldn't make heads or tails of it.

But when I went to put it back in its place on the shelf, I found a jar crammed full of Mercury head dimes.

I stood there for a good long while, just looking at those dimes, before I took the jar and placed it in a paper bag I found nearby and tucked the whole thing under my arm. Carefully, I walked through the house, listening for Lee or Mr. Chester, and sprinted up the stairs into the room where I'd been sleeping, and pushed the jar under the bed.

I knew it was wrong and yet I did it anyway, like I told myself it wasn't me that was doing it but some other person that only resembled me. Marie, and not Lilly. I told myself Mr. Chester wouldn't ever know on account of his not being able to see and the fact that he never went down to the cellar anyway and so therefore it didn't matter. But of course I knew what I was doing was wrong. True, they were only dimes and weren't so old, I didn't think, to be worth much more than the ten cents they were, but there was a reason Mr. Chester had collected them. So of course it was wrong.

But I hid them anyway. And even afterward, after I burned from shame for stealing from him, I didn't put them back. I had other plans.

꒕

Mr. Chester was lying on his bed not moving when I went to check on him. I plugged in the oscillating fan and let it run over him and then walked outside to find Lee sitting on the porch in just his underwear drinking endless quantities of water.

It has to be a hundred and five degrees, he said.

The heat made it so you could hardly think about anything at all— your name, your age, where you were even. It felt like a heavy blanket that settled on everything and wouldn't let you breathe. It was one of those heats where the idea of food is simply unpalatable. All you can do is drink. So I joined Lee and drank some of his water and we sat there for hours waiting for some relief that didn't come until the sun finally went down, and even then it was hardly much better. So we sat and didn't move and listened to the coyotes yelp in the distance.

Finally, I went back in and checked on Mr. Chester and he was fast asleep and so I joined Lee back out on the porch and we sat there some more in irritated silence until suddenly an entire army of fireflies—two, three, ten armies, maybe more—came and gave us a private show of such immensity it was as if the heat itself had made their lights and their efforts double. They flashed near our faces, some of them landing on our arms and legs, even one on my nose, and flashed so bright it blinded me for a second before it flew off and then we were in a different kind of silence. Just awe and wonder at what beauty this world is capable of at times. The whole sky was lit up with them and every time I tried to fix on one, one that might flash super bright near me, it streaked away and ten more took its place as if competing for my attention. Little pops of light everywhere before us, and the whole prairie, it seemed, alive with light bursts. It must be what heaven itself looks like.

It went on this way for near an hour before they seemed, one by one, to have tuckered themselves out, retreating to the very highest treetops and flashing there every now and again until they were too exhausted to flash anymore.

I forgot everything else during that show—who I was and why I was and what I was doing. Instead, I just *was*. And that was the gift of those fireflies. Because there are precious few moments in life when one can simply *be*, with nothing else to it. In the end, it might have been the most beautiful thing I'd ever seen. And I am certain to this day that I will never again in this lifetime witness anything near so glorious as that.

It was almost enough to make me forget completely the bad things I'd been a part of.

17

Independence Day had finally arrived, which wasn't soon enough for me. Or for Lee, for that matter. But for different reasons. For me, I was happy that it would finally be over and everyone could stop worrying themselves over it. Talk about being overhyped. It had been that way ever since Lee and I set out from Paris, more than a month earlier. Lee was excited because he felt he was living through history, something to tell our kids about. He said this over and over.

We're always living through history, every second of every day, I reminded him.

He told me not to get all philosophical on him.

This is the greatest country on Earth, he said. The only place where a man can be free to be what he wants to be, and it's worth celebrating two hundred years of that fact.

I reminded him that there used to be slavery, and Indians were massacred and women hardly counted as people and we're not as free as we like to think we are. When I said this I didn't need to remind him that he and I were on the run ourselves, but he looked at me mean, like I'd insulted his family or something.

Aw, go back to your poetry then or, better yet, move to the Soviet Union, you hate it here so much.

I let it go. It wasn't an argument I wanted anyway and I wasn't sure why I did it. It was a thing that came inside me at certain moments, this need to argue the other side of things. Besides, I reminded myself, what was the harm in letting him have his excitement? I mean, I did love it when he got all wound up like one of those jumpy things where you turn the little knob and watch as they hop around on their little plastic feet over and over in circles.

And there was another thing I had to admit: it *was* fun, once me and Lee and Mr. Chester headed into Haysville and watched the festivities. Everyone from everywhere nearby it seemed had come out, and they had little American flags in their hands and were all wearing red, white, and blue clothes. One old lady even had her hair dyed in red, white, and blue stripes and when I laughed upon seeing her, she looked at me, smiled as wide as the moon, and said, Happy birthday, missy. Happy birthday to us all! and continued on. It was clear that this day had allowed everyone to be whoever they wanted, even an old woman who made her hair up like a clown's.

The festivities began with a stunt flyer in an old-fashioned airplane. He did loops and once dove down straight to the prairie and then swooped up at the last second. Everyone gasped and some people couldn't even watch. For his last trick, his plane spurted out puffs of smoke that spelled out USA—well, sort of. By the time he finished up with the "A," the "U" was more like a smudge that didn't look like any letter at all. Still, everyone knew what he was trying and the crowd appreciated it.

Lee grabbed my hand and whispered into my ear: Baby, one day I'm gonna write *your* name in the sky. Then he kissed me on my cheek. The feel of him on me and his breath in my ear and the things he said to me; I could hardly stop my heart from pounding and I knew: I was just addicted to him. No other way to put it.

141

The three of us found a spot along the main street and watched as the parade went by. I narrated for Mr. Chester and at each description I gave, he nodded and smiled and it was clear from his face that he was enjoying it immensely and I wondered why it was I had ever resisted like I did. It was fun and, yes, I suppose there is something special about being around to witness your country turning two hundred.

The marching band from the local high school went by first and their playing was loud and very good. The musicians swung their trumpets and tubas and trombones back and forth and side to side as they marched and I marveled at the choreography. It really was perfect, each step in exact time to one another. It was clear they'd been practicing for a good long while.

Behind them came a long and very large Cadillac convertible and there was a man in it in a dark-blue suit despite the heat and he waved at everyone. I didn't know who he was, but he seemed important. Important enough to get his own car and driver and to smile like he'd just swallowed a canary and he waved at everyone, including me, even though there was no way he could have known me from Eve.

Then came another convertible car, a smaller one, and a pretty young woman sitting up in it, holding a big bouquet of flowers. She had a sash on and a tiara and lots of makeup. Some kind of pageant winner, it was clear, and when I described her to Mr. Chester, he smiled real wide, rubbed his hands together, and said, Woo-hoo. I slapped him lightly on the hand, told him to mind himself before I got too jealous, and he said, Miss Marie, no one can hold a candle to you.

There was a man selling ice cream from a little cart and we bought three and stood at our place on the sidewalk and watched the rest of the parade, which wasn't too much longer, but longer than I would have thought such a small town could muster: a bunch of boys in football uniforms, half a dozen baton twirlers, a few dogs gotten up in American flag gear, and my favorite: a man dressed as Uncle Sam walking on enormous stilts underneath his superlong striped pants. I couldn't even imagine how he did it. I was sure he was going to fall over. I could hardly watch and Lee had to take over the descriptions for Mr. Chester.

Last up in the parade were five soldiers who walked unsmiling and real stiff in their army uniforms and they got the loudest cheers of all and when I took back over the descriptions and told Mr. Chester what was happening, he stood at attention and saluted. Quite a few of the men in town were saluting also and everyone who had been wearing a hat now had it off and crossed over their heart. It was all enough to make me tear up.

Turned out the important-looking man from the convertible was the mayor of Haysville and he gave a speech in the town square after the parade. He called up the soldiers and everyone gave them more salutes and more cheers and it really was nice. Even Lee, I could tell, was a bit choked up about it because he gave each of those five men a salute and a nod and his face was so serious while he did it, more than I almost ever saw on him.

The mayor talked about how we were the luckiest people in the world to live where we did and he put in a nod for President Ford but reminded us that we were free to vote for whoever we wanted and no matter which way the election wound up, it was one more reason living in America was so special because there would be no riots in the streets or police and tanks but rather a free people taking part in another peaceful election, no matter the outcome. Mr. Chester clapped at this though he didn't share the same spirit, I noted, when he said he'd be damned if this country was stupid enough to elect a peanut farmer from Georgia. I thought it was an odd statement, seeing as how Mr. Chester was a farmer himself once. But maybe that was why he was qualified to make such judgments.

But all of that got lost anyway because just there, across the square, staring straight at us, was the old man from the river.

My heart jumped and my mouth went all dry.

Lee, look! I squeaked. I pointed across at the man. It was him, for sure. He had those worry lines in his head and that patch of discolored hair. It was higher up than I'd remembered it and it seemed that much of the rest of his head had gotten some white, too—or gray, at least. But it was him. I was sure.

What? Lee asked.

Look, over there.

I pulled Lee a few feet away.

What are you talking about? he asked.

Problem was, people kept walking back and forth and there were kids tossing a football now that the mayor was done and all those people were between us and the man and so now, when I thought about it, maybe he wasn't staring at us but rather watching the people between us. But it sure looked like he was keeping us in his sights.

The man from the river, I whispered through clenched teeth. The old man. You know.

I'll be damned, Lee said. That sure does look like him, doesn't it?

It looks like him because it is him.

No, that ain't him.

Yes, it is.

You're imagining it.

Look at that hair. I'd recognize it anywhere. You remember that patch?

I sure do. And I remember how black the rest of his hair was and that man there has a lot of gray.

'Cause his son was—

Hush up now, Lil.

Lee stared at him a bit longer before he said, I tell you: it sure does look like him.

Lee—

Let's get out of here.

We ushered Mr. Chester off and walked quickly back to our car. I kept looking back but couldn't see the man. If he was following us, he was either hiding himself real well or we'd lost him.

Still, I continued looking back, even after we got in the car and drove off. I kept my eye on the back window the whole way, just to see if there wasn't some car following us.

‿

What are we gonna do, Lee? I asked after we'd gotten back to Mirabile and I got Mr. Chester settled in bed.

What do you mean?

That man, Lee. What do you think?

I think you need to not worry so much. I say that wasn't him. It was just some guy that looked like him. All these Plains farmers look the same. All that time in the sun, their hands digging up the earth and rolling udders. They all wind up looking the same. It wasn't him and even if it was, he doesn't know to come out here and even if he did, there's nothing to tie us to his son and what happened. Now, get some sleep, okay?

Lee kissed my forehead and left the room.

I stared at the ceiling, following the lines of cracks in the plaster. After hours of this, I went to Lee's room and nudged him awake.

I'm scared, I said.

There's nothing to be scared of. It wasn't him and I'm going to take care of us no matter if it was. Go get some sleep.

He pulled his sheets over his head and turned away. And it was clear come morning, by the steely look in his eye, that there would be nothing to be gained in my pressing the issue.

After that, Lee and I didn't again mention the river man. And because we never talked about it, it eventually felt at times like a thing that didn't actually happen. 'Cause when you did think of it, and you reminded yourself it was a real thing, you had to accept the fact also that there was one less person walking this earth on account of it. No matter if you thought it was justified or not, that was the truth of it and there was no escaping that. So, I did my best to put it out of my mind. I'd tried that before, of course. And it was no easy thing.

And I can say this: despite Lee's confidence in the matter, I didn't sleep that night after the parade, nor very much for several nights after. I just kept waiting for that old man to come walking up to the barn and look right into my soul and ask me what happened to his son.

He never did, though. And in some strange way, that was a disappointment to me, almost as if I wanted him to come and find us, so I could finally be rid of it, once and for all, that thing that clung to me every step and every breath I took.

18

I continued to tell myself that the lives we were living were perfectly normal. And soon enough, we settled into a routine that made everything seem that it was, in fact, the case. Weeks went by, and then months.

Most days we were up not much after the sun. I made Mr. Chester's breakfast: eggs and flapjacks, along with sliced potatoes, and, of course, strong black coffee, and I took it in good cheer when he and Lee made fun of me for all the cream and sugar in mine. Later in the day, we got to work. The cows needed milking, which became my job. They needed to be fed, of course, and the house needed to be kept clean and neat. Otherwise, there wasn't too much for me to do. On Sundays, we didn't work at all, keeping the Sabbath rest, as Mr. Chester called it, even though he wasn't up for making the trip to church himself. I made sure not to sleep in late those days though and instead went out into the fields and sat quietly until I heard the chapel bells calling folks to church in Haysville. They went on for some ten minutes at least and it was a music more lovely than anything I could before imagine. It calmed me, which was something I sorely needed.

In the afternoons, I sat with Mr. Chester and read to him from his books—mostly about war and generals and all things military.

You serve, Mr. Chester? I asked.

Proudly. Not long after the Great War. I didn't do much, though. It was a peaceful time, that period between the wars.

Well, you're lucky for that.

All young men want to see action, he said.

But you're sitting here alive and had you served in either of those wars, well, who knows?

But then I wouldn't be sitting here talking about missing it, now would I?

I told him he had a point in that. Still, I said, I'm really happy you're here now.

He said, Thanks, Miss Marie, and like so many times before, I almost didn't answer, thinking he was talking to someone else, forgetting that it was me who was Miss Marie. I swear it, some days I couldn't get it through my head. What made it worse was that when we were alone, Lee went back to calling me Lilly. I'd given it all up, not calling him Lee or Jason or anything else really but communicating by look or by not talking at all. That wasn't such a hard thing to do, actually. We'd done so much living in such a short time that it felt like we'd grown to be like one of those old couples that's been together forever and knows nothing else. I suspect Mr. Chester and his wife had become like that. He hardly ever uttered a word about her. But I was certain he missed her. It was much nicer to think of things that way. It would have been better to have lost someone he truly loved and missed than to not miss her at all. That would have been a tragedy, and not something I could even imagine. Because surely Mr. Chester and his wife, when they were that happy couple in the photographs, imagined they'd be as in love for the rest of their lives together as they were on those days when they had those pictures taken that lined the stairs. Whenever Lee caught me looking at those photographs, he asked me what it was I found so fascinating about old photos, and I just told him I thought they were nice. He didn't need to know that I was thinking about us when I looked at them, and who and where we'd be when we reached the state Mr. Chester had.

Anyway, Mr. Chester thanked me—or Marie—and I came to and said, You're welcome, and tried to recall who I was and felt stupid that I couldn't seem to remember it so easily. But then again, I hardly felt like myself most days. Most of the time, I couldn't give any reasons to the things I was doing or the life I was living.

One morning, Lee told me he was going into town to get food from the grocer and silage for the cows. I asked to come with him, told him I needed to go into the pharmacy for unmentionables and a few other things. He didn't say a word to that, of course, only to blush and then say, Come on then.

Hold on, I said. I'll be right back.

I ran upstairs and grabbed the jar of dimes out from under the bed. I started counting them out but I could hear Lee yelling at me to hurry up.

We ain't got all day, he yelled.

I shoved about a dozen dimes into my pocket and ran outside to meet him at the car.

As usual, he held the door open for me.

It was a thing he did, holding the car door open, just like he always pulled out chairs for me, too. Probably the first twenty times he did this, I told him I didn't see the point in it, that I was perfectly capable of opening a door or pulling out a chair.

A man should have manners, he'd say.

I liked the ride into town. At first, there was nothing at all to see apart from the prairie but then, very suddenly, you came over the slightest rise and there it was: Haysville in all its glory. Don't blink or you'll miss it, Lee said the first few times we came in. But as we spent almost all our time on the Mirabile homestead and it was just us, Mr. Chester, and the cows, little Haysville had come to seem like New York City or something.

149

After Lee parked in the center of town, he went one way and I went another. Don't take too long, he told me, and I said I wouldn't, but I knew he'd be much longer than I would. And this was because he'd had to go to two places and I really only had one and it wasn't the pharmacy at all but instead the phone booth in front of it.

When I saw Lee turn the corner toward the grocer, I slipped into the booth, closed the door, and lined up Mr. Chester's dimes along the counter.

I was too scared to dial right away. So instead, I watched some towns-people going by with their private lives and private troubles and there I was in a glass booth walled off from everyone else with my own sets of troubles. But then I remembered that I didn't have much time, so I didn't waste any more of it and dialed the number. While I didn't think to hang up while it was ringing, there was a part of me that wished she wouldn't answer.

But then I heard her voice.

Mama?

And then I heard her crying, saying, Baby girl, baby girl. Where are you? Oh, my baby girl.

I'm fine, Mama. I'm just fine, I said. But I started to cry from hearing her voice and I didn't want to because she'd think I wasn't fine, so I told her I missed her and that was why I sounded the way I did, but that, really, I was perfectly okay.

Upon hearing this, she stopped her crying and now she was plain angry, yelling at me, telling me how I'd made her sick with worry and how would I like it, how could I even live, if she'd one day up and disappeared and I didn't hear from her months.

I'm so sorry, Mama. I really am. I'm not sure I can explain why I left except to say I did and of course Lee has a lot to do with it. But I promise you, Mama, he didn't make me go and in fact he takes real good care of me and he's a perfect gentleman. He always opens car doors and pulls out chairs for me when I sit, I added.

There's a whole hell of a lot more to being a man than opening doors and pulling out chairs.

I know it, Mama. But these are only some of the things. He's a true gentleman and he loves me, Mama. He does.

Where are you? she asked.

I felt a terrible tightness in my stomach and chest because I knew I couldn't answer. If I did she'd be on her way before I could even hang up the phone. And so I repeated that I was fine and she shouldn't worry.

Goddamn it, Lillian, she yelled, and this was something I'd never heard her say and I knew she would put her hands through that very phone and strangle me if she could. But this only made me feel even more sure I was doing right by not saying. It was one or the other: Mama angry enough to kill me for not telling her, or Lee angry at me for going ahead and telling her where we were. Lee was who I was with and I knew darn well no matter how angry Mama was at me, the minute I walked through her front door again, she'd be there with her arms wide open and give me such a big hug I wouldn't be able to breathe. She might have slapped me across my face right after, but the hug would be first. I wasn't sure I could say the same about Lee.

Where are you? she asked again, more control in her voice this time. But lucky for me the operator broke in at this moment and told me I needed to put in three more dimes, at the very same time I said: I don't know myself anymore, Mama. I'm just not sure who I am.

There was a clicking sound and the operator said something else but I couldn't hear her right. I asked her what, but I put in my dimes and it seemed she'd gone and then it was Mama's voice again and I realized she hadn't heard me.

I'm coming to get you, she said.

I could hear a man's voice behind her. I could guess it was Hank. I wanted to tell Mama that he was another reason I left, but I couldn't. It wasn't fair. He was all she had now and I couldn't very well try and turn her against him.

I don't want you to come get me, I said.

I called upon all the strength I had in me and I continued: I promise you I'm fine and I promise you that I'll be home again someday. I can't say for sure when, but I'll be home again. And I'm afraid you're going to have to accept that I'm with Lee now and that means accepting him, too.

You're asking me to accept a man who stole my girl away.

He didn't steal me away, Mama. I went on my own accord and I'm happy I did. You'll see: once you know Lee, know him like I do, you'll love him as if he was your own son.

How are you living? she asked. I mean, how are you getting on? What about food and shelter? Where do you sleep at night?

Right now we're working on a farm. I milk the cows, if you can believe that, and Lee fixes up the old house and barn. But mostly I take care of an old man who's blind and nearly deaf and his wife passed on last winter and he's all alone. Or was anyway until we came along. He's real sweet, Mama. And we get money and food and shelter and it's a fine life and I'm enjoying myself and I think I might have even put on a few pounds.

She was quiet for such a long time I thought maybe the line had gone dead, but then she said, in almost a whisper, You take care of yourself, Lillian. You make sure you get home to me in one piece.

Yes, Mama.

I'm serious now. You make sure you stay safe and healthy and you call me the very instant you're ready for me to come get you. I don't care if it's two in the morning and you're calling from Alaska. You hear me?

Yes, Mama, I will.

You get yourself home in one piece. And you call me from time to time, let me know you're okay.

I'll do my best, Mama.

I love you, Lil-Bear.

I love you too, Mama.

I said good-bye and quickly hung up because now I couldn't stop the tears from coming and I had to hurry to wipe my face and rub my eyes when I saw Lee striding up the sidewalk with bags in his hands.

Where're your things, he asked when he reached me outside the pharmacy.

Didn't have what I needed, I told him.

He looked at me. What's wrong with you? he asked.

Nothing, I told him.

Look like you've been crying.

Well, I haven't.

All right. Come on then, he said. We gotta pick up the silage. Man at the lot'll help us fill the trunk and tie it off so it won't fall out on the drive back.

I stood there.

He looked at me.

You hear me? he said, and he got in the car.

I'd been waiting for him to open my door for me, but in his haste, he'd forgotten.

19

I was still in a bad mood when we got back to Mirabile, but Lee didn't press me on why; I could guess that he thought it had to do with my lady thing, as he called it, and I didn't say anything to lead him from that conclusion. Sometimes it was a convenience.

I went into the house quietly and checked on Mr. Chester. He was fine and suggested that maybe later I could read him a few of my favorite poems. The Civil War guy. You know, Lincoln's friend, he said, as he'd come around to admitting his fondness for Whitman. Sure, Mr. Chester, I said, but I heard Lee outside calling for me, so I excused myself.

Help me with these, Lee said when I got out to him. He was pulling on the bags of silage from the trunk, hardly budging the heavy things. We didn't produce any of the stuff ourselves and didn't have the equipment to move the huge circles of it you saw in the fields on the farms around us, so we had to get it in smaller bags from the guy in town. But even the smaller bags were plenty heavy and even Lee, strong as he was, couldn't manage them by himself.

He parked the car near the barn and we started hauling out the bags. The first crop of it we took on had a nice smell, almost like molasses or tobacco or something earthy like that. But the stuff we got this day smelled kinda fishy, like it had gone bad or something. I complained about it to Lee, but he told me it was for the cows to eat and wouldn't wind up on our supper plates so it wasn't for me to worry about. He was in a foul mood and so was I, so we worked in silence. That was fine: talking to Mama had made me feel lonesome and sad, so I was in no mood anyway.

Occasionally, some loose grass found its way out of the bags and attached to my dress and my hair and I couldn't stand the feel of the stuff. Dry straw is one thing and easy enough to brush away, but the silage Lee got in town still held onto its wet and it felt slimy. It always made me shudder to see the cows chomping on it with their big dumb eyes and that stuff going round and round in their mouths and all that spit and snot gooing up their whole faces. I was no little girl when it came to most things, but I couldn't stand the sight of that. It was enough to make me feel sick.

Once we'd gotten it all stored, I told Lee I was going inside to lay down, that I didn't feel very well, and he didn't say a word but stayed behind in the barn.

I went up to my room but instead of lying down like I said, I stood at the window, which gave a view of the huge walnut tree with its mighty branches, a place where I was certain Barry as a boy must have climbed and played. I wondered, too, if at one time he had a swing there like I had at my home in Paris.

Part of the barn was visible through the branches and leaves, and every now and then I could see Lee moving back and forth. At one point, he stood there for a long moment and then moved again like he was unsure of something. I wondered what it was he was doing just standing, taking one step, moving back, standing still again. It was peculiar the way he looked all agitated but doing nothing about it, whatever it was. Then, all at once, he jogged out of the barn and straight into the house. I heard him on the stairs right away and before I even had time to get

155

myself on the bed and pretend that's where I'd been, he came into the room with his eyes all wide and his face full of sweat.

Come with me, he said.

What is it?

Just come on. Now.

I used to love it when he got like that, all riled up and hardly able to contain himself. Maybe it was my mood, or the phone call and the way it had to be hurried and my missing Mama, but whatever it was, I was full of irritation for Lee and I found myself staring in anger at the back of his head as he sprinted down the stairs while I moved at my own pace.

I realized in that moment that me and Lee had passed out of that phase where you're just plain fascinated by someone, by the mystery of them. I knew Lee now, through and through, and while that was something to celebrate, because he was mine and I was his, it was clear to me now that it was also something to mourn. 'Cause the mystery had gone out of things and with that mystery gone, a certain excitement had gone, too. Things to look forward to and be surprised by. So I was sad for that. I suppose nothing can stay fresh and new forever. But I just hadn't thought that its expiration would have come on so soon. And I hadn't realized either that when it did come it would mean that some of the things I used to love most about Lee could turn into the things I suddenly couldn't stand.

What's so important? I asked after I found him standing at the edge of the barn.

He looked around, all nervous, as if there was anyone within ten miles apart from blind Mr. Chester, who was at that moment sitting in the kitchen listening to the radio at high volume.

Look at this, he said, and he scattered some loose straw, uncovering a couple of planks on the barn floor. He pulled on one of the planks and it came right up and he placed it aside and then he got on his knees and reached down under where the plank was and pulled out a little box, which he opened and showed me.

156

Inside was more money than I'd ever seen in one place.

It's almost two thousand dollars, Lee said. I counted it twice.

So?

So? Lee asked. So? Well, what do you think?

I don't know, Lee, so why don't you spell it out for me.

It means it'll keep us in the black for a good long time and allow us to go somewhere, for real. New Orleans, Lil-Flower. Remember that?

But it's not ours, I told him. Mr. Chester must've buried it out here in case times got tough. Or maybe his wife did and he doesn't even know about it and would be real surprised and pleased to know it.

Lee looked at me. For quite some time. So we're standing there, looking at each other, trying to read the thoughts in each other's heads. Until finally he said, Lil, I don't think you fully understand the game here. Might I remind you that—here he lowered his voice to a whisper—that we killed a man and—

It was that stupid gun! I yelled. That stupid gun you brought along.

And if I hadn't brought it along, what would he have done to you, huh?

I crossed my arms and said nothing.

This is just like you, he said. Like all women. Want all the protection in the world. But if things get messy on account of that protection, well then . . . I tell you, first sign of something going awry and . . .

You're not finishing your sentences, Lee.

Far as I'm concerned this money is ours. It was their foolishness not to hide it in the house. Anyone can go poking around a barn. What if some tramp came through and bedded down here for the night?

Maybe it *was* in the house but when they started interviewing care-takers they moved it out for fear of someone finding it then.

Well then, that's their foolishness, not mine. They could have used a bank in town.

No matter why, Lee, it's not our money to keep. Their foolishness as you call it don't give us claims to anything that's not ours.

This money is ours, he repeated. And it'll stay that way. If you don't want to spend any of it, so be it. But remember that what I do, I do for us. And you will not tell Mr. Chester a thing.

Okay, I won't tell Mr. Chester, I thought. I won't talk to him at all. Or to Lee either.

I stormed away. But I turned before I got to the house and instead made my way onto the prairie. When I got far enough away so that the barn and the house and my life and everything else seemed really small and well behind me, I plopped myself down among the birds and the insects and decided to cry again. This time good and long and full and I realized that I'd only let out a little bit of it back at that phone booth in Haysville with those stupid dimes I'd stolen—dimes were one thing, not thousands of dollars, I told myself—and now no one would stop me from crying. I'd sit out there by myself on that prairie until I had nothing left in me to get out. And that is exactly what I did.

And before I knew it, the coyotes had joined in.

20

The one thing about crying the way I did was that it allowed me to sleep really deep that night. In fact, when I woke the next morning, the sun strong and already filling the room, I realized that the night before was one of the better nights of sleep I'd had since me and Lee set out. Strange, maybe, but true.

The new day began with the three of us in the kitchen listening to the radio over breakfast. We heard about a mysterious disease that struck an American Legion convention in Philadelphia. Almost thirty people had died from what we would later come to know as Legionnaires' disease. Another big news item was that some scientists found the skull of a boy in Africa that was more than a million and a half years old. It got me thinking again about all that stuff I hated to keep thinking of but couldn't help anyway: how we are all here and then we are not, just like that. And it was such a small step from thinking that to thinking *why* we are here, and what we are doing here, in the grand sense, and it was a terrible way to think about things because when you do, well, what good answer is there for any of it? It put me in a quiet mood, and when I got to thinking things like that and Lee badgered me to explain why I wasn't talking, that made me want to talk even less. It went on this way for several days, me not talking, with my head being too full to want to discuss any of it anyway.

Besides, I was still furious with Lee about that money and we spent each day's breakfast only looking at one another occasionally and not saying a word and I was glad of the radio's volume being a ready excuse for why we weren't talking. While I would have wished the opposite, the truth was that the more the days passed, the angrier I became.

One morning, while I cleared and cleaned the dishes, I actually thought about running away. Just taking off out the back door, tromping through the tall grass, on into Nebraska, and heading . . . somewhere. Anywhere but here with a thief. Then I considered telling Lee that I was going to stay at Mirabile and that he should go, go with all his new money. I'd stay and take care of Mr. Chester. Or maybe I'd simply pick up that phone and call Mama collect and tell her I was ready for her to come get me.

Still in my stormy mood, I headed out to the barn to milk the cows. When the heat was real bad, I hated that job because the cows would give off so much more heat and it was almost impossible to breathe in the barn, and to get up under them like you have to was pretty awful. But the heat had broken now and it was a lovely day, weather-wise, so I didn't mind it this time. In fact, there was something even nice about leaning my head into their sides while I got their milk. It was like I could have company, but I didn't need to talk to anyone.

So I was doing that and losing myself in my own thoughts, about that skull in Africa and about the money and about how mad I was and about the sick men in Philadelphia, when I heard a car approach and then stop. I was surprised to see it was Barry. He came into the barn and said hi to me real pleasant and I was really glad to see him. Maybe it was just a break in the routine. Whatever it was, I was happy and felt proud when he declared that the place looked great and he was amazed with all the work we'd done. He smacked his palms on the back of the cow I was working and said how healthy they looked, too, and I smiled at him and there was a feeling that flashed through me where I thought that I might like to *be* with an older man like him. It surprised me because it was not a thought I'd had before, not like that anyway.

I was still thinking it when he walked away into the house to say hello to Mr. Chester. But then I felt foolish to have those thoughts, especially considering how I must have looked a complete fright—unclean, my hair a mess, my clothes all filthy the way they were. Besides, I was certain he saw me as only a kid anyway and hardly a real woman, so I pushed the thoughts away and reminded myself how silly it was to even have them in the first place.

When I finished up with the cows, I went into the house and found Barry and Mr. Chester sitting at the kitchen table. When Barry saw me, he smiled at me again and said, Dad told me you've been taking real great care of him and things here and I'm very grateful for it.

It's our pleasure, I told him, and there was a real good feeling all around. But it changed when Lee came in, like in that weird way the wind has sometimes of shifting a day, bringing with it some warning. He had a hard and strange look on his face and everyone just stared and the air got a little heavy as Lee stopped, looked everyone over, and then said to Barry, I didn't know you were here.

Had business not too far away, about an hour or so. Thought I'd come by first, make sure you guys were doing okay.

Lee remembered himself, said, Of course, of course, welcome, sir, and removed his gloves and extended his hand to shake. The heaviness lifted a little, almost like the kitchen had been a balloon and someone unknotted the end and let out a bit of air.

We were in the kitchen another half hour or so, chatting and catching up, Barry confirming with us all the dollar numbers regarding pay and food and credit at the stores in town, and when the business side of things was through, he told us about his home outside Chicago.

I'd love to visit, I said. I've never been to a big city.

There are a million things to do, he said. You like museums?

I nodded. Yes, I said, though, truth be told, I'd never been in a museum. I could see Lee looking at me funny, kind of smirking, and I burned some more with anger. I love art, I declared, turning my full attention to Barry.

The Art Institute is considered one of the best in the country.

Well, I'd love to go there.

Lee was still looking at me out the corner of his eye—I could tell— as he sipped at his coffee. He drank it, as was his habit, standing up near the sink, like he was readying himself to flee any moment. Soon enough he excused himself, said he had to shower. Barry said he'd be leaving soon to get on to his appointments, so they took their good-byes and shook hands kinda roughly and because I knew Lee like no one else did, I could see it in his eyes that he hadn't liked this visit and was eager to see Barry go. It was there on his face and in his eyes plain as day, that hard look in him. I was sure he was worried about that money.

Well, Dad, Barry said, getting up, I see you're in good hands.

That seemed to signal that it was time for him to go.

Mr. Chester said, Yes, indeed, I am in good hands, and I cleared Barry's lunch dishes and took them to the sink for him. He thanked me and told me I didn't need to do that, while I filled the sink with soap and warm water.

It's nothing, I said.

We both stood there a second, me filling the sink and him behind me, and we didn't say anything and it was an awkward feeling, like neither of us knew what was coming next.

But then he said, Well, good-bye. I'm certain I'll see you again soon.

Okay, I said, with my back to him, and I heard him leave and I had the strangest feeling come over me. I pulled my hands from the soapy water and ran out after him and caught him as he was getting into his car.

Mr. Barry, I yelled.

Yes, Marie?

I came so close to telling him then that my name wasn't Marie at all, that it was Lilly, because I wanted him to know me, the real me, and I couldn't stand continuing the act with people I thought I could care about.

We found some money, I said, because it was the next thing that came to my mind and then it was coming out of my mouth before I could even stop it.

Barry just looked at me, so I continued: In the barn, under some planks. Nearly two thousand dollars.

That so? he said.

I nodded.

Can you show me?

I took him to the barn and to the spot and cleared away the pile of straw that Lee had put back over it and I pulled up the planks. Immediately I felt the coolness of the earth, rising from the spot.

Down there, I said.

Barry got on his knees and reached in.

There's nothing there, he said.

I didn't know what to say because I knew darn well where the money was. Or, more accurately, why it was no longer where it once was.

Thank goodness Barry didn't press me on it. He didn't ask me where it was or what happened to it. Instead, he put the plank back and got up to leave the barn. I knew what was about to happen, that he was going in the house to visit with Lee about it and it made me feel ill.

Please . . . I started to say.

You've got nothing to worry about. I'll leave you out of it.

And then he started his way to the house.

I had a real sick feeling shoot through me, like I might throw up. I moved to the far side of the barn, away from the smell of the cows, and sat there on a pail with my hands on my stomach.

It wasn't long before I heard Barry's voice again and Lee's and they were coming closer and then they were both there in the barn and I felt even sicker when Lee looked me in the eye, looking right through me it felt like, straight past everything on the outside and landing on my soul. I felt naked and wrapped my hands and arms even tighter around myself.

Barry cleared the straw from the hiding place and pulled up the plank, and then he just stood there, waiting. For what exactly I wasn't sure.

Well, sir, I don't know a thing about it, Lee said.

Has there been anyone else here besides you two?

Not that I know of.

Well, then . . .

I can't explain it, Lee said. Have you asked your pop where it might be? Maybe he moved it into the house.

I did ask him right now and he said that he put it out here long ago—and now he's quite upset because that was money my mother had saved for years and now it's missing.

Lee looked at him, then looked at me.

Then Lee said, How did you even know about it in the first place?

I almost cried out, but swallowed it instead and there it sat, at the bottom of my stomach. I could feel it, deep inside me, and it was a terrible feeling.

Barry didn't answer, for which I was grateful. Instead he said, I am going to tell you one last time to give it to me and I will restore it to its rightful owner, which is my father. And then you two can ship on out.

That's where things changed. Lee gave up the game, didn't bother pretending anymore. He got that smile of his, the sad one, like he was about to do something that gave him some little bit of pleasure but also made him feel bad, some terrible deed that needed to be done but, if he had his way, he'd just as soon avoid altogether.

He said to Barry, Well, sir, I'm afraid I can't do that.

Can't? Or won't? Barry said.

Lee smirked, like he liked the way Barry thought and talked. I remembered this same look on his face that day we left Paris, when Hank confronted him.

Lee said, I suppose it's both, sir. Can't *and* won't.

And then he pulled that stupid gun from the back of his jeans and pointed it not quite at Barry but at the ground near his feet, to sort of show him he had it and for now, at least, that's all that Barry needed to know.

But then—and I'll never understand, not until the day I die, why on earth Barry chose to do what he did next, but he got this real angry look on his face, and he turned all red, and he said, This isn't some damned game! and took some quick steps toward Lee as if he was going to try and wrestle the gun out of Lee's hands and that's when Lee lifted up the gun and shot him, right in his chest.

It wasn't like what you see on TV, where the person who gets shot staggers around, his hand over the place where the bullet went in, and says something real profound or something. No, Barry crumpled. Just fell over right where he was and took two or three breaths and then stopped breathing altogether and died. Just like that. The whole thing, from start to finish, took maybe five seconds and I could only guess that Lee got him straight through the heart.

I didn't yell out. I didn't throw up. I didn't get light-headed at the sight of it. And that was one of the worst things about it. I should have done any of those things, or all of them. But I didn't. Like what I'd just seen was little more than a bad movie.

Instead, me and Lee stood there looking at each other while the cows bucked and struggled from the noise of the gun before I turned away because I couldn't stand the sight of it and I hated him and I hated my life and all I wanted was to go home, to get in my bed in Paris and let Mama run a brush through my hair and turn back time and pretend I'd never left.

As for Lee, it was as if he remembered something suddenly and after he put a finger on Barry's neck he got up and hurried to the house. Don't tarry, is all he said to me before he left.

I sat there looking at Barry's body and it was the strangest thing. With it lying there like that, no longer moving, no longer talking, no longer breathing, it was like it wasn't even a real person anymore but a wax dummy or something, and I remembered what I'd once heard a preacher say a long time ago when we used to go to church, that the body is only a vessel, a pile of bones wrapped in a gray suit, once the soul has quit it.

It felt almost like I was floating as I stepped past that vessel and headed into the house. I wasn't even capable of feeling anything anymore, it seemed. Lee was wrestling with my case and he had another suitcase he pulled from Mr. Chester's closet, and he was filling them both with not only our clothes and possessions but also with items from the home: some silverware, a few hand tools, dried food, cans and such. And of course the box with the two thousand dollars.

I went to Mr. Chester's room and saw he was dead, too, and with the pillow lying next to his head the way it was, I could guess what happened. I sat down on the bed next to him. His eyes and mouth were closed and he looked very peaceful, like he might only be sleeping. I took some comfort in that. I put my hand on his and rubbed it a little, watching the veins roll over his knuckles.

I'm sorry, Mr. Chester. I'm sorry for it all, I said.

Then I got up and left.

You had to do that to him, too? I asked Lee when I returned. I whispered it. It was all I could manage.

Lee kept on packing in a fury and said, He ain't all deaf. No doubt he heard the shot. We can't have that. He was an old man, Lil. Don't get too bent out of shape over it. Hell, probably did him a favor.

I went over and slapped Lee in the face, hard as I could.

He looked stunned, stopped what he was doing, and stared me in the eye.

You didn't have to. You're evil! I yelled.

I hated him. I truly did. So I continued hitting him, pounding my arms and fists into his chest as hard as I could until he grabbed both my hands and held them, real strong, until I wore myself out trying to break free.

When I finally exhausted myself and he let me go, he said, quietly, That's your one free pass. It *won't* happen again.

Then he closed up the suitcases.

Take one last look, he said. Don't leave anything behind. You got five minutes. Then meet me out at the car.

He walked out and left me alone.

I turned off the radio. In the silence that followed, it was as if there came a double silence. Or more. The whole place was silent, with everyone having quit it. All three of the people who had lived there were gone now, and all within a year, two of them within minutes of each other. And now me and Lee were leaving, too. Out on the road. Again.

I felt numb. But I was glad for the numbness because otherwise it would have been too much. I was able to walk through the house that had been my home for months and not even look up the stairs or at the photographs I knew were there, or feel the need to go into that room again where the woman of the house left her memories and her presence and grab one of her handmade doilies to take with me. Because I knew those things were never mine to begin with and they were not mine now, even if I'd tried to tell myself otherwise.

When I got outside, Lee was leaning against the car. I took one look at him and while my love for him was still there, deep inside me, it was overtaken at that moment by something much darker and much larger.

I ran.

I ran as hard as I could, my legs pumping through the tall grass, the bluestem scraping up my shins, until I fell to the ground, Lee's arms around me, cradling me.

What's all this? he shouted. What?

I can't do this anymore! I cried. I can't.

Do what?

This. This whole thing.

Lee rolled on top of me and brushed my sweat-soaked hair off my head, and he kissed me, first on my forehead and then on my lips. Baby, you have to, he said.

I shook my head.

Yes, you do. Because you're all I've got. You're all I've got in this world. He kissed me again. You know that, don't you?

I nodded.

And I'm going to take care of you. Forever. That I promise you. I am going to take care of you.

Now the dizziness came on, unlike before when it should have. It felt like the whole sky above and the earth below were spinning at different angles, everything once connected now unhooked and spinning without any purpose or reason.

Without my hardly realizing it, we had walked back to the car. Lee kept his hands on me to steady me and he kept running one hand over my head. I love you, he said. I love you, baby. More than anything else in this world, my beautiful girl.

I saw myself getting in the car, like I was there but not there at the same time.

Lee started up the engine and we drove off, just like that. There was no peeling out or squealing away, more like it was simply time to leave and the worst we'd done was left behind a pile of dirty dishes on the kitchen counter. As if we hadn't left two murdered men behind.

I didn't look back at the house as we drove away, either, and this was on purpose.

I suppose you could say we had practice in ignoring the reality of things, or at least we'd been convincing ourselves that some things weren't real, going back to that first man, the one at the river. It was certainly true for me: I'd long ago made a habit of not accepting the reality of bad things. I did this when my pop left and of course I did it with the river man, too. Just refusing to believe the reality of it, the sad and terrible reality that we were killers. This time, my brain did it for me. A fuzz formed around all my thoughts and nothing real or lasting could take root there. If I tried to make sense of what had just happened, something blocked it, just pushed it all away until it was nothing but flashes, bits of this and that, and nothing real, nothing I had to reckon with.

But while it was true that my brain wasn't clicking like normal, my heart was working double. It thumped inside me, giving off a dull ache with every beat. I was so, so sorry about what happened. I held a real affection for both Barry and especially Mr. Chester. And it hurt something terrible when flashes of them went through me, even if the thoughts didn't stay long or form into something bigger. Just like it hurt when I allowed myself to think too much about Mama. Because when I did, it was all I could do to keep the tears from flowing.

So I went back to that thing I did, doing my best to keep the thoughts on the outside when they eventually started creeping back in, shutting myself down. I figured maybe I'd grow out of it one day and face the reality of things better. Maybe, I figured, when I was sixteen.

We were driving a good long while before either one of us spoke. When the silence was broken, it was by Lee.

I'm sorry for Mr. Chester, he said. He was a good man.

I nodded.

And I won't ask you how Barry knew about that money.

Again, I said nothing. He didn't need to spell it out for me: Had I never said anything to Barry about it, he'd still be alive, off to do whatever he was in town to do and then back home the next day to Chicago. And Mr. Chester would be sitting in the kitchen most likely listening to the radio and I'd maybe read him some poetry and we'd still be at Mirabile and not back out on the road just when fall would soon enough be coming and a chill would be setting in. It did occur to me that if I was back at home, I'd be gearing up for a new school year. But as quickly as the thought came, it flittered away, as if it belonged to a part of my life that was long gone now with no chance of getting it back.

Where we headed? I asked.

South, Lee said.

So when we approached the intersection just outside town, he turned, pointing the car south and soon the sun was setting and its warmth filled my face and I closed my eyes and let it wash over me and I told myself that this is what I signed on for. I used to find such comfort in it, the sun on my face back in that armchair by the window in the home I grew up in. The trick was finding it out there, too, finding it wherever I could. It was all I could do. We would take the road we would take. Mama had said about Lee that he was the murderin' type. I laughed at it then. Had I only known . . . But I can say this, hard as it might be to admit: had I only known, I most likely would have gone with him anyway. That's how deep my love was for Lee. I could hate him for what he'd done, and I did. But I couldn't, or wouldn't, hate him forever. No, my love for him was stronger than anything else.

For better or worse, they say when you get married. Well, Lee and I weren't married. But I calculated that by this point, we'd probably shared enough and done enough for most couples that married and stayed that way for a lifetime.

I cranked down the window and let the wind whip over me and the sun warm me and I floated away, floated away from it all and embraced my life for what it had become . . . something far outside of my control.

Kay surah surah. I think that's how you say it.

Springfield, Missouri, November 4, 1992, 5:00 p.m.

This is the hardest part. She already knows what he did; I've acknowledged that part of things. Plus, that's why the letter Lindsey found in the mail came from the South Dakota State Penitentiary in Sioux Falls. There's no secret there. But how much of what really got him there do I tell beyond what I already have? Do I confirm the portrait of a cold-blooded killer that the state of South Dakota did? It's a funny thing about South Dakota. I'm not sure I've encountered friendlier people anywhere, and that includes the Deep South, where people are supposed to be the friendliest in the country—at least that's what folks say. And yet when the governor of the state took office just a year after I left, in '79, the very first act he signed into law was a reinstatement of the death penalty, to be carried out by lethal injection, which never seemed very "Christian" to me. As for Lee, the jury found him worthy of the death penalty based on this statute, the wording of which I will never forget: "The defendant committed the offense for the benefit of the defendant or another, for the purpose of receiving money or any other thing of monetary value."

I explained this to Lindsey after we had our blowup and she had finally calmed down a little. "It was because of the two thousand dollars we took from the barn," I told her. "Turns out several people in town knew about that money, family friends, and once the police began with the investigation, all that came out."

I haven't told Lindsey my opinion of it, but I still feel that the punishment was too harsh, and not very accurate anyway. "It wasn't because of the money that Mr. Barry and Mr. Chester died," I told Lindsey. "I mean, had they never known about our taking it, they'd still be alive. It was because of the way Mr. Barry jumped at your father and then, well, he had a fear of witnesses. We both did."

Of course, if I paint too sympathetic a portrait of Lee, then Lindsey will get it in her head that she's lived her life without a daddy because of some injustice and who knows what kind of rebellion in life that will spark? Will she be one of those kids who searches out a man just like him, or what she thinks him to be, to take his place? It's a hard line to court. But more questions about her daddy and what he did to

Mr. Barry and then to Mr. Chester are coming. They have to be. And what to reveal then? I've got practice at telling myself certain things about my part in all of it. So much so that it's sometimes hard for me to tell anymore the reality and the otherwise, like it was all some crazy dream. But to tell her?

For now, she's turned silent in any case. Somewhere around Kansas City she retreated into herself. At first, she just watched the tall buildings of downtown glide past as we made our way to the central station. We don't have so many tall buildings in New Orleans, so I understand the attraction. Besides, she's never been this far north before. Never been much of anyplace, really. But I think it was an excuse, a way to pretend to be engrossed in something else to avoid the suddenly hard questions, things she wants to know but, maybe, doesn't at the same time. She's even slipped her headphones back on.

I let it go and don't push her, even after we'd left Kansas City altogether and made our way toward Omaha, where there really is nothing much to see outside these bus windows. It's a bit of a relief to me. I need this break.

I hoped she'd ask me some questions about Independence Day if anything at all, lighten the mood a bit. It seems after all these years, all that irritation I had for it then seems silly and immature to me now and I look back on it with real fondness, a certain end of innocence—before I got scared of that man, that is, which I see now as nothing more than my overheated imagination, a sign that I was far more scared than I allowed myself to believe at the time. But she doesn't ask.

I keep nodding off because of getting so little sleep last night and the sameness of the landscape. Funny how little it awakens in me some sense of "home." I suppose that South Dakota will always be a part of me because it's where I grew up and so many of these Nebraskan fields slipping by—the alfalfa and wheat and oats and rye—remind me of home. But I think I've always been too restless a soul to ever really consider any one place my true home, so there really isn't any charge or thrill or disgust or any strong emotion at all seeing those long flat fields. Instead, just sleep.

"You had a crush on Mr. Barry or something?" Lindsey asks, and I jolt awake.

I gather myself a bit. "I guess maybe I did," I say. "He was an older man and handsome and seemed he knew a bit about the world, in a way your father didn't. So, yeah, I guess I did."

Lindsey nods. Her earphones are off now.

"That's the part you want to hear about? Whether I had a crush on Barry?"

She nods again. "I think it's cute."

"But the rest of it, the killing?" I venture, hoping beyond hope that she's done with the subject, that I met my obligation, asked her what she needed to know and, hopefully, she's satisfied with what I told her and I'll be relieved forever after of having to revisit it. Maybe put it to rest once and for all. In this way, maybe this trip was the best possible thing that ever could have happened to me. It was a hope I had before we left but one I dared not place too much stock in for the potential disappointment.

"I'm not sure what you could have done about it," she says.

A burst of air comes from my mouth, unconscious and against my will. I run my hand across her hair. "Thank you," I say.

"I mean I couldn't have gone on like you did. I probably would have run away and called the police or something. I mean, it seems crazy to me. But if that's who *you* are . . ."

It feels like a cold poker jammed at my heart. The sweet and fleeting release of pressure now drops like a lead weight within me.

"I'm not sure what you mean," I breathe.

"You say you just got over it. Accepted it. I couldn't have done that. I wouldn't have done that. But, like I say, we're different people."

She's doing it to me again and it stirs up that old conflict inside me. There's a part of me that wants to straight slap her across the face, explain to her how easy it is to say things like that, to say what she would have done if she were there when she's sitting on her high perch after the life of comfort I've provided her.

But there's another part of me, that weight part that I fear will bog down inside me until the very last moments of my life, due punishment for all the crimes of this world in which I had a part. That part of me wants to beg her for forgiveness. I did the best I could. That's all I've ever done: the best I could. But how to explain this to a teenager? What does she know about the almost impossibility of forming and shaping memories so that they fit the view you have of yourself that you need to believe? Her whole life is still ahead of her, decisions to make and actions to take and only after, when looking back on it all do you then run through the ringer of regret for this, or beam in pride for that. For me, it's different. For me, everything is looking backward. There is no forward left for me. Will she believe me when I tell her that it has always been for her? No. She can't understand that, not unless I tell her everything, every last inch of the truth. But then I might just lose her even further. So I'm on that old balance beam again, shoving down this, conjuring up that, stealing bread to feed my starving family, as it were.

I take an enormous breath and then let it out. I know I'm not making sense.

"You want me to tell the rest?" I ask, keeping my anger in check. I need her to understand. I need, I need, I need.

She nods.

Okay.

I suck it up and plow on.

21

September 1976

Because we already had experience sleeping outside and we still had our tarp and Lee had taken several blankets and more bedding from Mirabile, we were able to remain pretty comfortable considering. Of course, it had been easy to get used to having a toilet and shower and a comfortable bed. But as we'd once done without those things, we managed it easy enough without them now. And anyway, what use was there in crying about it and missing what was already gone? And I told myself, tried to convince myself: this goes for people, too.

It was important to stay busy. So long as I had things to do, I could more easily keep the thoughts away and in doing this, I could tell myself once again that none of the bad stuff was real and soon enough, to my surprise, I was able to think only of the present moment, and I was able to not bother too much with what had been in the past or what might be coming in the future. I knew even then that the future is only an illusion because once it gets here, it's the present, and then all you have is the past. And the past is a thing you can't change anyway. So I stayed busy, best I could.

Still, try as I might, I couldn't pretend things hadn't changed with *me*. I felt like I'd aged ten or fifteen years easy in the last few days alone. Lee took notice of this. You haven't said a word, he said.

Nothing to say, I guess.

Not smiling or laughing either.

Not much to smile about. Or laugh neither.

After that, he just let me alone.

I stayed quiet and focused on what was in front of me and did what I needed to do and worried first and foremost about survival. All the rest of it, well, it was hardly worth even thinking about. I wasn't very proud about turning hard as I had, but I was grateful to find I even had the ability to do it. It got me through the days.

It wasn't difficult picking up our old routines again and after one day we found a good place to stop and set up camp. We were able to hide the car at a place where the trees and the prairie met, as if someone had come along long ago and planted a hundred acres or so and then abandoned them. Or maybe the other way around, that it had once been all woods and the rest had been cleared. Either way, those woods were a boon to us; there was no one around and even if there was, we were well hidden and the trees where we set up were pretty spread apart so it was easy to get up the tarp and lay down the bedding and it was certainly comfortable enough. We had our fires and we had water, using a bunch of old milk bottles Lee had taken from Mirabile. The weather was fine and warm and because there was a creek nearby, we could wash our clothes and, for now at least, we didn't want for anything.

After we woke, we were walking around looking over things, seeing what we could see, and we came across quite a sight: a mother cat and five of her newborn kittens. They hardly had any fur on them and their skin was pink and wrinkly and their eyes weren't even open. The mother cat was lying there, looking exhausted and hardly able to move, her swollen nipples out for the kittens to suck on.

We didn't want to disturb them so we just watched them awhile. The kittens squirmed around and buried themselves in their mama's belly, and she hardly lifted her head but only lay there with her eyes closed, and then we let them be to give them their privacy.

As we walked away, Lee kept shaking his head and whistling low and then finally said, We should help them.

What do you mean? I asked.

They all look so helpless.

Their mama knows what to do with them.

Lee didn't say anything but later that day he went down to the creek and the fishing he did had a weight and seriousness and concentration to it I hadn't seen from him before—fishing was not his favorite thing. But soon his seriousness explained itself: when he caught some small silver fish, he collected them up and carried them over to the mama cat and put them down near her face.

She blinked and stretched her neck toward them but she didn't eat.

Something's wrong, Lee declared.

Nothing's wrong, I said. She's just more concerned with her babies. She'll eat. Just leave them. Let's go.

That night, in front of the fire, Lee mentioned several times that he hoped everything was going well with the cats. He said also that maybe we could keep one of them as a pet for us so we'd have some company when we next hit the road.

Until we have our own children, he added, laughing a little.

I didn't really see the humor in it but I told him we'd see. I wanted to put his mind at rest, but I hadn't been able to completely let go of my anger over what happened back at Mirabile, much as I'd tried. But this was the other side of Lee, the one that got torn up over kittens, the one who loved me through and through. I knew I couldn't stay mad at him forever and even if he was foolish back at Mirabile and things could have ended up a different way, a better way, I did know that what Lee did—not all of it was right, I'll admit, but who is right all the time?—he did for me.

I think it's best we leave them alone for now and tomorrow morning we'll go down and check up on them, I said.

Lee agreed, but later that night, I woke up with an uneasy feeling and saw that I was alone. I think it was the noise of him leaving that woke me. He came back about twenty minutes later while I pretended to sleep. I knew he'd gone to look after those cats. It was sweet of him. But I didn't tell him I saw him for fear of maybe embarrassing him.

When we returned the next day, we saw that four of the five kittens were dead—one of them was even chewed up. And the fifth one was missing. The fish were still there but we couldn't decide if it was all of them or only some, as we hadn't bothered to count how many we'd left. The mother cat was gone, too, the only thing left of her the bent-down circle in the grass where she'd laid herself. It broke my heart to see them like that. But it was worse for Lee. I watched him as he crouched down and ran his fingers over the little unmoving bodies. He sat like that a long time, looking all around as if trying to solve the mystery of what happened. But then he got up and walked away without a word to me or to anything else and I could swear he had tears in his eyes. My heart broke for him. If Lee could get all choked up over those kittens, well, it told me what kind of person he was deep down inside. I knew plenty of people would call me foolish for thinking that way, but they didn't know Lee the way I did. For all I knew, it wasn't really the kittens at all that he was torn up about but rather he was just using them as a place to put his sorrow. I knew he couldn't be happy with having ended people's lives.

So to help make him feel better, I finally allowed him to pierce my ears, a thing he'd been after me about ever since he picked up those earrings for me in the pharmacy back in Haysville. I'd resisted it because I didn't trust him to do it right. What did he know about piercing ears? But if there was ever a time that he needed his mind to be on something else, some new project, that was it. I knew it would make him feel better to give me a gift and to see me wearing the earrings.

I knew you wanted them, he reminded me, 'cause I saw you holding them up to your ears.

So we went down to the creek and he filled one of our empty bottles with the cold water and held it against my ear. When he'd done this for five minutes or so, emptying it and doing it again twice more because of the heat of my ear and he wanted to make sure it was as cold as could be, he took the earring and pressed it to the lobe. It hurt like I don't know what. He had to push it really hard to get it all the way through. But I held it in and I thought about the time when I was a girl and I fell off a fire hydrant I was standing on and broke my wrist and how that hurt much worse.

But once it was through, it throbbed something terrible.

Give me that, I said, about the other earring, and I did it myself. Crazy, I know, but this one didn't hurt near as bad. I guess because the one hurt got all that started and a second isn't like double the hurt but rather just adding a bit to the original. Or maybe I was better now at taking pain—any kind of pain—when I put it on myself. We went back to the car and I looked in the mirror and told him it did look fine, those little silver balls in my ears, and he was smiling like a Cheshire cat.

He was like that sometimes. Could be down so low one moment and then up the next, with not much needing to take place in between.

～

We spent six days working our way southeast, staying clear of towns and main roads and navigating mostly by sun and stars and finally by an old map Lee picked up at a gas station. We figured state police from all up and down the middle of America were out looking for us. It was no secret we'd been at Mirabile and hardly one or two inquiries in town would have turned us up. The names weren't a problem—far as anyone knew we were Marie and Jason. But a description would be an easy match. So we stuck to the back roads only.

As had become our habit, sometimes we set up camp in the woods, sometimes we slept in the car. We got a real fright one night when we were awakened by a policeman who banged on the car window with his flashlight and asked what we were up to.

Just sleeping, Lee said. My lady here and I are traveling to see her sick mother all the way down in Alabama and, well, I didn't want to nod off while I was driving and cause anyone any injury.

I make him take frequent breaks, officer, I added.

It was amazing to me the way the fib rolled off so easily. It was fun playacting, and I think it helped because the policeman looked at me and then at Lee and said, Well, you two be careful. Make sure you remember to wear them seat belts, too. Then he looked me straight in the eye and said, I hope your ma recovers fine, miss.

Thank you, I said, and Lee said, Thank you, officer, and off we went, wide awake then. It was almost too easy, and the more time went by it wasn't so much relief I felt but a building nervousness.

That was scary, I told Lee.

He waved me off.

I'm serious. That was too close for comfort.

Actually, seeing how easy it was to get off, it should help put your mind at ease.

I don't know, I said.

Listen, if we're ever brought to account for the killings, you need not worry.

Lee . . . I said.

Far as I'm concerned, you had nothing to do with anything. You're with me against your will.

He held up the gun and waved it around.

Well, now, you know that isn't true, I said. And put that thing away. It's not funny.

Sorry, he said. But it's true: should we ever be held to account, it was my gun. And as far as I'm concerned you've never even touched the thing.

I didn't like that bit about my mama being sick, I said. Superstitious, I guess, that if you say it, it'll happen.

Yeah, I'm sorry about that. The truth is, it came to me because my own mama is sick and that's where we're headed next.

What do you mean, that's where?

Just as I said. We're out of food and we can't go into towns and shop for it. So we gotta go somewhere.

Don't you think this is something you should have talked to me about? Decide together? You've hardly said one word about your mama since the day we met.

It came to me as I was falling asleep and I was meaning to tell you when we woke. But the officer got to us first.

I didn't much like the idea of it, meeting Lee's mama. I'd heard very little about her from him and what I did had been pretty bad. But stopping and resting and getting food did sound good to me. The idea of a mother, even one other than my own, sounded pretty good, too.

We drove all the rest of that day, stopping only to eat the last of the food we'd taken with us. We sat on the hood of the car and it warmed us nicely and we watched as the sun set. The sky was all pink and blue and orange and red, like a fire that had jumped places and smoldered here and there unattended. It was one of the most glorious sunsets I'd ever seen: the way the sky and the earth met in a perfect line on the horizon and the dried grass of the southern plains reached up to blur that line in places and the sky, with its colored clouds, reached back down, too, like they were lovers unsure of themselves.

Look at that, I whispered, in awe of it all.

None of it was lost on Lee, either. He was more than happy to take the time, take it in, knowing sunsets don't last forever, especially ones like that. So we sat and didn't talk and watched as the colors got darker and then started to fade and the air in my chest had stopped fluttering and I no longer felt as if I could cry from the beauty.

That was truly . . . something, I said. Something.

Lee said, "The heavens declare the glory of God, and the firmament shows his handiwork."

What?

"The heavens declare the glory of God, and the firmament shows his handiwork."

How do you know that? It sounds biblical.

My mama, and it is.

This set my heart racing again, for in the beauty of that celestial show, I'd allowed myself to forget where we were headed and now this reminder made the nerves and flutters come back full and complete, despite the promise of rest and food.

Makes me nervous, I said. To meet your mother.

No need for that.

What if she doesn't like me?

Chances are she won't.

That's a terrible thing to say. Now I really don't want to go.

Either way it doesn't mean a thing; she doesn't like anyone. And that includes me much of the time. But it's a comfortable place to stay. And we need food. And, well, I should say my good-byes.

What's that supposed to mean?

She's sick, Lil. I wasn't making up that part.

What's she got?

Cancer.

So she's dying.

Lee nodded and hopped off the hood.

That why she a religious woman? Or was she always? I asked.

She never had religion when I was young. But somewhere around my fifteenth birthday, after my pop left for good, one night she went to a Tupperware party in some woman's trailer and afterward she came out a Jehovah's Witness or a Latter Day Saint or something like that. I can't keep it straight. Jehovah's Witness, I think. I don't know. She might be something else altogether now.

What's that?

Tupperware?

Jehovah's Witness.

He shrugged. I'm not sure I know enough to explain it right, he said. But I suspect she will if you ask her.

Come on, he said, and he got back in the car. We'll be there, I reckon, by morning.

22

The woman who opened the door sure wasn't one I would have pegged for Lee's ma. I hate to say it, but she was a homely thing. Her hair was all stringy and tied up in a greasy bun and there was no excuse for that like me and Lee had as we'd gone days without clean water. Though I hadn't yet been inside, I could assume from the outside that she at least had running water in the house.

It was a run-down looking place, for sure—made my own house in Paris and those around ours look like mansions or something. But it surely had modern amenities. If nothing else, I saw no evidence of an outhouse or anything like it. The impression was more of plain neglect: flowers and weeds run all over, a hanging section of gutter, some roof shingles torn off and not replaced, the mailbox off its wooden stake and instead plopped on top of three stacked cinderblocks.

As for Lee's ma, she had enough extra pounds on her to make me question Lee's claim that she was sick with cancer. I began to wonder if this was maybe just another tactic. Keep us out there, for some reason. Away from New Orleans. Away from any kind of settled life, a life where I might question things, and demand things. It was harder to do that when you were always heading to somewhere else, always moving on to the next thing.

Of course, whether she was really sick with cancer or not wasn't something I would have ever questioned out loud, awful as such a thing is. But she looked sick only of her own making, the way her belly rolled out over her filthy jeans the way it did. And when she opened her door, and saw her son standing there, and said, My word, the prodigal returns! I had full view to the wretched state of her dental health. Whole gaps here and there, so much I wondered how it was she managed her meals.

I couldn't believe it. Looking at her, and then looking at Lee—Lee, the most handsome man I'd ever laid eyes on. How could they be of the same cloth? It was a rude thought, and I knew it, but what's the harm if it stayed in my head? So I didn't allow myself to feel too bad about it and when Lee said to me, this here is Maybelline and then said to her, Ma, I want you to meet my girl, Lilly, I held out my hand and did a little curtsy as if I was meeting royalty.

She declined to shake my hand, snorted instead, and then said, Well, don't just stand there lettin' in the bugs. Get on in here.

And that was my introduction to Miss Maybelline.

I love that name, I told her once we were inside.

It's stupid, she said. Call me Maybell instead.

I told her I would indeed. One thing I could say, seeing her the way she was, all disheveled like that, was that it had the effect of taking away most of my nervousness about being in her presence.

We sat on a ratty couch and Maybell brought us water in chipped porcelain mugs. I looked around at the place and felt in a little bit of shock at the state: piles and piles of old newspapers and magazines, so many that I figured they acted as a substitute for proper furniture, as I saw little of that in evidence. Also, it seemed there was hardly any light at all in the house, despite the bright afternoon, as if the sun simply refused to let itself in. What else I didn't see, at least from where I sat on the couch, were any pictures of Lee whatsoever, or of anyone else. Except for one, a framed photograph of Maybell and some other woman, the two of them laughing as if they'd just heard the funniest thing in the world.

So what brings you 'round, Lin? Maybell asked.

It took me a second because I was still looking around the place, but I realized that she hadn't called him Lee, that she'd given him some other name, one I assumed was a nickname or something. She continued to call him Lin the whole time—when she called him any name at all, that is. Several times, she instead called him This One, and she jerked her thumb at him when she said it, like, This One runs out on me with no warnin' and then shows up unannounced expectin' . . . what is it you're expectin' now, Lin, you ol' bastard?

Tongue, Mama. What happened to your religious awakening? he said.

Gave it up, she said. All hooey. I didn't like the way they say one thing when they mean another and then pretend otherwise. Just last month, I was out there mowin' the lawn on a Sunday—now keep in mind my neighbors are always after me about keepin' the place up— and the next day old Mary Bogart said, Oh, I saw you mowed your yard yesterday, as if it was just a friendly observation, but both of us knew perfectly well what she was gettin' at, that I was workin' on the sabbath. So, no, no more church for me.

They told you you couldn't drink? Lee asked.

No drinkin', no swearin', no cussin' of any kind, no tobacco, no pork, no shellfish, no music. Well, no *good* music anyway. The list goes on and on. Things I can't even understand the reasons for: no sayin' the Pledge of Allegiance or singin' "Happy Birthday" or even salutin' the flag. What is the point to salvation after you die if you have to spend this whole life without doin' anythin' fun? I can't say for sure if there's an afterlife, but I do know I'm here now, so why not live my life to the fullest?

She smacked me on my knee and said, Ain't that right, darlin'?

186

I suppose that sounds right, I told her.

You dang right it's right, she said, and then she let out an ear-splitting belch.

I found it funny that Maybell had given up the church because it asked things of her. It wasn't my place to judge, but it seemed to me that maybe she was one of those people who just wanted all the good—salvation, grace, charity, that stuff—and none of the sacrifice that was required of it. I did share some of her skepticism about it all though. I remember clearly, when I was old enough to start having some ideas of my own, the discomfort I felt in church before we left it for good. I couldn't take my eyes off the Jesus on the cross at the front of our church. When I was really little, it scared me to no end. I think I even had a few nightmares about it. He was all bloody and there were thorns sticking out of him and long spikes through his hands and feet and so much sadness in his eyes. It was too much to look at, with all that blood coming from his crown of thorns. I never understood how that image of suffering was supposed to be any kind of comfort.

I must have expressed such a thought to the preacher one day in Sunday school and he smiled and corrected me and said that we didn't celebrate the suffering but rather the *resurrection*, the delivery from suffering. He called me my dear when he said this.

Well, I asked, why don't we have the *resurrected* Jesus out there then?

The other kids laughed but I didn't mean it as a joke. The preacher, he sure didn't laugh. Instead, his face got red and he sent me to the corner, where I sat through break and lunch and all the rest of that day in fact. That was the best answer he had, to punish me, which, of course, was no answer at all. It wasn't all that much longer that Mama declared that we were through going to that church anyway. I believe, if I remember correctly, we tried another church or two, probably some towns away. But then the car we had died and so we stopped going altogether.

Hey, Maybell said, jumping up off the couch. Let me get you a beer.

As she went to her kitchen, she kept on talking about the church, trying to convince us that she was right to leave, I guess.

Worse yet, she said, coming back with three cans of Pabst Blue Ribbon, They want ten percent of all I got, money-wise. Let me ask you, she said, looking at me. Take a good look around here: Does it look like I got one spare dime?

That's a question that's impossible to answer in the right. You say no it's an insult. You say yes it suggests she's holding back from the church. So, I just said, You keep a fine home, ma'am.

Hoo-weeee! she bellowed. I like this one. Knowin' how to lie with a straight face is a useful skill, my darlin'.

Lee looked downright mortified. This made me laugh. A few sips of beer and my head started swimming and it wasn't long before I was enjoying myself and if I was not doggoned, but I found that I liked Lee's ma. She was full of life, and how can you not like such a quality as that? I finished my beer and Maybell forced another on me and because I had so little experience with drinking, I was good and drunk by the second one and Maybell called me a lightweight.

But the beer served me well during dinner because I'm not certain how I would have stomached it otherwise. Maybell made a casserole, and the only things I could recognize in it were green beans from a can, mayonnaise, and some kind of crispy noodle on top. But I was hungry and it was food and I'm sure it was prepared with something as close to love or affection as Maybell was probably capable of mustering up, so I ate everything I was given. Dessert was better: strawberry pie with Cool Whip.

After dinner we went back to the couch and talked some more and Maybell embarrassed Lee with stories of his boyhood shenanigans.

Member that time you tried to shave the neighbors' cat and it scratched you and laid you up with cat scratch fever for two weeks? she said. Hooo-wee. You deserved that one.

Maybell rolled around the couch with laughter and when her laughing got too much she grabbed at her side in pain.

Ma . . . will you stop it? Lee said.

It was stupid kid stuff. Still, it was funny seeing him embarrassed like that and if it wasn't for the beer wearing off and the headache taking its place, I could have stayed up all night and watched them two.

But I asked if I might lie down, let the two of them catch up properly, and when Lee and I were alone, I confessed to starting to feel pretty terrible. I was to be set up in the back room, next to Maybell's, and Lee was to take the couch.

In this room, too, there was nothing of Lee, even though it was the room where he'd spent his boyhood. No pictures, no baseball gloves, no clothes left behind. It was as if he'd either never lived here or once he'd left, Maybell had wiped away all evidence of him.

While Lee put the sheets on the bed for me, I finally asked him what I knew he'd been waiting for:

Why'd she call you Lin?

'Cause that's my name, he said, not looking at me but instead acting as if putting on those sheets was the most delicate and difficult job in the world.

I thought your name was Lee.

And it is.

It's both at the same time?

My given name when I was born was Lindsey. So they called me Lin. Neither one of those names is a name for a man.

Where'd it come from? It *is* kind of funny for a baby boy.

It was my daddy's name.

Well I guess it is a name for a man then.

It ain't no name for a man, he said and then left the room, looking embarrassed or ashamed or both.

I was sorry to have upset him, but it was another one of those moments. How it is you can know someone but not know him at the same time? Had we not come to that place, had I not met Maybell, would I have ever known what my man's real name was? It was a thought that gave me great discomfort. We'd shared everything and I'd decided that

189

he was to be the man I'd marry and I'd have his children and everything else we'd talked about and yet all that time he kept a secret from me. It was a little one, and I could understand—seeing how his face got red and everything—but still, it made me wonder: what other things might he have been hiding?

23

I slept like the dead that night. I suspect it was on account of it being
my first night in a bed in some time. I'm sure the beer didn't hurt
either.

The morning broke clean and fine and I tiptoed my way out to the
back porch while Lee and Maybell slept. I've always loved the very early
mornings, when the sky has its first hints of blue coming on from the
blackness and it feels like the world hasn't awoke yet and the day belongs
only to you. It's like the promise of something fine before the events of
a day have a chance to come along and spoil things.

I stood in the morning chill and took it all in, the quiet and the darkness of the few houses I could see from Maybell's, and listened to the
birds calling to one another and I was out there for a good long while,
until the sun came up completely, just standing there with a blank mind.
There was a real relief in that, and a rare thing for me. I stared at the
neighbors' dog. It lay there with its head on its front paws. I could make
out the way he blinked at me occasionally. It didn't care if I was there or
not. So much better than having that thing barking at me and waking
up everyone within a mile.

The back door opened and out stepped Maybell. I was surprised to see her up so early and even more surprised by how it seemed the night had softened her up, as if sleep had ironed out a bunch of her kinks. Maybe it was the robe she had on or the way her hair was all loose from its bun and fell over her shoulders and made her look younger than she was. Or maybe she was like the morning itself and only gathered her roughness as the day went on.

Whatever it was, I found that I didn't mind the company and I liked the dreamy way she said, Beautiful day, ain't it?

I agreed it was.

She nodded and then lit up a cigarette. The smoke made me cough.

Oh, sorry, Maybell said. She moved off a bit and blew the smoke away from me.

It's all right, I said.

We stood in silence for a while and then Maybell excused herself inside and came back a moment later with a bottle of Maryland rye and poured herself a shot. She gulped it down and breathed out a smell like turpentine.

Breakfast of champions, she said and then laughed. You want? she asked.

No, thank you.

Yeah, I know it's stupid. But we all need our vices else we get boring and then what's the point? Need it to get my motor runnin'. It's my mornin' coffee.

I don't think you're stupid, I said.

She smiled at me and then ran her fingers through my hair.

You're a lovely child, she said.

Lee told me you're dying.

Yeah? Of what?

Cancer.

Not the first time he's told that story. Guess it gets him sympathy or somethin'.

So you're not sick then?

Oh, I'm sick, honey. We're all sick.

She took another shot of the rye, and I left it at that. Wasn't in the mood for riddles and it probably wasn't my place to ask anyway. Still, was Lee lying to me again? I wondered if that was a thing that men just do. But Lee loved me. Was his telling stories or holding things back a way of protecting me? I hated that I had so many questions and hated even more that I could never bring myself to really ask him most things I was curious about, afraid of coming off as some crazy dumb kid or something.

Your ear's all red, she told me, looking at me real close and then taking my left ear in her fingers. When she did, it hurt something terrible.

It's a new piercing.

C'mere, she said. She dabbed some of the rye on her fingers and put it on the earring. It stung like crazy.

Should help, she said. Keep the alcohol on. You don't want it gettin' infected.

I told her I'd look out for it.

We came back inside and by this point Lee was up and loading the washer with our clothes. Two things that shocked me about this: my man doing a load of laundry and the fact that Maybell, in this house of disrepair and untidiness, was the owner of a new and beautiful washing machine. I couldn't even imagine where she got it, or how. Life is full of little mysteries.

The phone rang, and it startled me and Lee. It had been easy to forget, somehow, that we were basically fugitives now—if we hadn't already been since that day down by the river—and it was easy to pretend we were leading some normal life, just visiting Lee's mother like people do. But then something simple like this happened—the phone rang—and it brought it all back to me that things could go terribly wrong at any moment.

But our fears were soothed when Maybell said, Hi, Shirl, and it was clear it was only a friend of hers. But then she said, What's wrong? Honey, stop your cryin' and tell me what's wrong.

There was a silence as Maybell listened and then she picked up a pencil from the counter and wrote herself a message right there on the wall next to the phone, a thing that shocked me at first until I realized that it was just one more thing that made Maybell Maybell and because of that it was one more crazy thing that made me like her all the more.

She said real soft, Okay, honey, we'll be there, and then she hung up, shaking her head.

What is it? Lee asked.

Shirl's beagle died. She's havin' a funeral.

Lee laughed out loud and Maybell's face got red.

And you're comin' too, she said. And you'll treat the affair with the respect and decency it requires.

Lee held up his hands like he was surrendering and said, Okay, okay. Fine. We'll come.

But he kept on laughing.

ᕲ

We climbed into Lee's car and drove a short distance before stopping at a nice-looking little ranch-style house. The front door opened and there was Shirl.

I was surprised by her, considering how Maybell chose to present herself to the world. Shirl was a beautiful woman with long gray hair she let fall over her shoulders and she wore nice clothes and makeup and even smelled of some flowery perfume and I realized that I recognized her from the photograph Maybell had in her house.

When she and Shirl met, they embraced in such a way I suspected they might have been more than friends. Maybell offered her condolences, said, Barney was a fine dog, and Shirl, through her tears and with a crumpled tissue balled in her fist, nodded her head in agreement.

I was touched by this, but Lee rolled his eyes.

Hi, Lee, Shirl said without the slightest hint of warmth, more like obligation than happiness at seeing him. And Lee gave it right back in the same tone of voice: Hi, Shirl, he said. It's nice to see you. But the way he said it made it clear he meant the exact opposite.

And who is this? Shirl asked.

This here is Lilly, Lee's girl.

A girl she sure is, Shirl said, looking me up and down like I was on auction or something.

How old are you, honey? she asked.

Never you mind, Lee said before I could answer.

Shirl shot Lee a look, then said, Well, you ready then?

We followed her to the backyard, where there was a hole in the ground with the dirt piled up next to it, a shovel, and a lump of something underneath a red-and-green plaid blanket. This, I guessed, was Barney the beagle.

When Shirl laid her eyes on it, she let out a wail as if it was the first time she'd seen him like that and Maybell put her arms around her and rubbed her back and whispered in her ear.

Lee stood away, looking off into the distance, muttering to himself and generally being rude, but it didn't matter in that neither Shirl nor Maybell saw him or could hear him through Shirl's wailing. It got even worse when Shirl picked up Barney and placed him in the hole. Her grief was so real and raw that it was impossible not to be affected and I found myself getting teary over it, as crazy as the whole thing was.

Once the dirt had been piled on and the ceremony was over, I was glad to see that even Lee had found his heart, and I smiled at him when he came over and helped Shirl off the ground and then said, I really am sorry, Shirl. I'm sure he was a good dog and I know you'll miss him.

Thank you, Lee, she said. Thank you. She threw her arms around his neck and he hesitated a moment but then hugged her back and rubbed her shoulder.

You're a good boy, Lee, she said.

When they were done hugging, she looked at me and said, He's turned into a fine young man. And quite a looker, too. In the end, you'll discover what every woman does: that there ain't a man alive can be trusted farther than he can be thrown. But that's something you got to learn in time. For now, while you're young, you enjoy all the things being young and in love can offer you.

Yes, ma'am, I said because I couldn't think of anything else to say.

Well, Shirl said, smiling now and wiping the last of the tears from her cheeks. That's that then. Soapy's?

You know it, Maybell said.

Oh, Lord, Lee said.

⌒

Soapy's, I came to learn, was a honky-tonk in town that looked like I imagine it did the day it was built, some forty years earlier according to the sign out front, without any attempt to update it whatsoever. But it was a place full of good cheer, the kind of bar where it seemed everyone knew everyone else. When we arrived, people greeted Maybell and Shirl almost as if they were Jesus returning from the dead.

We were there hardly one minute before Shirl ordered drinks for her and Maybell. She offered one to me, too, but I declined. She didn't bother with Lee and I didn't think he minded it any as he just pulled up a chair and set himself down and sulked.

I didn't blame him. The place was noisy and hot and the darkness didn't do all that good a job of hiding the rough edges. I saw mice running all around and roaches, too. So me and Lee sat there and watched the activities, which consisted of a bunch of old men and women getting drunker and drunker and louder and louder. And it wasn't long before Maybell and Shirl were completely schnookered and the focus of everyone's attention as word of Barney's passing got around and more drinks were offered as a tribute.

Shirl went to the jukebox and put in her dime and played some old-time song I never heard of before and the place went wild and everyone was egging on Maybell and Shirl, who were in the middle of the floor with the tables pushed to the sides and they were dancing and generally going crazy. I couldn't help but smile at it because it was downright funny but Lee looked more and more put out by it all. I could understand that. It was easy enough for me to enjoy but if that were my own mama out there, acting completely crazy, I'm not so sure I would.

Toward the end of the song, like it was some old practice or something, everyone yelled out this verse—and I'll admit it, it is pretty funny: "My wife died on Friday night / Saturday she was buried / Sunday was my courtin' day / Monday I got married"—and then they screamed and laughed and hollered and carried on like it was the end of the world. I never heard that song again, but I still remember those verses.

Right after the song ended and before another started up, I saw Maybell and Shirl kiss one another on the lips and it confirmed my suspicions from before. I felt the same way after as I did when I first saw them embrace, which is to say it wasn't any of my business if some people decided to go that way. Who was I to judge? I understood even then that people should be left to find their happiness where they could, and anyway it certainly was no skin off my nose either way.

But Lee looked downright disgusted by it and he said to me, 'scuse me, and just up and left.

I followed him out and even though the difference between the outside and in was the difference between a shout and a whisper, I could still hear the place rocking even after the front door closed. There were a ton more cars than when we'd arrived and the parking lot looked like a jigsaw puzzle with all the pieces thrown every which way. I couldn't even imagine how everyone would get their cars out when it was time to leave. But there was Lee, already doing the geometry he needed to figure it out.

You're welcome to stay, he said. I can come back and get you later on. But I can't take it no more.

I'll go with you, I said, and he smiled at this, looking relieved.

I love you baby, he said. I love you so much. I'm so sorry for all that's happened.

It's okay, I told him.

He kissed me real soft on my lips and took my forehead in his hands and kissed me there, too. These are things he would do probably a thousand times a day when we first set off, but hadn't in a while. I didn't ask what was going on with him, but I could guess that he was pretty torn up about all that had happened, how things hadn't gone as he had planned. And now, being inside Soapy's, watching his ma acting the way she did, maybe he just needed a reminder that there was at least one person left in this world who was on his side.

And so I didn't pester him with my many questions, why he did this thing or didn't do that. Lee needed me, and I needed him too. And when he kissed me the way he did, well, I'll say it: I was pretty powerless to doubt him about anything.

24

We spent another five days at Maybell's and all that time I liked it very much. The food was sometimes difficult—Maybell had a thing for bologna sandwiches—but I was grateful for it and of course I didn't complain. I liked having a bed to sleep in and I enjoyed being able to spend time in the house or on the back porch doing nothing other than trying to let my mind go blank.

Twice I walked into town and went to the library, where I read a book of short stories by Raymond Carver that the librarian told me everyone was reading called *Will You Please Be Quiet Please?*, a title I loved, and I parked myself the entire day in the same chair and nobody said a word to me. While I sat there, at least ten different people came in and asked for *Roots*, but each time they were told the library's copies had been taken out already.

I'd almost forgotten how much I enjoyed the simple pleasure of sitting down and reading something; unfortunately, my books had been left behind in the rush to leave Mirabile. After we'd been at Maybell's a couple of days, I went on the hunt for books there. I thought that with all those newspapers and magazines lying around, I'd find plenty to read. But it proved otherwise. The magazines were all really old, at least a year or more, and some older than me, so I didn't bother with them.

I did find Maybell's Bible on the floor near the couch. When I opened it, the spine cracked a little and it was clear to me that no matter what Lee or me might have thought about her religious life before we arrived, Maybell hadn't done too much of the reading one would think would be required of it.

I wasn't so much interested in the contents, either. At least not in any religious sense. But it's a book of great stories and there's plenty of poetry there, too, so I flipped to the Psalms and read over them and delighted in how lovely so many of them were. I can understand why people turn to the Psalms in times of joy and sadness both. I liked the ideas there, such as the one that says a person is like a "tree planted by streams of water, which yields its fruit in season, and whose leaf does not wither." There are far worse things to be compared to, I think, than a fruit tree.

So this became something of our routine—hanging around the house, reading, talking at night—and it was nice. It was a wonderful feeling to live a normal life again. But there was a danger in it, too, of course, which was that it became that much harder to leave it. So when Lee started to hint at our departure, it upset me. But it eventually got to the point where there was little choice in it anyway.

It started one day when we went to town together. While Lee headed into the pharmacy, I stood out on the sidewalk watching people going by worrying about their lives and passing without any interest in me. But then this guy came up to me, asking who I was and if I was from around there because he'd never seen me before.

And I'd sure remember you, he said. Pretty girl like you.

I suppose I blushed at this, which is a natural enough thing when someone pays you a compliment. But it wasn't like I was interested in him or anything, at least not in that way.

I told him I was just passing through, here with my fiancé, and we were on the way down south where he had a job waiting for him.

Well, he sure is one lucky fella, the guy said. But then he added, You sure you're engaged?

I nodded.

To be married?

What else? I asked.

Well, it's just that I don't see no ring on your finger.

It's being sized, I told him.

Well, he sure is lucky, he repeated. You tell 'im, tell 'im he don't treat you right, some other man's gonna come along and steal you away.

It was nice getting that kind of attention. It wasn't a thing I was very used to from boys.

But then Lee came out of the store and he marched up to us and put his arm around my shoulder and he looked at the guy and said, pretty mean, too, Help you, fella?

You the fiancé? he said.

Who wants to know?

Well, the guy didn't answer because as he asked it, Lee raised his arms a little so his shirt rode up and it gave view to the gun tucked in the waist of his jeans and he held his arms like that to make good and sure the guy saw it.

So the guy started backing away, saying, Easy, buddy, and then turned and walked real fast away from us.

Who the hell was that? Lee asked me.

And how should I know?

You were talking to him.

He was talking to me. I was standing here, waiting for *you*, and he came up and started talking. I can't help what other people do.

What'd you tell him?

That we were just passing through, that I was with my fiancé, and we were heading south.

We need to be careful, Lilly.

And I was.

We don't need to call attention to ourselves. You know that.

You mean like waving a gun around?

Waving? Hardly. And I wouldn't need to if you kept to yourself.

I reminded him of what I already told him, which was that the guy came up to me, not the other way around, but I was too angry to talk to him anymore, acting like I was some dumb girl who didn't know better. So I stormed off to the car and he was calling me back but I kept going anyway until eventually he caught up and we drove back to Maybell's in silence.

When the next day came and he told me he was going back into town again and did I want to come, I told him no, I didn't want a repeat of the day before. Besides, my ear was bothering me and it made me irritable.

Fine, he said.

But when he got back, he told me that everyone was looking at him.

That's crazy, I told him.

I'm not crazy.

You're imagining it. Why would everyone be looking at you?

Why you think, Lil? You seem to forget we're on the run. Whether you like it or not. I can't imagine it'll take any decent officer too long to discover we were working the Mirabile farm and then it's just a question of them looking for me and you. And from there, well, you start with relations and—it was dumb of us to come here—so word gets around and, I don't know, Lil, everywhere I went, people were looking at me and some of them were pointing and talking to each other.

They know Maybell and they probably remember you from growing up here and, well, what do you want to do about it anyway?

At that very moment, Maybell and Shirl came back from their day out. Me and Lee tried to act natural and the four of us sat at the table and drank coffee and talked and I will say this: Shirl did ask a lot more questions than I would have expected and it was enough to make even me a little suspicious, even without Lee constantly looking at me and saying with his eyes: *You see!*

So, where were you kids coming from before you washed up here? Shirl asked.

Things like that.

Lee told her we were at my mama's in Iowa, which was a lie of course.

And you come straight here afterward? she asked.

We got work in Sioux City, he said. Lilly was a waitress and I cleaned dishes in the back and bussed tables. You see, Lil's pap died and her ma's getting remarried and so Lil finished up her high school equivalency and we set out. We'll settle down soon enough, but figured we might have ourselves something of an adventure beforehand.

Well, I can understand that, Shirl said.

But I'm afraid it's time we move on. I've got a friend in Texas has a job in the oil fields waiting for me. Might be where we settle down, Lee said.

That right? Shirl said, and she did look more than doubtful at this. Even Maybell just squinted out the corner of her eye, blowing cigarette smoke in a steady stream each time anyone talked, as if that blowing out was her way of adding to the conversation and in so doing making it very clear she didn't believe a word of any of this. So I saw where Lee was coming from and perhaps it was best to move on.

So after Shirl left and we were getting ready to turn in, we planned it this way: that we'd go to our beds as usual but Lee would come get me sometime after midnight when we knew Maybell was asleep and Lee would roll the car down the drive so as not to start the engine and we'd set off under cover of darkness.

It all went as planned at first and I was relieved when Lee came into my room at a quarter to one because I wasn't sleeping anyway in anticipation of it and because my ear was really hurting me now, something real terrible. But I didn't complain as we had enough to worry about.

He told me he already had the car out to the street and our things packed. So we tiptoed out and simply left as if we had no connection to the place whatsoever. Except after we got out to the car and Lee was about to start the engine, here came Maybell running out of the house and if the circumstances weren't what they were, I'd have burst out laughing for how she looked, with her hair flying all wild around her head and her huge unharnessed breasts flopping all over as she ran. But as it was this was no laughing matter.

I'll give Lee credit for this: I think if it was me behind that wheel, I'd have taken off no matter if it was my mama chasing us down, considering the circumstances and what we had planned and all. But he just sat there and let her catch up and even gave her a minute to catch her breath as she stood at the driver's side window huffing and puffing.

Finally, she said, Son, I can't pretend to know what your story is, what you two have gotten yourself mixed up in, but I do know you're my boy and you always will be.

Thanks, Ma, Lee said.

If I wasn't seeing things, I could swear he got a tear in his eye.

I don't know what you're runnin' from or what you're runnin' to, Maybell said.

I told you already, Lee said, meaning nothing and nothing.

But Maybell just looked at him.

I don't know what you're runnin' from or what you're runnin' to, she repeated. And anyone comes askin', that's exactly what I tell 'em.

Lee nodded. Okay, he said. Thank you, Ma. I love you.

I love you too, son. I wish I'd have been a better—

Lee cut her off by waving his hand and that was the end of that line of talk.

You take care of this one, Maybell said, pointing at me. She's a downright angel.

I know it, Ma. I do.

The three of us sat there a moment in the silence of the night and then Lee said, Okay. We gotta go.

Maybell didn't say one more word, just took a few steps back to give us room to go, and I watched her through the rearview mirror as she got smaller and smaller and at that moment I surely did wish I would see her again.

And I'll say one more thing about Maybell: I was sorry I ever thought unkind things about her because looking at her there in the middle of the street in the middle of the night, watching us drive away from her—the only family she had (unless you count Shirl, of course, which I would be inclined to do)—at that moment she looked to be one of the most beautiful people I'd ever seen.

And I realized another thing: try as I might to convince myself otherwise, I sure missed my own mama.

25

There was no use getting upset over the cold hard facts of it, which was that we were on the road again and who knew whether we'd ever again get to some place comfortable like Maybell's. So I didn't bother worrying about it. Instead, I tried my best to enjoy the feeling of freedom. That hadn't gone away entirely, thank goodness, and it allowed me to carry on the way we did. Besides, it surely didn't seem any real hardship to stop somewhere and set up a temporary camp and sleep out in the woods under a tarp as we'd done it so many times before. Lee even went back to sleeping with his shoes on, as he used to when we first set out. I thought that was funny at first, and I teased him about it, but he only looked at me like I wasn't thinking and said, You always need to be ready.

Ready for what, I didn't ask. But now that he was "ready" again, there was comfort in that familiarity, too.

One complication, however, was that my ear was truly infected now. The infection had caused the lobe to swell up so much you couldn't even see the earring anymore and it oozed this terrible puss and felt awful. I told Lee we needed to do something about it, go see a doctor or something, and he told me there was no way we could do that, and what doctor was I hoping to see anyway?

Well, what are we supposed to do? I asked.

I'll take care of it, he said.

What do you mean by that?

Without saying another word, he went in through the back of the lobe and yanked the earring through that way. It hurt so much I cried out and felt like I'd almost pass out from the pain. He put his arms around me and hugged me real, real tight.

I love you, baby, he said. I had to do it that way. Get it all done at once instead of slow. Shhhh, it'll be okay.

He did his best to soothe me like that while I cried from the pain and waited for it to go away.

And eventually it did go away, or at least got less and less. With the earring out, the swelling went down a little and one day, as we passed through some small town I never did get the name of, Lee parked and ran into a pharmacy and got some ointment to put on it while I waited in the car.

Then we took off again and left the town behind like it was hardly even a real place and we were back on the road yet again, but this time with medicine to help my ear finally heal properly. He even got me more tampons, a thing that no doubt embarrassed him to pay for. But it was yet another way he showed his love for me.

Of course, we couldn't keep on this way forever. Someday Lee *would* have to get a real job—that story about the oil field and the friend in Texas was a lie, of course. But we needed more time for things to settle down, he said, and every day that came and went and put itself between us and Mirabile, the better the chances were it would be something we'd successfully outrun. In the meantime, we had money to keep ourselves in food and gasoline and other things as needed. I knew where that money had come from, of course, but I tried not to think too much about that, either. And to that end, Lee told me that he still had plenty of his own money he'd arrived in Paris with and he'd mixed it all to-gether and so while it was just a mental game, it was true that anytime we spent any money at all, it was impossible to say the source of it and it might as easily have been his that he earned honestly. I know it was only a trick, but it worked and when he did hand over cash to, say, fill up our gas tank, I told myself it was Lee's money and not Mr. Chester's.

So we continued on this way and the days passed and the nights, too, and it all became normal once again and there weren't many things to interrupt what was routine and boring, which was a good thing. The sight of a dozen police cars with their lights turning and sirens going, coming over a hill or around some bend and speeding to us—that would have been anything but routine or boring and no good thing be-side, obviously. So, boredom, that old luxury—I'd take it. I didn't even bother to bring up New Orleans anymore; the more time went by, the more that entire city and everything it represented to me seemed less and less a real thing. Now when I looked at that map Lee had grabbed from some gas station who-knows-where, and put my finger on New Orleans, it was just a dot with words a bit bigger than the ones around it but without even a star to mark its importance. That honor went to the capital, which I'd always thought New Orleans was. Truth to tell, I'd never even heard of Baton Rouge at that time, and didn't even have any idea how to pronounce it.

I supposed one day we'd make our way to New Orleans after all, but I knew better than to pin my hopes on it happening very soon. For now, we kept on our wandering ways.

But it wasn't as if nothing happened. From time to time, something occurred I'd not expected and was entirely new to me. We were some-where in Missouri, for example, six days out from Maybell's, when we first saw the Mississippi River. It wasn't something I ever could have imagined, that river. It was so wide I couldn't even see across it.

We stopped the car and walked to the edge of it and stood there looking for a long time not making a sound until Lee let out a whistle.

It is something, ain't it? he said.

Mm-hmm.

I walked along the muddy bank by myself and it seemed Lee understood my desire to be alone with my thoughts because he didn't follow.

So I kept walking and thought about how this river could be like an ocean for as big and wide as it looked and I knew that it was Illinois on the other side—or maybe Kentucky, I wasn't sure. Both were places I'd never been and I wondered how many more places I'd never been I'd wind up going to. Already we'd done more and experienced more and traveled more miles than I ever could have imagined back in Paris. And if I used to think my town was small when I was living there, well, I saw now how very small it was and how very big a country this was. And of course this is only one country in the world and there must be hundreds more and I wondered if I'd ever get to any of them aside from this one.

And as I was thinking all this, I accidentally kicked what I thought was a rock but when I bent down to pick it up realized it was actually a seashell. This seemed a natural enough thing at first, but then I remembered that of course this wasn't the ocean I was walking along and it seemed odd that a seashell should be there. I was pretty sure such things aren't found in the Mississippi River, so I guessed someone must have abandoned it there, or lost it by accident.

By this point Lee had rejoined me and seeing what I had, he told me to put it up to my ear and I'd be able to hear the ocean.

But we're nowhere near the ocean, I reminded him.

That's the whole idea, he said. That the ocean carries along in shells no matter where they travel. That's the power of it.

I listened inside the shell and all I heard was a noise like the static between radio stations.

Listen again, Lee said. You're not holding it completely over your ear. You're not doing it right.

I did it again and just a nothing kind of sound, a weird wash like I was hearing the inside of my own ear or head or something.

I turned and tossed the shell into the river and watched it disappear with barely even a ripple to mark its place.

What'd you do that for? he asked.

'Cause they're all just fantasies, aren't they? I said. These things you tell me.

I walked away. I wanted to be alone.

We never did cross to the other side of the Mississippi, and as we drove away I pictured it as if we were hemmed into Middle America— no river, no ocean, nothing else but what we were and, I suppose, where we belonged.

I'm not sure I completely understood it then, but it was the same feeling as being trapped against your will.

～

We slept that night in the car and the next afternoon found a secluded place well off the main road where we could set up our makeshift camp for a few days. It was a patch of woods near a nice river that I guessed fed itself into the Mississippi, probably seventy miles off or so, judging from the driving we'd done. Lee said we were in Arkansas, but I missed the sign telling us that fact.

They don't bother with signs on the kinds of roads we're traveling on, he reminded me. They save those for the highways and interstates.

While I was setting up our camp, I felt a terrible pain below my stomach, which signaled that my time of the month had come again. Usually, it wasn't so bad, but every now and again it made me feel just sick. This time, it felt like a knife being turned in my stomach.

After I got our tarp and bedding and catch basins set up, it was all I could do but sit and ride it out, my legs up against my body pressing hard against my chest. I sat there like that, hugging myself and wishing it were over. Mama used to tell me there wasn't anything more beautiful in this world than a woman, and there were times I believed it. Sometimes I caught sight of myself in the reflection of a river and saw how

210

my hair fell down over my face and, well, I never thought of myself as all that pretty, even though Lee said I was the most beautiful girl in the world, but there were moments I could see what he meant. But times like these, I felt plain rotten about being a woman, period, like there was something terrible inside me begging to get out. And then there was the matter of the blood and, well, certain days I hated it.

But Lee was a man and he didn't care about the blood or anything. The first time it happened, he said to me, Baby, it's you. I don't care if your blood gets on me. It's all through your body, after all. Who cares if some of it gets on me.

Sometimes I loved him all the more for his feeling this way, like it meant that he really loved me through and through. But other times, depending on my mood, it came off to me as just plain selfish. And this was one of those times.

He came over and put his hands on me, and I pushed him away, told him I was bleeding and we had that old conversation again, he didn't care, it was only a little blood, he said, and he could easily wash it off when we were through.

Have you ever considered that I might care? I asked him.

Well, I suppose I hadn't, Lil. I'm sorry.

He got up and walked away and did that thing he did sometimes where he sulked, all crouched over and knees bent and pulled up to his chest so his chin rested on his knees and his arms were wrapped around himself like he'd never had anyone in this world to love him. It was funny because that was the way I was sitting, too, and so we were like miserable mirror images of each other. It even made me feel a little bit sorry for him. Still, I wasn't about to give in first. I let him sit like that awhile before he finally came over and I let him put his arms around me and tell me he loved me.

I know you do, I mumbled.

Sometimes I felt stupid for how easy it was for him to get back into my good graces and how I would usually forgive him for just about anything. But this time I told myself that I would make him suffer, at least just a little.

But it became clear to me pretty quick that he wasn't the only one suffering. While I wasn't keen on making love, despite the fact that the cramps had subsided a bit, I realized later, under the tarp, after he'd gone to sleep, ashamed of himself for how I'd made him feel, I felt all alone without his arms around me, how we'd otherwise have laid there all quiet and content and I'd listen to his breathing near my ear and pay attention to that way we had where our breathing synced to each other's, rising and falling at the same exact time. That was when I loved him most. Had we made love, had I let him do what he needed to do as a man, I knew what waited for me afterward: the way he stayed awake and didn't fall off to sleep right away, how we would lay there all quiet, and he would run his fingers along the length of my naked sides. That journey of his fingers took forever sometimes, the way he did it so slow, up and back, and so long. Longer than the length of my favorite song, or of my favorite poem. Longer, even, than my own dreams.

⌒

I was the first awake in the morning and, as I always did when I woke before Lee, the first thing I did was look over to him, see if he was still there or something. And he was, as he was always, his underarm up-turned with his wrist over his eyes like he always did. He was pretty smelly. But I decided I could wait a bit and we could go to the river to bathe together. So I lay there and tried to enjoy the stillness of the morning. It was the time I liked best, a time where even though I was with someone else, I could be alone. So I lay there and enjoyed it and it wasn't long before I heard the buzz.

It was a fly, I realized, buzzing the inside of the tarp, banging against the plastic again and again like it didn't have the sense to know there was no busting through it. It beat itself over and over until it seemed to have exhausted that idea and then it came to rest right on Lee's chest. It was a delicate maneuver, crawling over those little curly hairs and holding on like it did, managing it so that it didn't even wake Lee. He barely stirred. Course, Lee could sleep through a freight train rumbling right across our path. Many nights I lay there wide awake, staring at the tarp or the stars or the branches of trees or whatever the situation presented, while he was out dead to the world, that gun near his side and his hair over his face.

The fly took little hops from this hair to that and still it didn't wake Lee. And then, as if the thing had spent that time figuring out what should have been obvious to it all along, it flew right under the tarp and out. Just like that.

As for me, I remained sitting there looking at Lee's chest hair, marveling as I often did how something could be itself one moment and then be something so different the next, even when it didn't change at all. There were times when that hair felt so good against my bare skin, so much like silk and warmth and protection. And then other times it felt like nothing less than pins and needles, poking into me and scratching me. I suppose it was my mood that dictated those things as the hair was just hair and didn't change. I guess it was me that was changing.

It often felt to me during some of those long days that I was changing minute by minute. My thoughts, my moods. One moment happy as could be, excited with the freedom and the adventure, the next moment scared, lonely, missing Mama, missing the cats, missing Paris even, something I never would have thought possible. And of course I thought of Barry and Mr. Chester, too. I almost never gave voice to any of it for I knew Lee often had a way of seeing everything some other way, and in any case I knew also that I usually only needed to wait a little bit and whatever was the opposite of what I had been feeling would come soon enough to be the new thing.

And, of course, there was the matter of that first man, too, the one by the river. It seemed each time I thought about it, I could piece together a little more of it. At first, in the immediate days after, it was all a blur and I truly couldn't remember anything of the main moments, only the before and the after. But more and more it seemed I was able to add a little piece to the event, a few seconds here or there, and I hated it. Someday, I assumed, I'd be able to replay the whole thing, remember it as it was, and I couldn't imagine that was something that would give me any comfort. And as for Barry and Chester: forget it. I kept that as far out of my brain as possible. Otherwise, I wouldn't even have been able to live with myself.

Well, enough of all that. Too much time, sometimes, doing nothing other than sitting and thinking. It was bath time, for both of us, so I poked at Lee until he woke and, like he always did, he opened his eyes and first thing grabbed his gun.

Come on, mister, I said, feeling playful. Let's get to the river.

All right, he answered, all groggy.

It's hot, he said, looking really uncomfortable. I'd pretty much gotten over mornings like those. In the beginning, when I'd wake with leaves and little twigs in my hair and who knew what else, I didn't want to even think of it. But it all seemed so normal by this point and there were times I could hardly remember what it was like to wake up and go to a bathroom with a sink and toilet. It should have been strange to wake up under a tarp, or drink rainwater, or eat wild rabbit, or walk to a river to bathe. But it wasn't strange, it was all rather normal, and I poked at Lee again to get him moving.

All right, all right, he said. There's no need for all that.

I bundled up our cleanest clothes and carried them with me as we walked down to the river. When we got there, I poked my toes in.

The water was cold, as I knew it would be. The river upstream from where we were ran fast, and that meant cold. But because it'd been so hot and stuffy under the tarp, the cold water felt wonderful. But the more I got in, and the further it crawled up my thighs, the harder it was to take. Goosebumps broke out all over me, but the grime of the past few days was washing away, too, and it was a good trade-off. I removed my dress, which I had kept on and held above the waterline. I still had a little bit of the shyness about me and I couldn't easily stand there totally naked like that. Once it was off and I tossed it to the bank, I quickly lowered myself under.

This was always both the best and worst part. Going under like that at first it was so cold and a surprise even though you already knew what was coming. When people use that expression about taking your breath away, well, that's actually what happens. And there's little pleasant about it. But the other part of it, the part I loved, was the light and the way it came through the top of the water and when I lowered myself and ruffled up the water and created a million little bubbles in doing it, and the way the light floated in waves all around me—I could honestly say there are few things in this world I've seen more beautiful than that. It got me every time.

So I stayed under a bit, swallowing my breath and trying to calm myself for the cold, and I opened my eyes and looked at that light and those bubbles and it thrilled me, my own private little heaven and I didn't even care anymore about the cold. Nor did I care about my bleeding, for I could see thin wisps of it coming from me and mingling with the water and I liked that idea, too, like I was part of the water itself, part of nature, and maybe Lee was right, that it's just blood and a part of me, and there wasn't much more to it than that. And when I came back up, I saw that Lee was in the water now, too, and there we were, like Adam and Eve, naked as jaybirds, and it was moments like those that it was very easy to be in love.

But then the oddest thing happened, something I couldn't have even imagined. It started with a really strange noise, a kind of humming that soon revealed itself to be singing, low and trancelike. And then the source of that noise came right after. They seemed to come out of no-where, all these people, emerging from the trees like they were part of the forest. They were already at the water's edge and entering, some dozen of them, before I even remembered that I was as naked as the day

215

I was born and so I had to lower myself to hide my bare chest. I was almost crab-walking to keep as much of me under water as I could, and I made my way to the edge where my clothes were laid out on a big rock and I put my dress back on. But I could see soon enough that it didn't matter what I did. I could have just as easily stood up in all my nakedness and waved my arms for all they'd notice. They paid me not the least bit of mind, so in tune as they were to their humming and singing.

I looked over at Lee. He was observing them with as much amazement as I was. As we dressed, we watched as an old man, obviously the preacher, went in first, walking about twenty paces out, until the water was up over his waist, no reaction to the cold at all, and then he turned to the rest to address them: two women who were clearly his helpers, walking out after him as if they'd done this a hundred times before, and once they came close to the preacher, they turned toward the bank and watched as the other ten or so of them, all in white robes, took their steps into the river, unsure about it, feeling around with their sneakers. Those that had on dark underwear, it became visible, but clearly they had no interest in hiding that or being embarrassed by it. They kept up their humming and the lady helpers continued their low singing and I stood there and watched it all, amazing as it was. I couldn't make out what it was they were singing. But soon enough this stopped anyway, at some unseen signal from the preacher, who started a little speech: "From Acts 2:38, Then Peter said unto them, 'Repent, and be baptized every one of you in the name of Jesus Christ for the remission of your sins, and you shall receive the gift of the Holy Ghost.'"

One by one the pilgrims stepped forward and each time, the preacher said, This is Rose—or Michael or Tessa or whoever it was—and she comes today to be baptized into Christ.

Then he invited each person to recite what he called the Good Confession: "I believe that Jesus is the Christ, the Son of the Living God, my Lord, and my savior."

The uninitiated then came forward, inched along by the women up front, who handed the person over to the preacher, who proclaimed, I

216

now baptize you in the Name of the Father, and of the Son, and of the Holy Spirit, for the forgiveness of your sins, and the gift of the Holy Spirit, and then the person closed their nose with their fingers and the preacher dunked the person under completely.

Some came up shocked, looking like they didn't know it was coming or they were afraid of going under and had barely survived. Others came up smiling, as if reborn, which, I guess, was the point. And some, well, nothing. No change at all. Gone under one way and come out the same from the looks of things.

It was all I could do but to just stand and stare. Of course, I could see the appeal: wash away the sins and all that. I'd had my fair share of thoughts to that end, about what sins Lee and I had committed and which ones would stay stuck to us forever, no matter what we did or didn't do. It wasn't anything I ever talked with Lee about specifically because I knew he didn't believe in the idea of sin to begin with and believed also that we hadn't done anything to be ashamed about. What we were doing was honest and pure and we had set out on the run, as it were, only because we lived in a small world that didn't understand us and we needed to see as much of this world as we could now so as to find a place where we could be left alone to live our lives. And the tragedies that came were thrust upon us and not things we asked or wished for but things we did only because we had been forced to, and those things didn't change the fact of our love for each other or the purity of our spirits joined in that love.

At times, I agreed with all that—well, most of it anyway. And so it was a surprise even to me that I found myself walking toward the people in the river. I was already right at the preacher before Lee's calling after me registered in my ears. But by then it didn't matter because I was being thrust under the water. My eyes were open and I watched the sunlight dancing along the surface and the tiny bubbles on every side of me and it was as beautiful a thing as the fireflies I'd seen at Mirabile. Even though I was only under for maybe a second or two, it felt like a day or more and when I came up and sprayed the water from my mouth and nostrils and wiped it from my eyes, I felt a lightness I hadn't felt since I was a little girl—or maybe hadn't felt ever.

I wasn't myself in my own body anymore. The sun and the preacher's hands and then his helpers' hands and my clinging clothes, even the rocks on the river bottom—one by one these things registered in my head as real only as I took steps toward the bank where Lee was. With each step it was like I was reentering the world somehow. And even with Lee on that side of things, standing there smiling, but not a happy smile, smiling and smoking and shaking his head, squinting his eyes for the reflection on the water, I wasn't so sure I didn't want to stay in that other world, the one I had just left, where everything was light and free and warm and comfortable.

Just one look at Lee and anyone could see that he thought we were all downright stupid for what we'd done. Sure enough, he said: No amount of river water is ever going to take away all you've done in this lifetime. And it's plum foolishness to think otherwise. Whatever it is that sends you looking for salvation in the first place is part of your record and there's no wiping that away until you die.

Well, I don't believe that. I choose not to, I said. No matter what you've done in this life, there's always the chance for salvation. You've got to believe that.

I don't got to believe anything, Lee said, and he stubbed out his cigarette in the mud and headed back to our camp.

I stayed and sat down and watched as one by one the people left the river and, resuming their humming and singing, walked back into the woods from where they'd come, disappearing like they were nothing other than ghosts. For a moment, I even allowed myself to think that maybe the whole thing was just a figment or something. But no matter how much I told myself that maybe they weren't even real, there was a big part of me said I wouldn't mind going with them.

And something else: no matter what Lee said, no matter what anyone said, I told myself that I'd done my soul some good. Maybe the record wasn't wiped fully clean, but maybe it wasn't quite as dirty as it had been.

And this would be an idea, a hope, that I would cling to every single day from there on, and I knew it even then: every day for the rest of my life.

26

There ain't no do-overs in life, Lil, Lee said when I returned.

I ignored him and started cleaning up our campsite a bit. I wanted to stay busy and I had energy to spare. The whole walk back from the river I felt almost like I was floating.

You may as well pack it all. We're leaving.

What do you mean we're leaving? I asked.

Not with all those people around.

They paid us no mind at all. You saw. And I doubt they're even coming back. Seems to me they got what they came for.

Whether they're coming back or not. Whether they paid us any mind or not, it isn't safe to stay, Lee said.

And so we broke everything down and moved on once again. I hated the idea of it because I'd done my best to make it as much a home as I could. In fact, I tried my best to make every place we stopped a home to us, even though I knew it would only be for a short while. And I'd done a pretty good job in that particular place and thought it creative the way I set up the tarp and all our possessions in an open spot that caught the sun and reflected the light. I could sit next to a tree with my back against it and close my eyes and feel the sunlight on me reflecting from the tarp and imagine myself in my armchair at home near my window, which had become in my mind the sight of some of my happiest and most peaceful moments.

But I probably should have known it wouldn't last, as if there was some sign pointing against it because when we first arrived, after I'd got everything set up such as the catch basins, and helped Lee with the rabbit traps along the deer paths, and set up the tarp and gotten firewood, the clouds came out and by the time the sun returned, it had taken up high on the tree and I couldn't catch it anymore. And so it was gone to me and I could only hope for it to come back again the next day. But now there wouldn't be a next day.

It was times like these I needed to recall my old sense of adventure and put it to good use. A raven can be no blacker than its wings, Mama would say, meaning, You have to be true to what you are and no attempts to change that core part of yourself will ever stick for long. She was right about that part. That day back home I'd gone walking to get to that distant rise was one such occasion. Seemed almost every week I'd be dragging myself home way past when I was expected because I was off somewhere and would lose all sense of time and surroundings because there was one more bend in the river or one more lizard to discover hiding under a rock or one more loose plank in an abandoned cabin that I'd have to pull up, see if there wasn't some buried treasure or something. Or maybe a simple piece of home life long gone now and well past use but that hinted at people come and gone.

And so off we went again and it was here for one night, there for another, none of them the right place in Lee's eyes, too close to that or too far from this—it grew tiresome. It was a funny thing how all I looked forward to most days was to settle in one spot, and what I was thinking of was a spot somewhere in the woods and not an actual home or even a motel room, like any sane girl my age, or any other age, would.

At one point, Lee said, You know, most girls would have tired of this by now. He was smiling when he said it and I knew he meant it as a compliment. In fact, he'd said this to me before.

Yes, most girls would get tired of it, I said, and while before I felt myself better than those girls, whoever they were, now it made me think there might be something wrong with me for not feeling that way and maybe I should think about trying to make my way back home and live the normal, secure life I'd always imagined for myself—even if secure and boring sometimes got mixed up and could mean the same thing. But Lee didn't seem to notice any of that.

We did finally hit some bigger roads, roads big enough to have signs for St. Louis. This made Lee nervous, so back to the smaller roads we went until one day, without any warning, we came across a baseball game. Out of nowhere: a narrow two-lane road, open field in every direction, and then, without any sign of a proper town, a mess of cars pulled to the side, parents and kids sitting in the grass, and a bunch of boys who looked to be around our ages playing baseball.

We stopped to watch and as we walked toward the field, Lee said, I used to play.

This was another thing I didn't know about him. But this time I liked the idea, that we could still surprise each other with little facts about ourselves. There was still plenty to discover.

Yeah? I said.

Lee nodded.

Shortstop. Kind of like the captain of the infield, he said. Least it was on the team I played.

He looked around, took it in: the way the dirt was all chewed up around the bases; the smell of ground-up earth all deep and rich; that unmistakable sound of the bat on the ball, the pop of it that can only come from this game; the cheering of the spectators; the boys themselves—all seriousness and sweat and effort, as if their very lives depended on the outcome.

I would have thought when we stopped at the game we'd stay at most an inning or two, take in the free show since we rarely got such a thing, and then leave. I knew how Lee was about being around too many people. But we stayed even after a half hour had passed. Seemed he couldn't tear himself away and I wondered if in his head he was reliving some glory years or something. As for me, my mind started to wander. The game itself wasn't all that interesting. Way too much standing around. I couldn't imagine it if I was one of those players who hardly ever moved. One of the outfielders, say, who spent an inning out where the grass is a bit taller and doing nothing because no balls came his way and then spent the next half-inning doing nothing on the bench because it wasn't his turn to bat. But none of them seemed to mind. They all sat or stood around chewing gum and making bubbles or eating sunflower seeds and spitting the shells everywhere. But like I said, it was free entertainment so I guess, all things being equal, I was happy enough to stay and watch.

I realized then that I'd spent a good chunk of that time messing around with my ear where it had got infected. It almost felt like the earring was still there because there was a thing like a little ball I could feel in there, under my skin. I often rolled it between my fingers when I was lost in thought. So much so that Lee would say, You're doing it again. But it was strange: it was like a souvenir or something, a war wound, I liked to think, and later on when I looked at it in the rearview mirror I could see also that I'd got a little scar and I decided I liked this, too. It was character. As for the other ear, that got all closed up as if I never had anything there.

But finally some excitement came, though I can't say I felt very good about being happy for it: seemed the shortstop on one team took a ball right in his wrist and it swelled up something terrible and he had to leave the game. For some time, I had no idea what was going on because the game didn't start back up. Instead, everyone just stood there looking around, even after the boy who'd gotten hurt sat down on the bench and took off his hat and glove. Then suddenly a few of the boys walked over to us. My reaction was to run for it—I don't know why—but Lee stood there and when they asked if he played, he got that smile on his face, the

223

one that could beat the world, and said, Yeah, sure, I've played some, and he took the kid's place at shortstop. I was surprised at how careless he was being, Lee who was always reminding me we couldn't be around people. But it seemed he didn't even think twice about it and before long I didn't think about it either for how much I enjoyed watching him play.

For three innings Lee played—man, he was good. Everything that came his way in the field, he gobbled it up and threw out the runner with a mile to spare. They didn't have a chance. I loved watching him, loved seeing my man show them all how it was done. I loved the way he had of just shrugging off their congratulations as they ran in after an inning, all of them slapping him on the back and him just barely even reacting like what he was doing was the easiest thing in the world. And the team he joined, you could see it: it was as if they had just landed the biggest ringer in the state—whatever state we were in.

And when he got up to bat—well, I thought my heart might just about pound out of my chest. Very first pitch and Lee sent that thing so far I thought it might never land. It was like a rainbow over the boys in the outfield and he ran around the bases so fast that he was home before the ball was back into second base. Was that something! I understood why women loved athletes. Just watching your man be better than everyone else, I could hardly stand it.

It was time for Lee's side to take the field again. I hadn't even realized that anyone was keeping track of anything, but apparently this was the final inning and Lee's team was winning by one on account of his home run. It was all so exciting.

The other team came up to bat and got two outs right away. So only one out to go and it was over. But then they got a hit and then a walk and that was followed by another walk before they got a new pitcher to come on and try to get the final out with the bases full. He got two quick strikes on the guy and again it seemed Lee's team would finally win it, but the batter hit the next pitch—a grounder that went straight at Lee. I knew then this thing was over. But just like that—and almost impossible to believe—the ball somehow went right under Lee's glove, between his legs, and on into the outfield. Everyone on his team just stood there and watched as the other team's guys came racing around the bases and into home plate and won the game, like they couldn't believe it was happening. The other team celebrated at home plate jumping all over each other while, slowly, one by one, the guys on Lee's team came over and slapped him on the back and shoulder and told him not to worry about it.

That didn't help any. Lee just handed the glove to the kid who'd gotten hurt and came back over to me. But he didn't even stop, just kept right on past me to the car and I had to hurry to catch up with him. When I got in, he started the car and drove off, spreading so much dust and gravel that everyone on the field turned to watch us go.

We were quiet and there was a sadness to us both that was plain enough but that neither one of us spoke to. I could guess easily enough that for Lee this sadness was probably because he missed a life in which he could do such things as play a simple game and not have to worry so much about anything else, where making an error—even if it cost your team the game—was the worst thing that could happen. When I thought about the things we'd set for ourselves that required worry—or at least required deep thought and careful planning—I imagined the idea of worrying about whether you'd get a hit or scoop up a grounder was a luxury Lee might have liked to go back to, if only for a day.

For me, it was something different. It was hard to watch all those people and know that when the game was done, they'd go back to their homes, wherever they were, and make their suppers and probably bow their heads in prayer and thank Jesus for their meal, and then tuck themselves into proper beds and wake the next morning and have their regular people worries and lives: school, work, prom dates, baseball games, and all the things that at the time seem like the normal pieces of a life but when you no longer have them can seem almost like glorious dreams.

I wanted to try and make at least one of us feel better. It's no big deal, I said. Heck, that team only had a chance to win because of you, because of your home run.

It was an error, Lil.

Well, I don't think it was such a big error.

No, that's what they call it in baseball. An error. When you don't make a play you're supposed to make.

So? It's no big deal, Lee. You were good.

He turned to me, his arm over the steering wheel. Don't you get it? he asked.

Get what?

It's like I told you: There are no do-overs. Not in any river and not on any field. No do-overs. Not in baseball and not in life.

27

After the baseball game, we drove in silence, each in our own little world of unpleasantness, while we looked for our next resting place.

So I was happy when we found the perfect spot. It was among the ruins of an old abandoned church deep in the woods with no path to it so we didn't expect any people to come, and it was beautiful, the way the sun came through the leaves and scattered itself all over and how the vines of some creeping flower twisted over the walls. We were lucky to have found it at all. Lee had to go to the bathroom and required privacy, so he'd walked deep into the woods and was gone a long time and then came back real excited, telling me what he'd found.

There was no roof and hardly anything left of the walls, either, and it was a tiny place, mostly just the foundations, but two of the walls were still standing all the way up to where the roof would have been and you could tell by the way it was so high and the pitched windows, too, that it was clearly a church at one time. It was pure blind luck to have stumbled upon it the way Lee did and it was funny how even old useless ruins could feel like a home just because it had walls—or what was left of them—and by the fact that they were built by human hands. And, of course, there was a time when people, whoever they were, congregated there, came together and sang and prayed and were a community. One had to wonder about it, how many babies were baptized, how many dead were prayed over, how many couples were married, all in that place that the woods had run over and would one day crumble to nothing more than a collection of old rocks.

How old you think this is? I asked.

I can't say as I have any idea, Lee said.

He looked around, as if he might figure it out, and said, Seems to me no one's been around here for a hundred years most likely. I suppose there was a town close-by at one time. At least enough to need a church.

We'd seen no evidence of people anywhere near and so I thought Lee was right, that maybe it was a hundred years or more easy when they were here. But who knew for sure?

What I did know was that it would become where we would stay for a bit and because of that I set to my routine. The ground was nice and flat and easy to clear and it wasn't long before we had our new home and even though I hadn't been in a church proper in years, being where we were lent something like a sanctified air to everything.

In fact, as I was coming back from collecting wood one time, I swear I caught Lee praying. I was sure of it, the way he was on his knees and his lips were moving.

Whatcha doing? I asked.

Nothing, he said, getting up.

Looks like you were praying.

That's silly.

I don't think it's silly, I told him. I don't think it's silly at all.

Yeah, well, so what, he said. Seems to me we can use all the help we can get.

I didn't know if he was playing a joke or what, for all his talk about not believing. But it sure didn't seem like a joke and I didn't think he knew I was there. Maybe those people getting baptized had some effect on him, after all, though he never did say another word about it.

228

The only drawback of our site was that it sat probably two miles from a creek. But even that wasn't so terrible for we'd reached that time of the year where the grasses were low and it was easy enough to make our way along. As I walked down to the creek, I'd have to climb over a fallen tree here and there, which was no big deal at all. It was harder for Lee when he fished. What with his makeshift pole and his lack of patience, he kept coming up empty. Then he'd swat at the water in frustration.

You're making it worse, I'd say. Probably scared every fish within a mile of this place by now.

He tossed the pole to the bank. I know how to fish, he said with a scowl on his face.

But he was on to crawfish by then. They were much easier. Lee would run his hand in the water slowly as the crawfish backed up step by step until Lee would steer the things into rocks where they couldn't escape. So long as you watched the pinchers, you could then just pick them up by the tails. So, that first night we had no fish, but did have three crawfish each.

The next afternoon passed easy, as it usually did when we were busy with work. First thing I did was mend our clothes with needle and thread we brought with us from Maybell's. By sunset, we had a fire going and Lee roasted a squirrel he'd caught in one of the traps. I much preferred rabbit and, honestly, didn't like squirrel, but it was food and I was hungry and so I ate it with gratification.

I even prayed before I ate it, silent and in my head, but I thanked the Lord for the meal, like we used to do back at home sometimes, even after we stopped going to church. Maybe it was being in a church of sorts again, or being homesick for an earlier time, or the fact that sometimes you just have to take an accounting of your situation and count your blessings. And there were blessings, lots of them in fact: the place was beautiful.

The moonlight fell over the church walls and the stars twinkled here and there, especially one, real bright and kind of blue in color.

229

That's Venus, Lee said, though I didn't know how he knew that and I wasn't so sure he was even right, but I didn't say anything. Even though the squirrel meat was gamey and greasy, our bellies were full and it was a warm enough night so we didn't even need much bedding and I was content enough as we fell asleep holding on to one another and it felt, crazy as this might sound, something close to perfect and for the time I was happy again. I didn't miss being at Maybell's, or even my own home. It had been a long time since I fell asleep truly happy, a thing I only realized once it happened.

～

We took trips to the creek to bathe and get water to drink, and during the day we told each other stories we made up—Lee's always had monsters in them and mine always had princesses, and we complained to each other about both, which made us want to tell monster and princess stories all the more until it ended up that he would tell me some story where a monster ate all the princesses in the land and then my story would have the princess defeat all the monsters and make them her slaves.

It was a fun time, like we were living some kind of break from the madness and difficulties, and we enjoyed each other's company again, like we had when we first set out, and we made a lot of love, which was how I'd come to see the act. Making love. There's no other or better way to describe it.

But of course I couldn't confine myself to this life forever. Within a few days of our settling in, I was heading out in every direction, seeing what I could find. Usually that meant nothing. But by nothing I mean to say more woods and some open grasslands at the edge of the tree line. That sort of thing. Eventually, my searches got more specific; I turned over rocks and watched little black salamanders squirm away and occasionally I caught one and rubbed its tail or flipped it on its back to see the streaks of red and orange on its undersides. Usually when I caught them, they did everything they could to get away and occasionally they dropped out of my hands and fell to the ground and then ran away under some leaves or another rock or something. But sometimes they just sat there like they trusted me or knew that I wouldn't hurt them. Of course they could have been playing dead, thinking that might be their best defense. But I liked to think that they trusted me and enjoyed the feeling of warmth from my palm.

So every day, after our chores had been done and we settled into that time that we liked to think of as free time, I set out to do my exploring. One day after we'd been there almost two weeks, a long enough time that we had to endure some chilly nights and rainy days, I found the graveyard. I must have walked right by it two dozen times or more, I figured.

Well, it wasn't a proper graveyard but rather a collection of stones that looked to have no real order to them. Maybe time had shifted them around some. They were all from the 1800s and the earliest of them had birth dates from the very beginning of the century. Poe was the name. Poe and Wilson and Rauch and a few other single names. But mostly it was Poe, seven of them by my count.

Several of the stones were scratched out and unreadable. But others were clear as could be, though they were all old, only one reaching into the 1900s and that just barely. I brushed the leaves and twigs from them and wiped off the dirt best I could. Seemed to me they should have had someone looking after them. The thought of all those bones beneath my feet didn't bother me. I knew it was the same fate waiting for me also, so why be creeped out by it? Besides, it's the soul that matters and that surely never gets piled under dirt. But while Lee and I were staying there, so close-by, it seemed only right I do what I could to at least see that what remained of them was properly looked after, even if it was only stone.

So while Lee was back at the church, I continued to clean the stones best I could. And in doing that I saw that three little stones, side by side by side, all had the name Poe on them and each one told of a life that hardly had a chance to get going before it ended. Theresa Poe lived 1885–1887; Thomas Poe was 1891–1897; and then there was one with no other name but Poe and only one date. That one was a puzzle to me.

I heard Lee coming and when he brushed through the tree branches and saw me sitting there, he stopped and took it all in.

Will you look at that, he said. Figured you were collecting wood.

Makes sense this would be here so close to a church, I said.

He nodded.

Come here, I told him, and I pointed to the one stone.

Look at this one. It only has one date on it. I wonder why.

I reckon it died the day it was born. Or came out dead.

He said it as if it was the most natural thing and there wasn't any sorrow attached to it for that fact. Just a part of the world. But the idea filled me with a great and terrible sadness. Hadn't even been alive long enough to be given a name.

How this mother must have grieved, I said, and I did so out loud even though I meant it to stay only a thought.

Lee just said, I guess, without any emotion.

Three children, babies, all dead and the oldest of them barely six years.

I ran my fingers over the damp stones.

You think it's worse to have the child for two years before it dies or not have it at all? I asked.

You're doing it again, he said, about my ear and the fact that I was rubbing that little knot in my lobe.

I asked you a question.

I really can't say, Lee answered. He kicked at the ground a bit. Come on, Lil, he said finally. Let's collect our wood before it gets dark on us. Besides, he added, no use in us grieving over these people gone long before we ever came around.

I suppose he was right. But, still, it got me thinking. Someday there would be nothing left of us but stones like these, too. And some people, not even born yet, would be standing someplace looking at our names and it would mean nothing to them. I liked the idea of someone I didn't even know, maybe someone like me, same age, same fears and dreams, out on some grand adventure, might come along my tombstone somehow, and stop what she was doing for a few minutes and brush the leaves and dirt from my name and wonder who I was and even say a silent prayer for my mortal soul.

While I collected more wood, I expressed some of this to Lee, even though, once again, I had no intention of giving voice to these thoughts. For I knew how he'd take them. And sure enough, I was right:

Why would it be any different? he said. It's the way of the world. We come and we go and there's no good reason to spend any amount of time worrying about it.

But wouldn't it be nice to think of some kind folks tending to us a hundred years from now? They might stand there and try to puzzle out the days of our lives, like we're doing here. Look at our names and our dates and wonder what all things we'd done.

Why would they do that? he said. Didn't even know us.

'Cause we'd be a reminder that no one lives forever, like these people here are reminding us, I said. It was making me angry this whole thing, why every time it seemed he needed to put all his logic into it when there were times to be dreamy and spiritual about things. Sometimes the best questions are the ones with no answers and the only thing to do about it was to air those questions and then leave them alone.

But he kept on it: I don't need any reminders to tell me no one lives forever, he said.

Sometimes you got to wonder about it all, I said, holding my ground. Like we're racing toward a stone. To end up nothing more than a name someone wipes dirt and leaves off of. I know there's little use in thinking about that. But when we do wind up here, I said, pointing to the graves, the question then is: What was it all for?

He just looked at me. Then he said, Let's go, Lilly.

Yeah. When you have no answers for me, that's what you say: Let's go, Lilly.

What else you want me to say?

I don't know, Lee. But don't you ever have any grand questions? Ones that keep you up at night, ones that toss around inside your head until you're dizzy: heaven and hell, for instance, or what purpose do we have on earth?

There's no use thinking those things. What good does it come to?

Well, I'm sorry to tell you, but I need things beyond just sex and all that stuff. Sometimes I want to just sit and talk. I mean, really talk. And not about collecting kindling for a fire or if we'll have luck catching fish or what Louisiana might be like in comparison to Arkansas or if Ar-kansas was in some way an afterthought in comparison to Kansas, name-wise that is.

Well, you want to talk, then let's talk. Go ahead. I'm all ears.

I just looked at him. Forget it, I said, and went back to collecting kindling.

I don't get it. You say you want to talk, about all the grand things in the universe. And here I am saying, Okay, let's talk, and now you want me to just forget it. Makes no sense at all to me.

You're right, Lee. You *don't* get it.

We went to sleep early; well, at least Lee did. I stayed awake most of the night. When I looked over at Lee, fast asleep, his body rank from lack of a bath, I grew angry at him. And while I hated to do it, I finally fell asleep with my anger and I was grateful that he didn't wake up in the night and put his arms around me, as he often did.

When I woke, Lee was already up and he took me over to a huge oak tree and pointed at it.

Look, he said.

Sometime while I slept, he must have taken his knife and carved our names inside a big heart right there on that tree. It was clean and deep and I could see the yellow of the tree underneath its rough bark. With tears in my eyes, I threw my arms around him and kissed his face.

Now, he said, that'll outlast us, too, and people can come by and marvel at it all they want. But it won't be stones they'll see. But rather there were two lovers who were here and are here no more and they can imagine that we're off together somewhere still in love. Which we will be, he added.

You make me happy, Lee, I said. You just do.

It was a moment of such great sweetness. I ran my finger along the lines he'd carved and even with the little sharp pokes on my skin, it still felt good.

But I couldn't help myself, even before I was done: I knew some dark thoughts would be coming soon enough, to get themselves all mixed in. It was a thing I did where even the best of times seemed to be infected with a certain sadness around the edges just because they *were* such special moments. It was like because I knew I'd remember something for its goodness and pleasure, it meant that when times turned bad sometime later, it would make it harder to remember the good for the pain it would bring. It was a beautiful kind of pain, I knew, but there just the same.

I didn't know where it would be, or when or why, but somewhere along the line the thought of that tree with our names carved into it would go from lighting me up with happiness to making me sad thinking about it. It was like we'd left ourselves to the same fate as the Poes and all the others under their stones. What Lee had said was right, that people would come by and wonder about us. But would they wonder anything different than they did about the Poes? In fact, as the fresh bark faded and grew old and gnarled over our names, they might even think that Lilly and Lee were Poes themselves.

As the days went on, more and more things like that made me sad. Things that earlier had made me happy.

28

We wound up staying at the church for six weeks before we left—just up and got out of there one day. It had gotten cold and we weren't fully prepared for that, so we needed to keep moving south. During those weeks, there were times I was bored, and at other times angry. Sometimes I felt like all the love I had for Lee was wiped away in a mess of irritation and boredom. Other moments I couldn't imagine being more in love or more in tune with another human being, what people meant when they talked about a soul mate. I never asked about New Orleans in all that time—I couldn't stand the idea of any more disappointment—but now, after so much time had gone by, and we were feeling pretty safe about everything, now we could get back to what had been our original plan.

So we were another several weeks traveling the byways of the American South, down through Arkansas and Mississippi and, finally, into Louisiana. As we headed south and toward our goal, I felt as if everything that had happened was just a necessary route to travel to get us here, and so as the miles clicked by, I felt myself growing more content and that made everything much easier.

It's a funny thing about the South and specifically the South as winter approached. The cold seasons, I learned, were far different than back at home. In Paris, you didn't even have to wait until the end of fall before you woke up mornings to see the grasses all crinkled up and stiffened with morning frost before the sun burns it off. But there it was almost December and it hit eighty degrees a couple of days.

But winter did make itself felt again. One night there was an ice storm and we had to sleep in the car with the engine running and the heat on. In the morning the sun was out and by ten o'clock it was already past fifty degrees and everything that had been coated with ice the night before now dripped off so much it looked like it was raining. The branches of the evergreens sagged with the weight of the ice and the spindliest of the branches snapped off altogether. It was a beautiful show—that false rain and the melting ice and the places where it hadn't yet melted glittering rainbows like tiny diamonds. I was sure such a show had occurred in Paris, but I couldn't remember any. That's another thing about being out on the road with no fixed home: you notice things you wouldn't otherwise. At home, you run through your days sometimes without your brain offering up one thought as to how or why. But then you're someplace new, and it seems that you have no choice but to answer those questions to yourself, to sit up and take notice of things.

As I said, Lee was more comfortable taking the bigger roads and so we stopped in little towns and we ate at diners and even on two occasions took a motel room. I asked Lee how our money situation was holding out and he said fine, we still got plenty, and he figured we could easily go another year before we needed to settle down.

It was a funny thing when he said that. A year. I swear it, how I regarded that figure changed minute by minute, even second by second. There were times I thought how exciting and wonderful it would be to live such a life as this for a year before we planted ourselves somewhere and started a family. But just as quickly, I thought how awful such a prospect might be, having to live that way for so long. But it became a moot point when we reached Interstate 10 outside Lafayette, Louisiana, and there were the signs saying east was New Orleans one hundred sixty miles and west was Houston, one hundred ninety miles. It was something for me to be that close to two major cities when my home was a thousand miles to the north and I hadn't been in any real cities before. We were so close now. We stayed in a motel in a little town called Adrian and the plan was to get into New Orleans early the next morning.

While we were unpacking our things, Lee said, out of nowhere, that we'd been on the run for exactly six months to the day. Six months—half a year since we'd left Paris—and I could hardly believe it. But then again, I wasn't sure I even saw much of a meaning in it. Six months. Eight months. Ten months. One year. Two. A week. What was the difference? When you've got no watch. When there's no clock to stare at. When there's no school calendar—no calendar at all—you not only lose track of it, you come to realize that time doesn't really mean much of anything. Sure, if you've got a plane to catch, or a train, or a job where you're expected at a certain hour, then, of course, time is a thing that you need to obey. But otherwise, it means about as much as the rings of Jupiter. Out on the plains, and in the great wide-open spaces of Middle America, running the length from Canada to Mexico, there are no appointments to keep. At least not for Lee and me there wasn't.

All this was brought home to us when we saw Adrian's huge clock, right in the center of town on the face of city hall. Its hands alone were probably as tall as me and when we walked past, I stared at it like it was an alien or something else I'd never seen before or seen only in a dream.

It was a shock to return to a place with time as we'd long ago stopped living in such a world. Time for us usually meant sunrise and sunset and long shadows or when the cicadas ceased their noise. But there it was, big as day, and it was yet another reminder that the life we'd chosen for ourselves was far beyond the reaches of what ruled other people's lives.

Lee parked the car and we hopped out and did this thing we did where we stopped wherever we were and looked around, taking stock and sussing things out, just to make sure all was clear. It made sense earlier, but as we'd now put months between us and the killings, it made less and less sense. Habit, I suppose. I only hoped it wasn't something we would wind up doing for the rest of our lives.

But we did act on guard, vigilant, as Lee called it, maybe to remind ourselves that we'd left a mess in our wake and we couldn't take any foolish chances or else it would all come back to us no matter how much time went by and we'd have more than enough to answer for.

So we stopped and looked around and, satisfied, carried on. We moved to the sidewalk real fast, not talking to each other and barely staying near one another, like we were trying to be invisible, get from this place to that as quickly as we could and then move on. Nuthin' to see here, folks, Lee used to joke.

Just down the street, under a big gazebo, there was a band and they were playing some old-time Dixieland, so we went over and listened.

Getting close to New Orleans, Lee said. Come on, let's hop into the drugstore real quick so I can pick up some razors.

And there it was.

Behind the counter: a calendar.

It looked funny enough on its own, simply because in my old life it was an everyday item. I'd see one all the time at home or at school. But it had been a good long while since. Mr. Chester hadn't had one in his home. Nor could I recall one in Maybell's house, either. So it had been since Paris. But that wasn't the issue. It was instead the realization hitting me when I took a good look at it, at the way the first nine days on that calendar, the squares of each day, had been crossed through with a big red X, and looking at the month, I realized that my birthday had come and gone and I'd turned sixteen and I hadn't even known it.

So I started to cry. Right there in the store. And I couldn't stop. When Lee saw me, he dropped his razors onto the floor and rushed over

239

to me. By this point, a man had already stopped and asked me what was wrong and did I need help, but Lee pulled me away and we were out on the sidewalk and I was still crying and Lee was telling me I needed to pull myself together, but I couldn't.

Sixteen. Sweet sixteen. While I wasn't into big parties or the importance people place on what are supposed to be big dates, truth was I'd been looking forward to my sweet sixteen ever since I was a little girl. Back then, I figured sixteen was the age where I'd be considered an adult and would get to do things I wanted to do and wouldn't have to get permission for things from Mama or anyone else. Of course, as I got older, I realized that I'd already been an adult in some ways well before sixteen and in the ways in which I hadn't, one turn of the calendar wasn't going to change that anyway. Still, it was a nice idea and Mama had always said that we would do something super special on that day.

But it had come and gone. How Mama must have been feeling! How for so long she'd been planning out something grand for me and I wasn't even home for it and what a terrible daughter that made me.

Lee was confused and getting anxious, looking around. You need to get yourself under control, Lil, he said. Now. We're drawing stares.

So what? I yelled. I don't care anymore.

You've got to calm down. Come on now. We can't have people getting suspicious.

The reality of that made me cry even harder, so Lee steered me to the car.

When he finally got me in, I told him I wanted to go home.

He looked like I'd kicked him in his stomach. His face dropped. His whole body slumped. His shoulders, his hands to his side. He looked weary, tired, like someone who'd played a whole football game or something, without a break, giving it his all, only to lose it at the very last second. Someone who'd come up just a little short.

But finally, after a long time, he spoke.

I always worried such a day as this was coming, he said, looking at his hands. I never said this out loud to you because in the end I figured you'd come around no matter what and realize that your fate lies with me and that together we're a team, something special that no one can tear apart. But separate, well, we might as well just give up the ghost, for one little person in this world doesn't stand a chance. So you need to think about what it is you're saying to me now. You need to think about it long and hard.

What I didn't tell him was that somewhere deep inside me, I'd been thinking I wanted to go home to Paris, and to Mama, and to my red reading chair, and to the cats, even back to school, to live the normal life that was my due—that I'd been thinking it, I realized now, almost since the very day we left.

Six months earlier.

29

It didn't take me much time to come to my decision. But I sat there a long while for the sake of appearances because I knew it would hurt Lee that it had come so quick. But eventually I did tell him: Yes, I want to go home.

He hit the steering wheel real hard with his fist. Then he jammed the gear shift into reverse and peeled out. He didn't even bother to look first and I heard the squeal of someone's brakes behind us and honking and cursing and I could hear it still even as Lee righted the car, peeled out again, and took off down Main Street going way too fast.

You do realize I can't go home with you, he reminded me.

I nodded.

So you're saying, then, that this is the end of us?

I'm not saying that at all, I told him, and I started crying all over again.

But what else then?

I want to go home. See my mama. Be normal for a while. Then I want you to come back for me. After you've got some proper and re-spectable job and we can settle down and go ahead with our plan to be a married couple with children.

He punched the steering wheel again. I wondered if he no longer believed in this plan.

I felt like he was slipping away from me, so I added another idea: We can pick a date, I declared. Let's say New Year's Eve, 1980. Or 1979. Whichever is the one for the new decade. You know what I mean.

But I knew I was making little sense because I was still crying and it was kind of a ridiculous idea anyway, one I heard people make in some dumb movie I saw once—at home or on the TV in one of the motel rooms we took, I couldn't say. And anyway, he didn't even respond to it.

I wished he would stop the car once we were out of town or something, pull off on the side of the road and put his arms around me and tell me he still loved me and that we'd be okay. I needed to hear those things at that moment, though I imagine it was him who was hurting worse than me because I was the one who said I wanted to go home. Either way, this would be no fun trip, heading through some five states or so, straight up the middle of the country through so many empty places. And if Lee had decided he was no longer talking to me, I wasn't sure I'd be able to bear it.

But soon enough he had to stop the car anyway because I threw up all over the place. It came on real sudden. I figured all the nerves and awfulness of everything happening had just been too much and before I knew it, it was coming up on me and I was powerless to stop it. So Lee squealed to a halt and I threw open the car door and vomited some more while he rubbed my back and held my hair out of my face.

We were sitting for a long time, not saying anything, waiting for me to get myself back together. I finally started to feel okay, all emptied out inside, and I was sitting there with my eyes closed, silence all around, heaviness coming in at every direction when I suddenly bolted my eyes open at the sound of Lee crying.

It came slow at first, just a few deep inhales of breath and a single tear running down his cheek. But then lots of tears and he started sobbing. I leaned over and held him. He buried his face into my chest and between sobs, he said something, but it was all muffled.

243

What did you say, baby? I can't hear you.

You're my best friend, Lilly. My best friend in the world.

I nodded. I felt the same way. But I couldn't talk. It felt like a hot iron poker had been driven right down my throat and straight through the whole of my body.

You're the only thing I have in this world, he said.

After a long moment, he asked, You know about the dodo?

Dodo?

Dodo bird. I read about it in a book, long time ago. It went extinct. When there was only one of them left in the world, it went deaf with the sound of its own mating call. I never forgot that.

I looked at Lee and wished more than anything else I'd ever wished for that I had something to say to him. Something to make it all better. But, I didn't. I didn't have anything to say at all.

We sat there for close to an hour, just rubbing each other's hands and we took turns crying and then composing ourselves and then crying again.

Then, finally, when it seemed he'd gotten out everything he needed to, he looked at me, long and hard, like for the first time he was trying to figure me out completely.

I guess sometimes I forget that you're a girl, he said.

The tone in his voice wasn't one I could read. He didn't say it sneering like, like he was saying I was *just* a girl and nothing else. Nor was there any regret or sympathy for the fact, either. It was more like maybe he'd only then figured it out. And it set me to wondering again. *Is* that what I was to him? I certainly didn't think so. When I thought "girl," I thought of someone small and young and without any independence or experience. And if the last half year hadn't given me more experience than even I'd have wanted for myself, well, I didn't know what. But it was true, there were parts of me—big parts—that still wanted to be a girl, to go home and crawl into my bed and have Mama put her arms around me and brush my hair for me and figure out some way to stay like that and keep age and the years away. I understood what it was Mama meant all those times when she said she wanted to keep me young and that if she blinked she'd come to see I'd grown up and I wouldn't be her little girl anymore. I thought it was silly talk then, but now I could see what she meant in it.

৹৲

It was a very long trip home. Never had I experienced something so full of hope on the one hand—I was going back home, to my bed, and to Mama, and, yes, even to Hank; he always was a nice man, a thing I'd only really begun to appreciate while far away from him—but there was of course real sadness to it, too. For every mile closer we got, through the wastelands of northeast Texas and on into Oklahoma and the emptiness of Kansas and the wheat fields of Nebraska, and then into my Dakotas, every mile closer meant one less with Lee and also the reality that our time together, at least for now, was coming to an end. At first, that idea made me too upset to even think about, and several times as we drove those long and lonely miles I had to bite my tongue, and I mean this literally in one case, in my desire to tell him to turn to the west and head to California instead, follow in the steps of the pioneers and find ourselves some little cottage on the Pacific Ocean and spend the rest of our days out there together.

The thought of me and him and palm trees and no winter: it surely was an attractive idea, made even more so in the emptiness of the heartland. But that heartland, well, it was my home. And I didn't think it was for nothing that it had the name heart in it.

I kept getting sick, too, which made the trip even longer. I thought at first it was food poisoning or a stomach bug or something. But then I guessed it was due to all those feelings and thoughts all jumbled up inside me and it was just too much. Probably half a dozen times Lee had to pull over so I could throw up. I kept saying how sorry I was; I didn't make it easy because I could never tell when it was coming and all of

245

sudden I'd be yelling for him to stop. But he never made me feel bad for it, only looked at me and rubbed my back. And then when I was done, we'd be back on our way.

We had little time left, little chance to have the deeper conversations that I often yearned for and that perhaps would have kept me out there if not forever then at least some time longer. But I knew it wasn't to be. I'd come to understand that Lee's avoidance of such topics wasn't on account of anything other than the fact that Lee wasn't settled about anything and certainly not so in his mind. And to wrestle around with questions that had no answers made him even more antsy than normal. He needed some time, in other words. To grow up a little. I did, too. And then we could be together for real, and forever.

And so as we crossed into South Dakota and I knew that at least for now our adventure was coming to an end, I decided it was all for the best. It wasn't over, of course. I knew that Lee and I were destined to be together—just not right then. That I knew because while people can wind up with any number of others in their lives, there is only one true soul mate and for me that person was Lee.

We *would* find each other again. Of that, I had no doubt.

30

I read a book once about a pilot whose plane crash-landed in the Sahara Desert and he wandered alone and close to death for two weeks before he was saved. He wrote about mirages, about how he'd be walking and see whole towns sprouting up from the sand and he'd believe he was saved and he'd muster up all his strength and run to it only to realize it never was there and instead it was only more sand. What would follow would be a desperation that was almost too much for him to bear. But before that realization and that desperation, the unbelievable joy that man felt was something wonderful beyond his ability to describe.

I can't say that coming into Paris compared to that, but as we reached the outskirts of town and I saw the familiar dusty streets, it did something to me on the inside that I could spend a lifetime trying to describe and still never get right. It was joy, yes, but mostly it was wonder, a feeling like it couldn't be real. Having spent so much time away from the only real home I'd ever known, it had the effect of turning that home into something that felt somehow unfamiliar even at the very moment that it was the most familiar thing I'd ever known. We came upon the streets I could walk with my eyes closed. And people I used to see almost every day and yet because I'd been gone and had experienced so much, it was as if the streets and the people and everything else about Paris had gone from one thing to another and in that transformation shrunk down to a size I could pick up in the palm of my hand and put in my pocket.

As we drove toward town center, I saw the bar where Mama worked—or still did, for all I knew. I saw Mr. Robeson's grocery, I saw the room above Mr. Olson's hardware store where Lee had stayed, and then we passed the school and there I saw the people who were at one time my classmates, one grade older now, all spilling from the school doors, the boys chasing each other around and the girls holding their books to their chests with their long skirts and trying to stay out of the boys' way. It was a funny thing to remember that life goes on in your absence the way it always has and nothing ever changes much. Before I left, I thought that was one of the problems, how boring life can be. But now that I was back, I felt a comfort in that reality. As we passed my schoolmates, some of them looked at us and, seeing me, stopped on the sidewalk and stared at me as if I was a whale or an elephant or Jesus himself back from the dead. For all I knew, some of them assumed I actually *was* dead. As it was, I guess I'd have to rejoin them there. But that was all right; it was only a matter of time before Lee and I would be gone once again, I figured, but doing it the right way, without just taking off and with Mama's blessing and ready to start our lives in a proper way.

We made the turn onto my street and Lee slowed. I think he didn't want to have it come to an end. We approached the Petersens' yard and of course there was the fence where I'd first seen Lee and as we drove slowly past it, I strained my eyes looking for the muddy mark he'd left there on that fateful first day. But of course I didn't see it. I was sure the wind and rain, if not Mr. Petersen himself, rubbed that away a long time earlier, probably even before Lee and I had been away from Paris a day.

248

So we continued on and that's when I saw them: three police cars right out in front of my house and one of the officers standing on my porch and he was talking to Mama and she was shaking her head back and forth and looking worried sick.

Mama, I gasped.

At that, Lee saw what I did and he stopped the car.

I need to find out what's wrong, I said.

Are you crazy? You can't go up there now. There's police all over. They'll haul us both in.

He was right, but my mind was a stew. I tugged at the door handle but Lee held me back. Calm down, he yelled. Calm down! They'll see us.

I need to go now! I yelled.

Calm down, Lilly. Calm down!

He put the car in reverse only to see another police car approaching from that direction. He peeled out and made a turn on the dirt track that used to be the tractor path between the Petersens and the Van Waggoners when there was a farm down there and without even knowing it, we were following the path Lee and I first took that night under the full moon when he came and pulled me out of my sleep and we went down to the creek and kissed for the first time.

Where's this head to? Lee asked.

We were bumping along and he was going way too fast and it was hard for me to even answer, but finally I said, The creek, and he asked if we could drive through it in a car.

How on earth I would know the answer to that, who knew, so I didn't say anything but just held on. There was a police car behind us with its lights and siren on and it was kicking up a cloud of dust and Lee continued driving, but harder and faster now.

Go right, I said once we were clear of the Van Waggoners' property because I knew of a small bridge over the creek. It had been out of commission to vehicles for years but as kids some of us used to climb on it and jump into the creek or fish from under its shadows on hot days.

I pointed it out when it came into view. Lee had enough sense to take it real slow as he drove over it. It was hardly as wide as the car itself and we could hear the thing creaking as we went. We were just about over when one of the tires fell straight through a rotted section and Lee had to gun the car and we spun out of it and banged against one of the metal railings but we got across as several other boards cracked through and fell into the water.

Once across, Lee set the car straight for the rise and we tore across the prairie with that beacon in our sights.

I looked behind us and saw that the police car was sitting on the other side of the creek, its doors open, with two officers looking over the bridge.

We kept on driving until we reached the base of the rise and it was clear to me now how it was that I never did reach it by foot, considering it had taken as long as it had by car. Lee drove around the side of it instead of up. Whether he felt the car couldn't make it up there, I didn't know, but it appeared a pretty gentle slope to me. Finally Lee stopped the car and he jumped out without telling me what he was doing and started running all over, his eyes to the ground, and then he fell to the dirt and clawed at it as if looking for buried treasure.

Help me, he screamed.

I got out and went to him, but I didn't know what it was we were looking for.

A rock, he said. We need a rock.

Right away I spotted one and handed it to him.

He immediately tossed it away. No, he said. A big one. Heavy.

So I looked around some more, but still I didn't know why, and I wasn't finding any big rocks until he said, Forget it, and ran to the back of the car and popped open the trunk. He pulled out our two cases and then took a few wrenches he'd had back there as part of his tool set. He got back into the car and turned it so that it was pointing away from the rise and away from Paris and away from the creek and away, if you want to look at it this way, from the thing that had been our lives.

Once he got the car where he wanted it, looking out over the prairie as if measuring something, he put the wrenches on the gas pedal all the while pushing down on the brake and the car was bucking and straining something awful and then finally he let go of the brake and the car took off, straight as an arrow across the prairie. Its setting off threw Lee back and he took a nasty tumble. When he righted himself, I could see he'd gotten a sizable gash across his forehead and the blood had already started dripping down his face.

Look at you, I said, and I went to wipe away the blood, but he waved me off.

It's nothing, he said, and he grabbed my hand and we ran back to where he'd put our suitcases and we each grabbed one and started to run up the rise. The car looked like a ghost rider or something, continuing on its journey without a soul in it. But very suddenly it took a sharp veer to one side and seemed to catch on something, and then it swerved back to the other side and popped up on two wheels and doing this must have loosed the wrenches because it slowed and came to a stop in a cloud of dust.

We continued running and running and in our haste we both slipped and tripped a few times and we lost our grips on the cases and decided without even saying to let them rest where they were and instead of holding those we held onto each other's hands and kept on running. Close to the top, Lee pulled the gun and the knife from his pants and tossed them both as hard as he could off the far side of the rise. Finally, we made it to the top and collapsed and tried to catch our breath.

I was still trying to catch mine when Lee rolled on top of me and started kissing me and telling me how much he loved me and how there was nothing in this world or any other he loved more and there never would be.

I didn't care about the blood or the dirt or the sweat or anything else. I kissed him and kissed him and held him to me and I swore I'd never let him go and we both started crying and now there was that mingling with everything else dripping from us but it was like we were combining the very souls of ourselves, with our blood and our tears and our sweat.

It's on me, he said. All of it. On me. You understand?

I shook my head.

No, you have to understand. It's on me.

We were so entwined in one another, like we were trying to merge our two bodies into one, that neither one of us registered the sound of the sirens right away and only when we did did we sit up and see what was happening below us: police cars, probably ten of them, two next to Lee's empty car and the rest racing toward the rise from every direction. We knew now: there was nothing left to do but wait.

So we stood, still holding hands, and we waited.

It was one of those moments, one of those things I used to do, where I could see myself as if I was outside my own body, and the way we looked, standing there side by side, holding hands, well, we looked like giants. I could see it then and I can still see it now.

As we stood there and watched those police officers running up the hill with their guns drawn and shouting words that the wind carried away, I imagined we might have looked like giants to them, too. Because the two of us had become one, and because we loved each other truly and honestly, we were much bigger than what we were, and we looked it. We were like lions or something. Lions, in the wild. Rulers.

So here they came, closer and closer, still shouting and they had their guns drawn and one by one they got to the top. It was coming to an end.

I love you, Lilly-Flower, Lee said.

I love you too, I said, and we squeezed our hands together a little bit tighter and we waited.

When the officers all got up there, a dozen of them easy, they screamed at us to put our hands in the air. As soon as we did, four of them came running over.

Two grabbed me, holding my arms behind me, while another two rushed Lee. One of them punched Lee right across the jaw, without

252

even a word of warning, and the other grabbed Lee and kicked out his legs from behind him and got him in a headlock and threw him hard on the ground. I started screaming and pulling and trying to get to him, but they wouldn't let me and somewhere during this scrap I got scratches across my arms and legs and even on my neck, from them or from my own struggles, I couldn't tell. It was hard to see with the hair falling into my eyes and the tears in them, too, and the fact that it felt almost like I might be dying. It wasn't possible to love someone more deeply than I did Lee at that moment and to see him getting roughed up and held on the ground like he was—one of the cops had a knee on the back of his neck and through strained and choked breath Lee was saying he could hardly breathe—everything, all of it, all of the times we'd had together over the past six months, it all came flooding back to me and I knew without a shadow of a doubt that Lee was the one and only person on this planet put here to be with me. And we were being held from each other and it was the most awful pain I could ever imagine.

They pulled me away and started me down the hill before they took Lee, and I could no longer see what they were doing to him. It was a torture. I screamed and screamed until they told me I better shut my mouth if I knew what was good for me. But I yelled out one more time: I love you, Lee. I love you.

For the first time in a very long time we were no longer together and who knew when we'd be again. But then I heard it. It wasn't easy but I *could* hear it, him, and he said, I love you too, baby girl, I love you too!

The walk down the hill seemed to take forever. I pictured that old oak tree back at the church, the one with our names carved into it and just as I feared, the thought of that made me almost want to die. But this image soon faded and what took its place was more like a long movie, like the entire time of our being together playing in my head, the way I guess people mean it when as they lay dying they say their whole life flashes before their eyes. But the weird thing about it was that when that movie was over, what was left was only one image, a time—I couldn't even remember where or when it was—when Lee and I had come across a sturdy old wood pole fence thicker than either of us had ever seen, sloped at the edges, and the way we walked up it and then across, our arms out to the sides for balance, to see who could travel the longest along that fence rail without falling and how I won every time. I suspect Lee was letting me win, though he denied that. But looking back on it, I was sure he was letting me win. He loved me.

And then we were at the bottom of the rise and there were probably fifteen cop cars waiting there. The prairie stretched out all around me and in the distance I could see the outlines of Paris and I did take some relief in knowing I'd see Mama again, but when I didn't know. My guess was that she probably took off sprinting across the prairie, too, when she realized it was us, but the cops forced her to stay behind.

My exhaustion had gotten the better of me now and I was calm, mostly because I couldn't muster up anything else. They put me in the back of the cop car and I sat there and then came the rest of them and they put Lee in another car. He was completely filthy and beaten up and his lower lip was swollen to double its usual size. But for a very brief second we caught eyes and he smiled at me and it looked, I swear it despite the changed circumstances, exactly like the first time he smiled at me, back in that other life of ours, when he was just some handsome stranger leaning against the Petersens' fence and I was just a girl who'd never done a thing in her life.

I smiled back at him. *This* time, I smiled back at him.

⌒

We were off, moving away from Paris. I figured it was because the police knew some way across the creek that I didn't and as it turned out that was exactly the case.

I looked behind me out the back window and saw the other police cars, though I wasn't sure which one Lee was in. Behind them was the rise where we were and it looked small to me now. But then again, everything looked smaller to me now. The whole wide world and everything in it.

A relief came over me suddenly, as if all this time there was some little part of me that was wishing to be caught already so that the fright of getting caught would finally be gone and not something I would need to worry about any longer.

The officer who drove me told me everything was going to be all right and asked if he hurt me. The "he" he was referring to was Lee, obviously.

Course not, I said.

Well, your ordeal is over now, miss.

Lee had told me many times that if we ever ran into any kind of trouble and were held to account, that it was all on him. But that hardly seemed fair or right.

There was a metal crisscross between us that separated the front seat from the back and it reminded me of those confession booths they have in Catholic churches, or at least what I figured they were like. I had a friend when I was a kid who went to confession every week and told all her sins to a priest and he'd give her prayers to say and then everything was back to the way it was before the sins. She told me she could do just about anything so long as she confessed for it and then said her prayers afterward. It never made any real sense to me, but the idea of it sounded appealing.

You know, I said, maybe it was me who shot one of those men.

Now why would you say such a thing like that? the cop said. Huh? When you know such a thing ain't true.

I didn't answer.

I was too tired now, just exhausted from everything and my head was swimming with it all.

We came to a proper bridge, which went right over the creek. It was amazing to me how such a bridge could be so close to where I'd lived my whole life and I'd never seen it before. It made me feel silly. But then I told myself that I'd seen enough in my time and more places probably than the officer who was driving me, and maybe all the rest of them, too. And it was Lee I had to thank for that and though he couldn't see me, I smiled to myself for the thought of it, and him, and I rubbed my fingers over the hardened bump in my earlobe, and I was glad it would be with me for the rest of my days, my reminder of him and of what we shared.

Of course, that was only one thing, and even if I didn't have it as a reminder, I would always have a million other things, living inside my head and my heart and my body. Like poems.

Separate, we were just words, aimless and floating. But together, me and Lee were a poem.

⌒

And you, Lindsey. There was, in the end, you—and that's what matters to me most.

Sioux City, Iowa, November 5, 1992, 1:20 a.m.

"So that's why you do that thing," Lindsey says.

"What's that?"

"With your ear. When you're thinking about something, you rub your earlobe and stare off into space."

I smile.

"Are you thinking of Dad when you do that?"

I'm taken aback. It's the first time she's called him Dad, ever, and it brings it home again just what we're doing here, and how we're so close now. It's well past midnight, meaning our second day on this bus, and we're in Sioux City, just across from the South Dakota line. Sioux Falls is hardly an hour and a half away. We'll stop and eat and get ourselves a room, catch a few hours' sleep maybe, before we start out to see him. No more trying to pretend this is something less than what it really is.

But it seems she's asking to better understand her family, that part of her that has never been in her life, a thing I realize now must feel like a huge hole to her.

"Whatever happened to Miss Maybell?" Lindsey asks. "My grandma."

I smile. "She was your grandma, yes, and it does upset me that you grew up without grandparents. As for Miss Maybell, I still think of her fondly. You know that awful phrase, 'white trash'?"

"Uh-huh."

"It's not something I would ever use to describe someone or a way to think about a person. If you ever wanted to paint a portrait of someone who was 'white trash,' you'd do well to paint that portrait to look much like Maybell, true. But the moment you do that, you've degraded and demeaned her. She had a heart of gold once you dug below the surface. Rough around the edges, sure, but someone with real humanity, and who knows what kinds of struggles or troubles she had to contend with?"

"I like to think of her in a good way."

"I'm glad for that."

"In some weird way, I almost feel like I'm getting that family I never had, right here, on this trip."

I take her hair into my hands and lean over and kiss her on her forehead, a thing I've been aching to do ever since she first learned of her dad. But I knew she wouldn't let me. Now, maybe, some of the edge might be wearing away. It's been a long, long day and she tastes like sweat and oil, but I love it. Love the way she tastes and smells. I can even catch a faint whiff of her underarms when she moves a certain way, and I love that, too. It's real and human. We spend so much time and effort covering up so much about ourselves, sometimes even our most essential selves. *Mostly* our essential selves, if we're being honest.

"She was a lesbian?" Lindsey asks.

"I guess she was, yes. You can only imagine how hard that must have been back then. Not easy today. But back then, in that place . . ."

Lindsey nods.

I hadn't even known she had any real sense about what a lesbian is. But I'm glad she seems to and glad she asked the question. It tells me she's interested also in the real about people and not just what we show the world.

But there's still a bit more to tell—that old millstone: how it was Lee ended up where he did and how I ended up where I did.

31

November 1976

Hank got a lawyer for me who took my case and did a good job, I suppose, in that I wasn't in too much trouble. Hank told me I'd been silly to believe it, but it did seem that Lee knew what he was talking about when he promised that all the trouble would land on him and none on me. I didn't get off scot-free because I was now on probation, which meant that I was only allowed to go to school by myself and other nearby places in Paris and if I went anywhere else it had to be with an adult—for the time, that meant only Mama and Hank, who became my stepdad not long after I got home; they were only waiting for me to return to get properly hitched. Mama said she couldn't do it without me there.

I couldn't go for my driver's license, either, and I had to be home by midnight every night unless I was with Mama or Hank. And once a month, they had to take me all the way out to Yankton, where I reported in with an officer. All this till I was eighteen.

But I got lucky. It could have been much worse. All the police officers' questioning at that time was about Mirabile and Mr. Barry and

Mr. Chester and nothing to do with that river man. Eventually, though, they'd made a match between the bullet that killed that man and the gun Lee threw that day we were finally caught. But that would come later and would only add to the case against Lee.

Your boyfriend insists you had nothing to do with anything, one of the officers said.

He says you never once even touched the gun, another added.

They nodded as they said it, as did my lawyer and Mama and Hank. It felt like we were all in on the same thing, which was making sure all the blame went to Lee, just as he said it would. Sitting there like that, with all those adults and authority figures, and Mama staring me down, I felt way too small and weak to even try and set the record straight about any of it.

He says that you told him many times to put that money back at Mirabile, one of the officers said.

It wasn't a question, so I didn't say yes or no. My lawyer said, That's right.

Of course, such an answer can go either way, like that's right that Lee said that. No one could ever accuse you of lying if you simply agreed that someone else had said something. Besides, neither of the officers pushed it one way or another.

I was underage, a thing they kept coming back to. It meant a lot apparently, along with the fact that Lee was himself over eighteen. Because I was underage, it meant that I'd get turned over to Mama and Hank, who vowed to keep me in check.

Well, it's our view that Lilly here was either unwilling to go along with Lee and fought him over it or she was powerless to break free, one of the officers said.

Or both, the other added. And they seemed satisfied by that, as did everyone else in the room. Of course, neither of those things was true, and in fact, as I pointed out to my lawyer back at my house, I was only back home because I'd asked Lee to take me and he obliged. But when I said that, Mama let out a sound like she was greatly frustrated and Hank said, Now, Lilly . . .

But my lawyer cut him off and told me very sternly that I was not to contradict the narrative even if it wasn't true. Now, I'm not telling you to lie, you understand, he said. But when we go see those police officers and eventually a judge, you are not to volunteer that you'd gone with Lee under your own free will. If such a line of thinking is offered up, I'll be forced to paint a portrait of you as a naive girl who'd fallen under the spell of an older man and who didn't have the wherewithal to get yourself out of things. Further, once the killings took place, you had no choice. You simply could not leave. He was driving. He was in charge. He was in control.

You promise you'll listen here, Lilly, and do as you're told, Mama said.

We know what's best for you, Hank added.

That made me angry all over again, but I promised, for Mama's sake. I knew I'd put her through enough already.

But as it was, I never did have to sit in a courtroom in front of a jury and account for my sins anyway because there never were any charges against me in the end. We avoided all that and instead sat with only a judge and my lawyer and Hank and Mama and they hammered out the deal. It was all done in an afternoon.

Of course, Mama was happy to have me home and would have accepted anything if it meant I'd be back with her. I'm so relieved, she kept saying over and over. I'm so happy to have you back in your old room that I can't even skin your hide for what you've done.

But after all the joyful reunion tears had been shed, she sat me down on my bed and told me she had something to say to me that she knew I wouldn't like to hear but believed it her duty to tell me anyway.

I haven't done my job as a mother in talking to you enough earlier, having the real heart-to-heart conversations that should be required of a mother and her growing daughter, she said. So some of this whole episode is my own fault, and I'm going to have to live with that the rest of my days.

No, Mama, that's not true, I said.

But she wasn't going to hear any of that from me. She vowed instead that she would start now, better late than never.

Lilly-Bear, she said, listen to me. There are all kinds of love in this world—a mother's love for her daughter, for instance. Or the love a good man has for his woman. The love God has for humanity. Even the meanest of animals has love for their offspring. Yes, all kinds of love in this world. But one thing there ain't: there ain't ever the same love twice. You understand what I'm saying to you?

You talking about Lee?

Well, of course I'm talking about Lee.

You think because I'm only sixteen I don't know my heart and that I'll grow out of all this.

I'm only saying that I'm older than you and I know what first love feels like and I know that nothing is forever, no matter what the romance novels and movies tell us.

Well, you don't know about this, Mama. You can't know and you can't be right. 'Cause if you are, well then, what is the point to it all?

She looked at me and shook her head a little. It made me furious, like I was some innocent thing to be pitied. So I didn't say anymore. And, anyway, I couldn't. The thing I would have wanted to tell Mama, but couldn't because I didn't have the words for it and it felt like it was all mine anyway and not something to share—the thing I didn't even try to explain to her—was this: Lee was my home.

Yes, I was back home with Mama. Home in Paris. But it didn't matter if I was in Paris, South Dakota, or Paris, France. Or any place in between. It was all pretty simple: with Lee, I was home. And without him—well, without him, I was not.

⌒

About a month or so later, I went to visit him. It was a long ride out to the penitentiary and I was grateful to Hank that he came along with me and that he'd bought us each the bus ticket to get there. At first, he and Mama forbade my visiting Lee. But I threatened to run off and go by myself, reminding them that they couldn't watch me every second of every day, and that I didn't care if that meant breaking the terms of my probation—they knew it was no idle threat and that I was perfectly capable. So, they allowed it, on condition that Hank come along. We had to wake up before dawn so we could make the three-hour trip and be there during visiting hours.

I used to think that Paris was in the middle of nowhere and of course me and Lee saw many places that could easily be viewed as such. But during the ride out to that penitentiary, I saw the true definition of middle of nowhere. About an hour outside Paris, we crossed a train track and then for the next two hours that was the only evidence of humanity we saw until this huge white building with tall fences and razor wire came rising up out of the horizon all alone on the prairie. The road, in fact, ended at the penitentiary. Had I realized this before, I would have spent some time studying the other people on the bus, seeing as how we were all heading to the same place. It was only as we approached the entrance that I noticed they were all women—Hank and the driver being the only men—and they were all doing the same thing I was, though by the looks of some of them, I imagined they were visiting their sons and not their beaus, like me.

Crossing that train track reminded me of the times Lee and I would do the same, when sometimes we'd sit there for an hour or more while those trains, miles long, chugged across the empty landscape, hauling coal and grain and whatever else, and it would give us the opportunity to stop and stretch our legs and backs and watch all those cars. Seems watching them go by would be about as exciting as watching sap run. But I never tired of it and I loved the sound of it, too, that rhythm they had. There was something about it I found romantic, some reminder we weren't alone out there even if those trains never stopped and we rarely ever saw a person on them.

When we got to the penitentiary, the big gates opened and we were let in. The bus stopped and a corrections officer came out and led us into a building, where we emptied our pockets and turned our possessions over to a different officer, who wrote down each item and our names and told us we could pick up our effects when we left.

There were only a dozen of us but this took well more than an hour and the line hardly moved during it. But finally we were finished and we moved into another room where there were six chairs in front of glass with phones on the wall separated by little barriers with the same setup on the other side. We stood some more without any direction or understanding as to what was going on until finally the door on the other side of the room behind the glass opened up and in they came, eleven men in handcuffs and matching uniforms.

I saw Lee right away. Some of the women near me started crying at the sight of their loved ones, but I was smiling as big as I'd ever smiled and that old feeling came back to me like it used to: where I'd look at him and my heart would start thumping around in my chest and my breath would catch for a moment before I could recover. Like jumping into cold water.

Despite my excitement, I had to wait as they only allowed six at a time to come to the glass and Lee was not in the first group. When I saw some of the men who did come, I realized that these older women who'd made the trip were not there to see their sons at all but rather their husbands, and I wondered how long this had been going on. I couldn't even imagine it.

One of the older women started crying when she saw that her husband was not one of the eleven men and when she asked some questions, an officer told her that he'd committed a violation and lost his visiting privileges. It was so sad to think she'd come all that way for nothing.

Finally it was my turn and I sat down and started jabbering away like an excited schoolgirl and Lee laughed and, holding the phone to his ear, pointed at my phone and mouthed for me to pick it up.

His voice sounded funny through the phone but it was nice to talk to him as it was the first time I'd done so in six weeks, ever since we were caught.

How you doing? I asked.

Just fine. How are you?

I can't complain. Hank came with me, I told him, and I looked to the back of the room where Hank was standing.

Please thank him for me, Lee said.

I have some news.

What's that?

I went to the doctor on account of the fact that I was late.

Late to what? he asked.

That's when I told him I had his baby inside me.

Well, then, he said. That sure is something. Then he smiled so wide. I knew it! he shouted. I just knew it!

Then he pulled the phone away and yelled out for everyone to hear: I'm gonna be a daddy! he shouted. Just like I said so.

Most of the men on his side of the glass cheered for him, even one of the officers, too, and a few of them came over and pat him on the back and looked at me and gave me a thumb's up.

I started blushing something terrible. There was a heat running all through me that started spreading across my neck and my ears and my cheeks. But it was in my heart and my belly, too. I could feel it there really strong.

Lee came back to the phone and he said, We've got a lot of planning to do then.

We do, I agreed.

We talked and laughed about diapers and midnight feedings and all of those things new parents go through. The other stuff—where we'd live, his needing to get a job, money—those things we'd talk about some other time. For now, I didn't want to lay all of that heavier stuff on the little time we did have together.

And it did indeed come to an end really quick. Before we knew it, our twenty minutes had gone—all that travel and that long day for such a short visit—and we were told to wrap it up. Everyone else around us did so like they had practice at it, but Lee and I were still talking when the other men started getting up out of their chairs and an officer hollered at Lee to hang it up. But he was still talking and he said, Hey, Lilly-Flower. Listen, baby, I need to tell you—but then the phone went dead and the officer was pulling Lee up and he did so in such a way that Lee couldn't even turn around to see me before he was shoved through the door and he was gone.

I sat there until Hank came over and helped me up.

We'll come back, Hank said. You'll have another chance to speak with him.

Maybe that was true, but it would be a long time off and I hated the way we'd parted.

Something made me stand and stare after him even though he, and everyone else, was gone. I couldn't leave yet. I watched as the phone Lee had been on swung back and forth on the wire below its hook. It hadn't been properly hung up in the scuffle and so there it swung, the only movement in the room.

I ran my hands over my belly.

One more life would come into this world and maybe begin to balance out the ones we took. I'd sure got my stories to tell her some-day. Yes, I just knew it would be a girl. A beautiful little girl, run through with the spirit of adventure and rebellion, just like me and her daddy. I knew how wonderful a thing that can be. But how dangerous, too. Just like my mama had said to me, so long ago. Everything runs in circles.

The phone had stopped now, and hung there like it was dead. It made me so sad. But I was tired of sad. And so I tried not think too much about it now.

Or about the upcoming trial or about the fact that maybe Lee . . . well, I couldn't think about any of that. I had to get back home and help Mama. The next day was Saturday and it was a big day for me. Mama had a whole thing planned. Yes, technically we'd missed my birthday long ago, but she planned a huge party anyway, pretending we'd got the right day. So there was plenty to worry about later, but for that moment . . .

As Mama said to me not long after I got home, big tears in her eyes: Lil-Bear, you only turn sixteen but one time.

Sioux Falls, South Dakota, November 5, 1992, 4:00 a.m.

We take a room in a Motel 6. I feel terrible about waking the proprietor, Mrs. Patel by the nameplate on the desk, but this is the occupation she chose. Still, she seems none too pleased about being woken up.

"We've been up for twenty-four hours," I tell her. "Came all the way from New Orleans by bus." But she doesn't respond, only leads us to our room in her old robe. Can't blame her; what does she care? Still, it would be nice to have some kind of happy greeting. I can almost convince myself at moments that Lindsey and I are on some good-time cross-country trip, just a kid and her mom, out for an adventure. But there's something about a north-south trip that just doesn't feel completely right to me, as if a real cross-country trip requires coast to coast, sea to shining sea. Of course, this is the same trip Lee and I made—and then there's always that: As much as I might try and work this into something else, I do know why we're here. And I know why it appears that my hands have gotten a bit of the shakes back.

We settle our bags in the room and throw ourselves on the beds. I'm keeping it together well, though I'm being quiet. After a time, Lindsey asks me: "Mom, when grandma told you that stuff about never the same love twice and all . . ."

"Mm-hmm?"

267

"And you said that you just couldn't believe in that, that there has to be soul mates in this world and people who are the only ones for us?"

"What about it?"

"You still believe that?"

I think long and hard, because this is about more than what I believe or don't. What I say to her apparently matters—or else she wouldn't be asking—so I need to answer honestly but keep in mind my job as her parent. This is the balancing act, the razor wire, I've been walking since the day I found out I was pregnant. And it hasn't stopped, not for even one moment—I know that now.

"I think my mama was probably right in the end," I say. "Grandma knew more than I gave her credit for at the time. It's the same thing here, with us. I'm sure given the same exact circumstances only if you were me and I was her, I'd be saying the same thing to you that she said to me. And I'd expect you to say the same things to me that I said to her. There's simply no substitute for growing up, living a little, and learning your fair share of lessons, often the hard way. There's just no way around that. But I can tell you this—"

"What's that?"

"I'm glad I believed. How cruel a world this would be if innocent girls didn't believe with all their hearts that their love is the most special thing in the universe and that no one else can possibly understand it. It might not be right, but it sure is sweet to feel that in your heart. It might even make learning otherwise worth it."

Lindsey gets up, pokes around the room some—opening drawers, turning on the TV, turning it off. Funny, I see myself in her once again.

"I'm hungry," she declares.

"Me too."

We head out to a little diner we saw a half mile or so up the street. Turns out they don't open till five, so we have to wait outside in the cold morning air and darkness for half an hour.

"You moved to New Orleans then?" Lindsey asks.

"Well, you know that part."

"Tell me anyway."

"I moved to New Orleans—guess I never got that dream out of me—when you were not even two. You don't remember anything of Paris?"

"No."

"No. You wouldn't, I guess. Mama got sick then, when you were still just a baby. And she never got any better. Died on your first birthday. But you know that, too. Hank started going out on long hauls again—didn't want to be in the house with us two alone and who can blame him for that? Eventually he met another woman and they moved to Hawaii. I visited Lee—your father—three times in the penitentiary. Once when I was still pregnant with you. But then I got put on bed rest and that put a stop to visits for a while. When you were born, Mama was pretty sick by then, so trips were hard. I took you one time and that was a nightmare. You were colicky and cried the entire bus ride there and didn't stop when we went inside, so poor Lee had to watch you screaming your lungs out from behind that glass and it was so frustrating I even gave up my spot before our time ran out. The next time I left you at home, but it was hard for Mama to take care of you; she was going through her treatments and feeling weak and awful. By then, Lee—your daddy—had been sentenced for what we did. It was a hard time."

Lindsey just stands there, staring first at me and then off in the distance and we're quiet for a long time before she suddenly turns and wraps her arms around me and we're standing there like that, holding on to each other for a long time, just holding on and not saying anything to spoil it.

I feel myself melting, everything just washing away, as if I've said all I can say, told her everything I could, and it's been enough and she understands. Nothing more needs to be said.

269

When I was pregnant with her, I used to think we had our own way of communicating. I'd run my fingers across my swollen belly and she'd tap back on the underside and we'd press our fingers toward each other, separated only by my skin. It almost feels that way now, like we're becoming one person again, sharing flesh and blood and life.

"Excuse me."

It's some little old woman. We move aside as she steps forward. She unlocks the door, heads inside, and then quickly locks it again behind her. Soon, the lights go on and we're getting real hungry and anxious for some warmth and light and food. A few other people show up—cooks and busboys, by the looks of them—and they head inside too, and it's almost too much to bear.

"New Orleans," Lindsey says.

I run my fingers over her hair, caress her check, stroke her as I continue. I can hear my own voice, like it belongs to someone else, all dreamy and somehow mine but not mine, right here but far away. "After Mama died, I sold the house. Because I'd turned eighteen by then the money was mine and so I picked up and came south. I had to start my life. Move away. Face the reality of things. Grow up, in other words. I got a job waiting tables and started dating the manager straightaway. He moved in and everything, but it only took a few weeks with him to know that wasn't right."

"Why?"

"Well, turns out he was still legally married, for one."

Lindsey shakes her head.

"There were other reasons. You don't remember him either, huh?"

"No."

"Just as well. Yeah, Mama was right about a lot of things; she once told me most men are real snakes. Not all, but a sure lot. It was okay. I just needed someone so I could find my way in a new place. But I quickly realized that I really just had to raise you up. That was the only thing I had to do. The most important thing and the only thing."

"You did a good job, Mom."

270

I smile. I can't see myself, but I can imagine it's the same dreamy, love-soaked smile I used to give Lee.

Lindsey turns and looks inside the diner, almost as if they'll let us in if we present a pathetic enough picture.

And sure enough, the old woman comes over and opens the door. It's hard to resist an innocent-looking teenaged girl. "Still ten minutes away," she says. "Kitchen's not quite ready, and I just put the coffee on, but come in and get yourselves warmed up."

We settle ourselves into a booth and soon enough the waitress brings us both hot cups of coffee, even though we didn't ask. "I'm taking the liberty," she says and walks off.

I can't help but smile some more—no matter how tired and hungry I am—as I watch Lindsey pouring in five sugar packets.

"You trying to make the spoon stand up?" I ask.

The waitress comes back and tells us they're ready and we give her our order. I watch her as she walks away. Must be seventy years old or more; could easily have been working in this place for fifty years. I think about the other waitresses we had when Lee and I were out on the road and about how so many women out there lead such quiet and un-distinguished lives and yet how they very well may be the most impor-tant people in the world. They're probably somebody's mother and even if they're not, they fill the role for so many people at moments like this. Lindsey and me sitting here, waiting for our food, occasionally glancing at each other and communicating more with our eyes than with words and how long has it been since we did that and how this trip has been a blessing, probably the biggest of my life since she was born, and how that waitress will come back soon enough with plates piled high with warm food and refill our coffee and for the short time we'll be here, she'll be like a mother to us both. Mother, and grand-mother, too.

The food comes and we dig in. The heat of it fills me and I savor each bite. It feels good. To be inside. To have hot food. To be here with my daughter.

271

I'll stay, I decide. In this place. This space where I've gotten Lindsey's acceptance and understanding. I watch her as she eats, slowly chewing on the right side of her mouth like she does. And when she sees me staring at her, she just smiles. I have what I need, and I don't need to tell her any more. It's settled.

I don't need to tell her how Maybell had pleaded with me to do something, testify, save Lee, save her son, and how Hank and Mama and my lawyer convinced me to stay off the stand. I won't tell her it was me who shot that man at the river, how he was running away and how I shot him anyway, how he was frightened when Lee picked up the branch and how he could have easily gotten away, how his back was to us when I pulled the trigger because I was scared and how it was Lee who fixed things up and made it out so I couldn't blame myself, and how it was me who insisted we keep that money at Mirabile, how I saw it as a way for us to stay out on the road together and how we'd be tied forever when I was worrying that Lee would get bored with me and how Lee shot at Barry only after Barry came after him as Lee was trying to give the money back, how it was really all a huge misunderstanding and Lee simply got scared and it was me who created the whole mess in the first place and how he then killed Mr. Chester out of fear and panic and how he just kept saying, "I'll keep you safe, Lil-Flower, I'll keep you safe," and how it was me who got all excited by it and me who pulled him down to make love right there on the floor of Mr. Chester's room and how I still can't even understand why I reacted that way, but I just did, and how it was Lee who was crying all the while. I don't need to tell her any of this, but how could she understand it anyway when I can't even myself?

I was a kid. I was scared and I didn't know what I was doing. Now I'm no longer a kid and I live every day with the things I've done and some days it's almost too much. Lee is where he is and I am where I am and I know the reasons for it, the justification for it. But still . . . It's her. It's Lindsey. She's the reason. She's here and she's real and I have to keep myself together for her sake and now it seems, for the first time in our lives, she understands me completely, and she forgives me for things she hadn't even known to blame me for, and she loves me. I can't tell her the truth. I can't. Her daddy took the full rap for me and now he's to be executed for the crime. How can she understand how it is I could have allowed that? Will she really understand what it was all for and why I did it: So she would have a normal life? So her mother could stay on the outside and be her mother because there was no one else?

"Hey, Mom?"

"Yes?"

"I don't think we should go."

I realize that I'm just staring ahead, seeing but not seeing, a haze covering everything—my vision, my brain, my soul. "Go where?" I manage.

"To see him."

"I don't understand."

"Why do it now only to never see him again? He never was any part of my life. It just seems kind of crazy."

I sit back, take it in. I can't believe what I'm hearing from her. "What's crazy," I say, recovering myself a bit, "is that we came all the way up here, on that bus. What's crazy is that you begged me to come and I really didn't want to. It took every single thing out of me to even get my head right to do it and take this trip . . ."

She's just staring at me. There's no use in arguing it. Her mind is made up. And when she sets her mind to something, the only person who can change it is her. Maybe simply coming to South Dakota was enough. Maybe my telling her the story was enough and so now she's ready to head back home, ready to get back on with her life. In truth, I don't even know why I'm arguing it. It's surely not something I wanted to do, seeing Lee and Lindsey together knowing he would be dead so soon after. I don't know what good could come of that for her. And yet I feel obligated to it now. So I keep pressing the matter.

273

"What about the old house? In Paris? You want to see that?"

"I guess I just want to go back home."

I excuse myself to go to the bathroom. Once inside, I lock the door.

A huge wave of nausea sweeps over me. I put my fingers over my mouth, as if I'll hold it all in and wait for everything to pass. I turn to the mirror, spotted in the corners as if the shine has been taken off. I look downright terrible. Hair a mess, bags under my eyes. I've been in so many bathrooms like this one and they all look the same: rust stains in the sink, the constant drip of the faucet, no soap or towels, a toilet scrub brush sitting in the corner.

Finally, the nausea passes and I splash water on my face and hair and head back out.

There's a busboy at our table and he's taking our plates and there's Lindsey, of course, and she's smiling and twirling her hair in her fingers and talking to him. He must be eighteen, nineteen at best. White shirt and apron tied on and he's carrying a plastic tub. He's got dark hair and blue eyes and his hair falls over his eyes and he pushes it back and smiles a lot: these beautiful white teeth, and, man, but he might be the handsomest kid within three states.

It takes everything in me not to rush the table. I want to get her out of here, take her away. Take her back home. I need to keep her the person she is at this exact minute, one who sees no reason not to love her mother, and never let her go. But I know I can't. Some things you just know.

Others, you have to learn the hard way.

Sioux Falls, South Dakota, November 5, 1992, 7:30 a.m.

Her eyelashes flutter, just like she's been doing since she was a baby. It means she's deep in sleep and it would take an airplane flying right through the room to wake her.

I leave her a note and slip out, catching the bus to the penitentiary as had been the plan all along.

It's little surprise to me how my body reacts when he comes in. Like it had from the very beginning: the shortness of breath, the flash of heat all over me, my heart bouncing around. But this I chalk up to nervousness more than anything else.

He looks good. He's aged, of course, though haven't we all? But apart from a few gray hairs here and there and a few more lines around the eyes, he still looks like Lee, only more muscular, which I suppose I can chalk up to his spending almost half his life in prison.

It's not like the penitentiary where he used to be, where we had to communicate by phone through thick glass. Now it's just him and me, and a corrections officer, at a little red hard plastic table inside a room with about ten other tables, everything bolted to the floor.

"No touching," the officer says and then he just stands there in the back of the room, watching.

"I suppose you don't have much interest in touching me anyway," Lee says, smiling. "Dead man walking."

"Please, Lee," I say. But I don't have anything more to say.

Here he is. This is him. Once the center of my universe. And sometime tomorrow he'll be gone. What I can't seem to get past, what sticks itself in my chest and lodges there, where I am certain it will cling until I, too, am dead and gone, is the stupid, sad reality that people change. It's him, but it's not him. My soul mate, my galaxy, my sun and moon and stars, my everything. And now what is he to me? A handsome man who I once loved and who I love no more. I can't even say I know him. So sad. Sad the way the world works.

We stare at each other for a good long time, as if saying nothing is the only way we can say everything. I realize after a while that I'm rubbing my earlobe. It will be with me the rest of my life, no doubt.

"Where's Lindsey?" he finally asks.

"She didn't want to come after all. I'm sorry."

Lee shrugs, gives a sad little smile. "I suppose I can't blame her," he says.

"She wanted to, but—"

"I understand," he says, but the look in his eye, a bit of light going out of them, tells me he probably doesn't.

"I want you to remember me as a good man, Lilly," he says.

I nod.

"I tried my best."

I feel a hot sting burning behind my eyes and then the tears spill out down my cheeks.

Lee reaches out and wipes them away. The officer stares at us, but he doesn't say anything. Lee nods at him and the officer nods back. I wonder if Lee had made friends in here or if this is just the kind of consideration men get who are considered suitable to die for their crimes but then, when that death is on the horizon, they're treated with a certain kind of respect.

"I ran so that they'd catch us," Lee says. "You understand that, right? I was driving. I was older. I was the man. And I told them it was all me."

"But that wasn't true," I whisper. "I'm the reason you're in here. We both know that."

Lee shakes his head and waves me off. He takes a quick glance at the guard, but he isn't paying us any attention. It looks like he's at the end of his shift and just wants out of there.

"This is who I am, Lil," Lee says. "This is where I live. Is it where I belong? Who knows? But it's not for nothing that I'm here. On some level, I've known it all along. From the very beginning. From when I was a little kid, when I came to understand where my daddy was, and where his daddy had been for a time, too. It's the path that's always been there for me. Blame you? Blame my daddy? *I* brought along that gun. Me. I knew it all along."

"But why? After all that happened," I ask. "Why did you always insist it be all on you?"

And it occurs to me now that this is really the only thing I need to know, the only thing I never asked, and it's the only real question, in a slightly different form, that Lindsey asked me, too. I guess it's the only thing that really matters anymore.

"You remember, a few days before we went back, you were sick all morning?" he asks. "Happened again a few days later? You blamed it on bad food. Well . . . I knew. And the only way that kid was going to have any kind of fighting chance was if one of us was out to raise her. And that one of us should always have been her mama. And I have no doubt you've done one heck of a job, Lilly."

I nod, the tears coming hot and fast now. Of course this was the answer. I've known it all along and it was the very thing that has allowed me, all these years, to swallow it whole and live my life. For her. Keeping it in. You can condemn me for it, sure, and many people would. But it would be impossible to condemn me more than I have myself.

"I've done the best I could," I say, wiping away my tears.

"I don't doubt that. And because you did, there's a piece of me out in the world. And it's a good piece. And between the two of you, you'll do more good deeds and take away so much bad that it cancels out all I've done in this world."

I shake my head. "No, Lee, you never were bad. It was me, Lee—"

"None of that now. Not one more word on that, Lil-Flower. You're our daughter's mother. And it'll never be anything different. We did one thing right then, didn't we?"

I smile at him. "Yeah," I say, nodding. "I guess we did."

"And she's a good kid?"

"Yeah, I guess she is."

"All right then. Now I can go out with my head up."

He gets up and the officer leads him away. "Bye, Lilly," he says.

I try to respond, but nothing comes out.

I sit there for a long time, alone. I can't move. I'm unable to pull my feet from the floor and put one in front of the other and head back to that motel to get Lindsey and then go back home. I'm rooted.

277

But finally they make me leave. "Ma'am?" they say. "Do you need us to call someone for you?"

I shake my head.

The walk back to the bus station is a long one. But during the time it takes me, my head clears a little with each step, each step back into the life I'd always been destined to live. I have permission now. I've been waiting for that half my life.

So now I know who I am. If nothing else, that. For good or bad—or maybe a little of both—I know who I am.

Acknowledgments

Thanks to early readers when *Independence* wasn't yet even in draft form: Elizabeth Evitts Dickinson, Christine Stewart, and Gregg Wilhelm. Thanks also to copyeditor Michelle Wing and the good folks at the University of Wisconsin Press: Sheila McMahon, Kaitlin Svabek, Jennifer Conn, and especially Dennis Lloyd, who believed in the novel and shepherded it through. Appreciation for three more of my writer friends, experts in various genres, Marc Lapadula, Tom Swick, and my midwestern resource (but great Baltimore guy), Frank Starr. Thanks also to the wonderful administrators and colleagues at the Community College of Baltimore County, who make my working life a joy. Most especially, thanks to my wonderful families, biological and nuclear, most especially the three terrific ladies who live with me and who I think the absolute world of—I would be a tenth of who I am without them.